Prologue

28th March 1984

'Knock, knock.'

'Who's there?'

'Interrupting cow.'

'Interrupting co...'

'Moo.'

'That's not funny.'

'I know.' Henry stood up and straightened the sheets on the side of his mother's bed. 'That's why it's funny.' He had a plastic bottle half-full with her urine in his hand. 'I'll empty this thing and be back,' Henry waved the plastic bottle. 'Do you want anything?'

'No, I'm alright. Thanks love.'

'I'll bring some milk in a thermos though shall I?'

'Thanks.'

When he came back, Henry's mother said, 'You haven't had much of a birthday have you?'

'It's been great,' Henry smiled. 'Day off from school. Couldn't ask for more.'

'No, I mean, you're sixteen, Henry, you should be out with girls and...'

'I'm happy, Mum. There'll be plenty of time to catch up with girls later.'

'You should be out there with...'

'Ah, go on,' his voice rose. 'I had a really good day with you. You and me, down the Mumbles. It was perfect. There's no one I'd rather spend it with.' He slid a wedge shaped piece of foam between her knees. 'Alright? So, I've drained your bag, buffed the pillows, given you all your meds.' He glanced at the digital thermometer on the bedside table. 'Even got the temperature bang on. Do you need anything else, or will you be OK if I go down now? I'll be back in a couple of hours to turn you.'

'How's the homework?' Henry's mother said. Her rosary had grown sweaty in her palm, so she released it, letting it dangle and then clawing it back up again nice and safe.

'Blah,' Henry shrugged.

'Your O Levels are really important. They might be boring but...'

'Yeah, yeah, I know. Don't worry.' He bent to kiss his mother's cheek. 'I'm doing fine.' He gestured towards the hoist and shower chair in the corner of the room. 'You know with all this stuff, it's made biology a doddle.'

'Well I'm glad it's been worth something.' She rested her hand on Henry's arm, speaking slowly and clearly. 'I mean it, love. I'm glad. You've had to experience real life so young. But it could've been worse. I could've had something that'd taken years, you know, not...'

'You'll be around for years, Mum, don't be daft.' The rosary beads pressed into the soft flesh on the back of his arm.

'No, I mean it, I...'

'Look, I'm not having a talk like this on my birthday,' his tone hardened. 'Seriously,' and he looked away from her.

'You dad didn't send a card or anything?' She noticed the shape of his face change as he clenched his teeth and slid behind his defensive wall.

''Course not. I'd have told you, wouldn't I?'

'Right. Sorry. Well, what I mean is, what I want to say is, that this thing I've got,' she dug her fingers into his forearm to stop him as he tried to interrupt, 'this thing I've got has made you more of a man than he ever was. It mustn't matter what people say about him, you know, when the time comes. You're not your father's son. You're nothing like him.'

'Ah, go on. I've seen the pictures of him my age. Fair-haired six footers, both of us. We could be brothers.'

'Not like that, Henry. I don't mean physically like that. I couldn't ask for a better son than you.'

'Not tonight, OK? No talking like this. Not on my birthday.'

'I mean it. I know we weren't close when your dad left, you and me. I know you blamed me...'

'I didn't understand...'

'I know that. Of course I know that. You were thirteen. How could you possibly understand anything? But I accept why he couldn't handle me getting ill. I'd have probably been the same if it was reversed. I've seen how strong you are, and the man you're going to be. How brave. I wish it hadn't happened, but it's making a man of you.'

Henry nodded wearily. 'Do you want any more cream for the sores?' he asked.

'On my back, just a little. Thanks.'

'OK.' He opened a tub of chamomile and calendula, dug in his fingers, scooped some out and slid his hand down the back of her nightdress. 'Just there between your shoulder blades?'

'And on my shoulders. Perfect. Thanks.'

'S'alright, love.' He put the lid back on the tub and looked at her again. She watched his mouth smile, but saw that the smile had not reached his eyes.

'Look, Henry,' she said. 'I want to ask them to stop the treatment. I've been thinking about it and this is no good. It's not fair on you and...'

'Don't talk like that!' Henry shouted, his fury sudden but quickly passing. 'Don't ever talk like that,' he hissed. 'Don't blame it on me, alright. I can handle it. I can take care of you till you get better.' He wiped spittle from around his mouth with the back of his hand. 'If you want to stop the treatment, then do it because you want to. Because of the pain, or whatever, but...' His voice lowered. 'I'm sorry. You do what you want, but just don't blame it on me.'

'You're just sixteen and...'

'And I'll be seventeen next year and I'll still be emptying your urine bag just like I did last year, and I'll be doing it again every year after until you're better.'

'You don't get better from Hodgkin's,' she said. 'The treatment only delays the inevitable. You know that.'

'I've read the same rubbish you have, but I've also been to Lourdes. You sent me there year after year with church,' he said. 'And why? So I'd develop faith? Well I did develop some faith and it's amazing what faith can do. Isn't that right? You always used to say that if you've got faith you can move mountains. Well I've got faith that they'll find a cure and that you'll get better and we'll dance at my wedding, you and me, one day,' he smiled, his eyes blazing at her. 'There'll be a happy ending, Mum. They'll find a cure for everything in the end.'

'There'll be no happy ending for me, Henry,' she said firmly, trying to smile. 'There is no cure for Hodgkin's Disease.'

Henry put his hands over his ears. 'La, la, la, la,' he said. 'Can't hear you, and even if I could I wouldn't listen.'

'I'm not going to be here next year, love.'

'La, la, la, la.'

'It's a fact.' She struggled up onto her elbow and reached to pull at his arm. 'I'm so tired.'

'La, la, la, la.'

'I'm just so tired,' she said, slumping back down on the bed. 'I'm so sorry.'

Henry sat with his hands in his lap. He looked at his fingers resting crossed above his thighs, like a choirboy at prayer. Tears stung at his eyes, but he squeezed them away. He turned to his mother, his lips drawn into a tight smile. 'I'm sorry, Mum,' he whispered.

His mother sighed. 'This rash, Henry. When I moved. I'm sorry; with the cream it's sticky on the material. Could you, you know, hitch my nightie around a bit?'

Her body was as nothing in his arms as Henry reached around his mother. 'OK?' he asked.

'Lovely.'

He stood and walked to the door. 'I'll see you later then,' he said. 'You OK? Don't need anything?' She shook her head. 'Right. Try to sleep now, yeah?'

'Happy birthday, Henry dear,' his mother said, the rosary beads running slowly through her fingers. 'Happy birthday.'

Chapter One

11.30am 14th February 2007

'Are you sure you don't make a change, Dan?' Henry asked. 'I don't want to try to talk you into anything, but Carlo and Cathy have a spare room in their house and I could get you in there easy. Supported tenancy, no problems. Or somewhere else if you'd prefer. You just have to say the word?' He turned to face Dan. They were sitting side by side outside Marks and Spencer's on Swansea's Oxford Street. Henry perched on a bench and Dan hunched beside him in his wheelchair. 'Face it Dan,' he said. 'Your missus is a nutter.'

Dan didn't say anything. He just smiled.

'OK. You're the big boss,' Henry said. He reached to release the breaks on Dan's chair. 'You're the boss, big man, same as it ever was.'

It was a busy day in the commercial zone. Shoppers came and went and babies were silent in their prams as they stared at the gargoyle-grimace of the old man in the wheelchair.

Dan smiled at the babies, or at least he tried to, his MS making his intention and the result very different. One mother glared at him as her infant son began to cry, so he looked away, along the road to the approaching sound of gangster rap and the boy-racer in a Fiesta who squealed to the curb in front of them.

'Booming bass, sunglasses, baseball cap,' Henry murmured as he stood up and took hold of Dan's chair to leave. 'Cliché, eh,' but Dan raised his arm to stop him. His eyes narrowed as he watched the kid springing out of the car, bopping across the pavement, twisting to fire his key fob automatic-locker back at the car and then, shifting his cigarette across his lips, spat heavily as he headed off in front of Dan and Henry and away up the street.

'HEY NUMBNUTS. YOU FORGOT YOUR PERMIT!'

The boy stumbled as he stopped to turn back to them. 'You what?' He glanced at Dan but spoke to Henry, looking up at him, shaping up in front of him, ready for action, though he was eight inches shorter and four stone lighter.

'HEY NUMBNUTS. YOU FORGOT YOUR PERMIT!'

'Not me, Sunshine,' Henry grinned. 'I didn't say a word.' He rested his hand on Dan's shoulder. 'He speaks for himself.'

'YOUR CAR. YOU FORGOT YOUR PERMIT FUCKWIT!'

'What are you talking about?' The boy glared at Dan who was tapping away on the keyboard of his talk/touch communication devise. He had pre-programmed sentences ready at his fingertips, but it took longer to write new ones.

'YOUR CAR. YOU FORGOT YOUR PERMIT. YOU DO HAVE A PERMIT, DON'T YOU NUMBNUTS?'

'What the...?'

'It's a disabled parking bay,' Henry explained, 'and you're parking in it.' His voice was calm, his expression friendly. 'You forgot to put up your blue badge permit, if you've got one, if you are disabled, that is?'

'Fuck off,' the boy said, turning to go. 'Do I look like a cabbage?'

'No permit? Well you shouldn't be parking there, son.'

'So what?'

'So what? Well it's not complicated,' Henry laughed. 'It's the law and it's quite simple. No blue badge - no parking.'

'Nobody's using it and I'm back in a minute.' He threw down his cigarette, twisting it beneath his heel. A few pedestrians had stopped to watch.

'You can pick that up too,' Henry said pointing at the squished butt.

'What are you? A fucking Womble?' the boy said.

'WE'LL DO YOUR TYRES IF YOU STAY THERE!'

'What the fuck?' the boy's voice trembled as his confidence faded. 'I'll just be...' he glanced at Henry who shrugged, '...the cash point...'

'You do what you want to do, son,' Henry said. 'You know the right thing to do though don't you? We always know the right thing to do.'

'Ah fuck off,' the boy said as he went back to the car. He climbed in, wound down the window and NWA boomed on the stereo as he turned the ignition. 'I'm glad you're in that fucking thing,' he said as he gunned the engine, and then at Henry he yelled; 'You too. Soon.'

'FUCK YOU!' said Dan.

'Yeah, whatever,' the boy jeered and the Fiesta sped away along the road.

Henry sighed as he watched the little car slow and turn left onto Dillwyn Street, heading off towards the sea.

'PATHETIC!' said Dan.

'Hey ho.' Henry sat down again. He reached into the sports hold-all hanging from the back of Dan's chair, fumbling for tissues to wipe the foam from around his friend's mouth.

'CHEEKY FUCKER,' Dan typed, letter by letter, and he made a noise that sounded like pain but which Henry knew to be a laugh.

'Damn right,' said Henry. 'Tell you what, though. It's exhausting doing this parking bay vigilante shit. We're going to take a beating one day. We both are.'

'BRING 'EM ON. I'VE TAKEN DOWN BIGGER MEN THAN YOU IN MY TIME.'

'That I know, Dan,' said Henry, and then he laughed. 'Fun, though, isn't it.'

'LET'S GO HOME.'

'Really? Home?'

'YEAH.'

'OK,' said Henry, taking hold of the handles. 'Just remember, though, you can leave the moment you want to. The moment it's too much with Ruby.'

'NO!'

'OK, Dan,' Henry laughed. 'But calm down. Your hands are shaking. Calm down, eh?'

'JUST PUSH YOU FUCKING WOMBLE. PUSH,' and people turned to look as Dan's groaning laugh rang out louder than the cars that moved along Oxford Street.

Chapter Two

11.30am 18th February 2007

Four days later, Ruby Franken walked out on her husband, moved in with a man who stacked shelves in the supermarket. She left Dan in a filthy bed, unshaven, hungry and furious. 'Some man you are,' she screamed as she left. 'Pretty fucking useless you've always been to me, and look at you now. Pissing pathetic.' A hanging stream of saliva clung to her chin.

The next-door neighbour spent that day peering through her voile curtain, waiting for Ruby to return. When she hadn't come back by late afternoon, the neighbour called Henry, who rushed round to Dan's house, shouldering his way in through the door and ending up on his face in the hallway.

In the bedroom it looked like the cupboard and chest of drawers had vomited their contents all over the floor. Soiled clothes crusted in the centrally heated closeness.

Henry scooped Dan up as if he were a child. He carried him through to the bathroom while the neighbour made some tea. Henry spoke tenderly and washed Dan clean of his filth. He dressed him gently in clothes bought years ago which were now far too big for him, shaved his chin and fed him packet chicken soup through a straw as there was no other food in the cupboard. Then he changed the bed linen and tidied up the house while Dan watched television with the neighbour in the front room.

Henry stayed there that night, and the following day, when Ruby had not returned, he loaded Dan into his Doblo and drove him across town and into supported tenancy with Carlo and Cathy.

'Do you remember when I first came by?' Henry asked as he pulled away from the kerb. 'I couldn't believe it. I was so excited. You were a hero to me when I was a kid. Was about four years ago, wasn't it?'

'Multiple Sclerosis,' Ruby Franken had said as she let Henry in and led him along the narrow hall and into the lounge. 'You know how it is. Had it years, he has.' She glanced down with disgust at her husband, his head and shoulders poking out above the blanket. 'Do whatever it is you're going to do. Assessment, is it? Fucking needs it, assessing. Should be on more benefits than he is.'

'That's something we can talk about.'

'Talk? Ha! Whatever,' she said. 'I'm going to town. Just let him do what he wants, or whatever,' she flung her arms up. 'I don't care. He's going to try to, no matter,' she rolled her eyes and slammed the front door as she hurried out.

Henry glanced at Dan and Dan glared at Henry. Henry looked away, noticing the yellowed walls and stained carpet. And the smell, good grief, the smell!

'Nuther, fucker,' Dan said, he twisted in his chair away from Henry. His voice was fading, but he could still speak back then. 'Nuther social worker fucker. All front, no bollocks.' He reached for the mug of tea that his wife had left him just out of reach on the coffee table. When Henry stretched to help him he snapped, 'Fuck off, I kin fuckin' do it.'

'OK.' Henry sank back into the sofa. He laid his folders unopened on the floor. 'No notes, Mr Franken. It's just you and me,' he said. 'I know you get through social workers faster than syphilis through a Swansea Valley rugby club, but you and me, we start from scratch. Clean slate, right?'

'Pah,' Dan spat. The mug trembled in his hand, inches from his mouth. 'Nuther fuckin' social worker. All the same. Most are girls. You a girl?'

'I remember you years ago.' Henry stretched his legs, crossing them at the ankle. 'When we were kids you were my hero.'

Dan stared at him over the mug, his eyes cold and black.

'Rugby, right?' Henry said, smiling. 'I wanted to be you back then. 1981 or something. You hit JJ Williams in one game like a 125.' He clapped his hands together so suddenly that they stung and Dan leapt in his chair, the tea flipping up over the edge of the mug. 'It was like watching Martin Williams these days, though you were a bit slighter than Nugget, of course.'

'Not ginger, neither.'

'Not ginger, that's true enough. Swansea against Bridgend it was. Or maybe against Maesteg? I can't remember, but I do remember that it was a hell of a cold day. Anyway, we used to call you "Nails", me and my mates. Wanted to be tough as Nails, all of us did.'

'An' look a' me now,' Dan growled. 'Tough as strained shite.'

'You trained us one time,' Henry ignored him. 'Under twelves. I played a bit, see. Rugby was all that mattered to me and my mates back then. We played cricket too in the summer, but rugby was the main thing. I had to stop when I was about fourteen. I didn't have the time after that. Anyway, you were coaching us up on top of the hill. You remember? It sleeted the whole session. Sheets of the stuff coming in off the sea. And you told us about being tough. You said it's in here that matters,' Henry beat his chest with his fist, loudly, making Dan jump again. 'In here toughness grows. Not the muscle on your thigh but the courage that's in your heart. I never forgot that.'

'So,' Dan hissed. 'Wha's tha fuckin' point o' sayin' tha' now?'

'Just that I remember you, that's all,' Henry said. 'That I remember who you are.'

'Who I was.'

'Who you are. In here.'

'Pah!' but Dan's eyes had softened.

'You were magnificent on the rugby field, Mr Franken. Should have played for Wales, people said.'

'Face din't fit.'

'People said that too. We all thought so, me and my mates,' Henry said.

'Yeah?'

'Yeah.'

'Got clumsy later,' said Dan. 'Dropping stuff. Easy passes. High balls. No use then.'

'Yeah?'

'MS, see. Makes you clumsy.'

'Of course.'

'Bastard thing, MS. It can come to anyone. Any time.'

'Yeah, I guess so,' said Henry. 'Listen, there's the Ireland game in Cardiff on Saturday. I'm taking my daughter.'

'You got a daughter?'

'Karina. She's eleven. She loves the game, and I just happen to have a spare ticket. Her mum was going to come, but she doesn't want to now. Changed her mind, so do you want to come? There's no way we'll beat France in Paris next week, so the Ireland game's our only chance to miss the Wooden Spoon.'

'You workin' on a Saturday?'

'Not working, but that doesn't mean I can't take an old friend to a game of rugby does it?'

'Friend?'

'Why not?' Henry shrugged. 'I mean, if you'd like to come, and if Mrs Franken hasn't got plans for you both.'

'Tha' bitch,' Dan laughed. 'Haven't done nothin' together for fuckin' years.' His mouth looked like an old tin can with his few stained teeth rusty in pallid gums.

'She could probably do with a break from you, eh?'

'Yeah.'

'And you from her?'

'Sure.'

'So you'll come?'

'Righ',' Dan nodded. '2.30 kick off?'

'I'll be here by 10 and we'll get the train up.'

'Righ'.'

'And here we are,' said Henry as he pulled up outside Dan's new home.

'OK?' he asked, but Dan said nothing.

Chapter Three

7.00pm 23rd February 2007

Henry stood in the doorway of the Odyssey. It was seven in the evening and the wind raced up Wind Street. 'Hey, Gareth,' he said, watching the rain drip from his coat sleeves.

'Henry,' Gareth glanced towards him as he stapled an advertising poster to the board beside the door. 'Good to see you.'

'Nuclear Pussy,' Henry read. 'Any good?'

'Don't much matter if they are any good,' Gareth sighed. 'It's the name that'll bring them in. Some blokes'll hope it's literal. Anyway, three for two on spirits tonight, so we'll be busy no matter how shitty they are.'

'There'll be fighting and tears later for sure.'

'No doubt. Last week we had a McCartney tribute band in called Bingo Wings. Bunch of fatties who met at Weight Watchers. They were truly shite, but three for two on spirits, we were busy as fuck. That's when Jimmy Ullman got a hammering and now I'm short on door staff.'

Henry looked back out onto Wind Street. He wrapped a chewed piece of nicotine gum in a small piece of paper and dropped it into the bin by the door. He looked up at the neon sign. 'I kind of liked it more when it was still called Nog's, mind' he said.

'Me too,' said Gareth. 'Still, had to change the name to go with the change in everything else.' He stood next to Henry. They were both remembering Gareth's dad, Big Dave Turner who'd run Nog's for twenty years. 'I don't know how Dad made it pay. No idea. We had to make changes just to survive.'

Henry followed Gareth into the club, past the bar staff filling the fridges and the DJ, with oversized headphones looped beneath his chin, nodding in silence behind the decks. Three orange girls sat round a table, shivering over glasses of diet coke.

'Alright girls?' Henry called and Gareth laughed when they ignored him. 'Nuclear Pussy, right?' he asked and Gareth nodded. 'Class.'

When they got to the office, Gareth sat behind his desk and Henry slumped into the chair opposite. 'It's good of you to help me out,' Gareth said, tossing him a can of Red Bull. 'With Jimmy gone, I'm short on muscle.'

'It was a compliment,' Henry said. 'Good to feel needed.' He held the can away from himself as he popped the ring pull, slurping at the drink as it spewed over down the side. 'Flattering that you think an old git like me's worth his place on the door.'

'It's the only way I get you round for a chat, mate,' Gareth said. 'These days you never come in.'

'Well, you know,' Henry said. 'I never was much of a dancer and this isn't really a place for a quiet drink anymore. I'm sorry, mind.'

'It's been a while since we talked.'

'It's funny,' Henry signed. 'I always had a pint and a fag in a pub when I was out. The three things seem to need to go together, and then they stopped smoking in pubs, it's hard to sit still and have my hands idle. Anyway I'm chewing these nasty strips of muck now so everything tastes horrible. Even beer tastes grim so it's best to get as drunk as possible as fast as possible. Beer's OK and wine is fine, but liquor's quicker.'

'You could still come in for a word anyway, yeah?'

Henry laughed. 'Yeah, I should, and I will. It's nice to know you missed me.'

'I wouldn't go that far,' Gareth smiled.

Henry gestured towards the door. 'Nice new chairs out there I saw. You've tidied things up a bit.'

'It's 2007, mate. You need more of an upmarket feel if you're going to survive! I was amazed when the bank approved the loan. I never thought they would. Didn't think the figures were strong enough, but still...'

'First the stage and the DJ booth,' Henry laughed. 'Now new security cameras too.'

'Now those are dummies. Three for two at the Pound Shop,' Gareth grinned. 'You should go there, Henry boy. Bargains galore.'

'Can't say fairer than that,' Henry nodded. 'Now, how's your mum?'

'Better than ever,' Gareth stood up and stretched. 'We all are. It was tough getting her settled, but she's better off now than she was with us. Good advice that, mate.' He sat down, spun his chair and flipped on a kettle. 'You want a cuppa?'

'Just doing my job,' Henry nodded, grinning. 'Tea would be great. Red Bull's alright, but it's nothing on a cuppa.'

'Strong and milky?' Gareth asked.

'That's it. Got to support the farmers, right?' He took another slurp of the Red Bull, crushed the can and rested it on the edge of the desk. 'She's alright then, your mum, up at the Sancta Maria?'

'Hell, yeah. The nuns are top. They put on a good show; make a real fuss of all the old ones and they don't sedate them like they did at that other home; that first place your colleague suggested.'

'The Blessings?'

'Yeah. A proper dump. They had china mugs for staff and plastic beakers for the residents. Never sat right with me, that one.'

'I'm so sorry, mate,' said Henry. 'I hate to think of your mum in a place like that.'

Gareth waved him away. 'At least she had family to keep an eye out for her. It's those on their own that I worry about, but I guess it's up to folk like you to take care of all of them.'

'There are quite a lot of people on their own.'

'But Mum, yeah, she's happy now. And you'll never guess who's in the next room to her; David Kelman's mum. You remember him from school? He kicked the crap out of you a few times.'

'I remember,' Henry sighed. 'And yeah, I knew she was there.' But he didn't know where David Kelman was. Living rough up in Cardiff, someone had said, but no one really knew. He'd had a breakdown after his wife and son died in a house fire. David's mother had been living with them. Molly had Alzheimer's and David was her primary carer. One night Molly got out of bed, went to the kitchen and tried to roast some potatoes in a metal tray in a microwave. She wandered out into the garden to pick some daffodils and stood there in amazement looking back at the house as the microwave exploded, taking the ancient gas boiler and half the house with it. David had got out. He'd been asleep on the sofa downstairs, but his wife and four year old son were trapped upstairs.

Everyone had tried to help David, but one morning he went out for a walk from the sheltered unit he and his mother had been placed in, and he never came back. He was somewhere out there alone in the night. His mother was fine now. She was staying with the nuns up at the Sancta Maria, oblivious to pretty much everything.

Henry and Gareth had been in the same year at school as David. Not friends, exactly. It was funny how things work out. David had been much bigger than everyone else in their year. Bigger and harder. He was clever too, and Head Boy. He was that sort. He was going to conquer the world, and he had the warmest, kindest mother imaginable. And then... and now.

'Anyway,' Henry said. 'How about your brother? How's Dwayne? Is he coming to terms with his accident?'

'Doing alright. Well, no, actually. He's not doing too well. The little fucker's so angry since it happened that he's coiled tight all the time. Ready to go off like a sprung cobra or something. He's talking about getting another bike and... Fucking idiot,' Gareth sighed. 'He'll never ride a motorbike again, and he knows it. It makes him angry when he thinks of everything he's lost I guess.'

'Angry?' Henry asked and Gareth nodded. 'Right?'

'Drinking too much, too,' Gareth shrugged. 'Can't keep himself off the pop.'

'That's not going to help with his meds.'

'I don't know what we can do about it...' his voice trailed away as he saw a smile creep into Henry eyes. 'You got an idea?'

'Well, I'll have to have a think, but yeah, I might have.' He shifted in his seat. 'This anger is natural, see. Think of everything he had that he's lost, just like that.' He flicked his fingers.

'He doesn't come in here anymore. And he was always in here. Always after some girl. Now, nothing.'

'No interest in that? In sex and stuff?'

'The opposite. He talks about it all the time.' Gareth stood up to sort out the tea as the kettle came to the boil.

'Right. Well, mate. I'm no pimp or anything...'

'Right?'

'And it's all legal...'

'Oh yeah?'

'Yeah. There was this service that started in Australia and then some places in America to help people in Dwayne's situation. In Brighton too. It's sort of like a complementary therapy, I guess, but it's a bit unconventional. We Brits are a bit tight about sex. Best if I don't tell you too much until... Well, I need to have a chat with an old friend of ours. We'll see if it works out, alright?'

'OK,' Gareth laughed. 'You know what you're doing. Anyway, we'd better get a wriggle on.' He passed Henry a mug. 'You can leave your coat in here.'

'Got a shitty name tag for me?'

Gareth chuckled. 'And a fucking awful tie. They're behind the bar.'

'Delicious.'

'OK,' Gareth said. 'Just like old times, yeah?' He held out his hand. 'Thanks for doing this. For doing everything, mate.' Henry took his hand and Gareth pulled him into a hug.

'Get off, you big puff,' Henry said, laughing as he pushed him away. 'I'm glad to help, mate. Serious. I'm always glad to help.'

Chapter Four

9.30pm 23rd February 2007

'Alright, love?' Henry said, and that was how it started with Sadie. That was how it usually started.

Henry leant against the wall outside the Odyssey, watching her as she climbed out of her Mercedes, lithe limbed, orange hued. She glanced at him as she locked the doors. She saw the way he was looking at her, and nodded to herself.

'Alright,' she said. She smiled as she approached him; her dress a sheer silver sheath stretched taut across her thighs. He was lulled by the intoxicating swing of her hips, the fabric's smoothness against her body. 'Any good?' she asked, nodding towards the adverting hording behind him.

'Nuclear Pussy?' He drew a last, hot breath from his cigarette and sighed as he exhaled. He looked at the cigarette guiltily and dropped it at his feet. 'They're an Atomic Kitten tribute act.'

'And are they any good?'

'They have their attractions,' he said and she laughed. 'Their musical ability is not one of them. They're pretty much as shite as you'd expect them to be.'

'Tidy! Nice to know nothing changes round here.'

'Yeah,' he said. She smiled from her eyes, Henry noticed, and it was nice, and she didn't cross her arms as she faced him. There were people watching her; judging her, but she was used to it and she didn't care. It showed confidence that she could stand there like that, and that was nice too. She must be cold mind, Henry smiled, with just that slip on.

'You're a bouncer here?' she asked.

'Security, that's right,' he nodded, straightening his thin purple clip-on tie over his shiny black shirt. 'Wouldn't wear this get-up otherwise. Helping out a mate and tonight's the last night I ever do on any door I hope. I'm getting too old to stand around in the street in the middle of the night. Daytime I'm a social worker.'

'Yeah?' her eyes widened. 'Social worker?'

'Pays the bills, doesn't it,' he said and she laughed. 'I haven't seen you here before.'

'New back in town, me. Used to come here lots,' she glanced up at the building, 'when it was Nog's.' She looked up at the sign, eyes narrowed in the neon light; her face as enchanting as a pixie. 'Is the Odyssey any different to the Nog's?'

'A very different beast.'

'I wasn't really legal when I used to come in before.'

'Right?'

'I spent my sixteenth birthday minesweeping the dregs of other people's pints in there.'

'Good times.'

'Yeah,' she laughed. 'Bit old for a bouncer, you?'

'Some say,' Henry pressed his hands together in front of his chest, making his biceps bulge and his forearm muscles tighten like knotted rope. 'They don't say it twice, mind.'

'I'm Sadie,' she said, and she offered him her hand.

'Sadie with a Mercedes. Nice.' Her hand was tiny in his. 'Henry,' he said. 'Henry Antrim.' He patted his chest with his fingers. 'As it says right here on the name tag. Listen,' he leant towards her, lowering his voice. 'You've parked in a disabled bay there, love. People find their tyres let down if they park there when they shouldn't.'

She glanced at him and turned to face the car. 'Oh,' she said.

'Just thought I'd let you know,' he leant away from her.

'Right?' She looked back at him.

'You're not disabled or anything?' he asked.

'What d'you think?'

'No need for a mobility badge then, I guess?'

'No.'

'So what're you going to do about it?' he asked.

'What am I going to do about it?' her eyes widened.

'Well, I've warned you. The next move's yours.'

'Right,' her lips shone as she ran her tongue over them. She looked up at the bright orange light above the pub doorway; Odyssey spelt out in a tight Old English font. The neon shone in her eyes, on her lips, on her skin.

'Well, Henry Antrim. If someone was to let my tyres down while I was inside, would you help me change it later?'

He leant back against the wall, coughed a short laugh and said, 'I'd sooner you just move it now, love.'

'Would you?'

'Sooner you moved it? Yeah, I would.'

'No. I meant would you help me if I had a flat tyre?'

'Yeah, I'd help, but I'd sooner you just move it now.'

'Well I'd sooner you kept an eye on it and see to it that I didn't get a flat tyre.' She planted a kiss on the tips of her fingers and pressed it gently onto his lips. 'See you later then, Henry Antrim. I like the sound of Nuclear Pussy.'

'It's every man's dream,' said Henry as he watched her go. He slid his hands deep into the pockets of his jeans. 'Jeeze,' he whispered, rocking from one foot to the other. 'She must be freezing. She's hardly got anything on.'

Chapter Five

6.22pm 1st March 2007

Henry stood in the doorway of his flat. 'Don't worry mate,' he said as he turned back to face Dwayne. 'You look great.' Dwayne dabbed his cheek where seeping from his rheumy eye had left a salty trail. The briefest of smiles touched his cheeks and was gone. 'I'll be just out there in the car if you need me, right.' He came back into the room, rested his hand on his friend's shoulder. 'I mean, you won't need me, but if you do, I'll be there anyway. OK?'

'I just come to the window,' said Dwayne.

'That's it. And I'll be right up.'

'OK,' Dwayne nodded.

'OK.' Henry looked up at the clock on the wall. 'Right. I'd better get a wriggle on.' He nodded towards the kitchen. 'All that lot should be ready in ten minutes or so.'

'OK.'

'And you'll wash up after?'

'Yeah,' Dwayne's hand came to his cheek again. 'Pans and everything.' He ran his finger beneath his eye, smiled and scratched his ear. 'And when it's all over I'll change the sheets. Put them in the machine and turn it on. I got it, Henry. I got it.

'Good,' said Henry. 'I'll be off to get her then.'

'And you'll be at the window, Henry?'

'No, I'll be in the car,' said Henry. 'If you need me, you come to the window.'

'Yeah. Right,' Dwayne said, frowning as he nodded. 'And I'll change the sheets after.'

Mansell Street was busy as Henry eased the Doblo along it. He pulled over outside the tattoo parlour and checked the time. In his mirror he looked back up the road at the pebble-dashed buildings. In a moment he saw the narrow door open, and a girl stepped out into the street. She waved as she fumbled with her key and then she bounced along the pavement towards the car. She had her dark hair tied back in a pony tail, wore a tight cream singlet, tidy jeans and pink Converse trainers. With her olive skin and large almond eyes, she used to look like a young Cheryl Tweedy. Nowadays she looked more like Cheryl Tweedy's mum. But anyway, there was nothing intimidating about her. She looked like a woman who might live next door. Not like a hooker at all.

Henry reached across and opened her door. 'Hey Maddie,' he said. 'You're looking good.'

She swung her bag onto the back seat, leant towards him and kissed his cheek. She smelt warm and clean and lavendery.' You think I'll do?'

'You'll do fine.'

'Not too much, you know?'

'Just right.' Henry checked the mirror and pulled out into the road.

'How's Dwayne doing?' Maddie asked. She flipped down the sun shade, checked her mascara in the mirror.

'Better,' Henry nodded. 'Off the pop, pretty much. Sticking to his meds.' He turned right onto Craddock Street joining the rush hour as it trundled through town. There used to be a cinema here, he thought. I saw Swallows and Amazons with my mum. It was derelict now. Large white walls and boarded up doors. He shook away the reverie. 'Yep, we're quite positive about him just now,' he said.

'Excellent.' Maddie flipped the shade back up and clapped.

'He's got something to save for now, see,' said Henry. 'He's decided it's a waste if he goes on blowing all his cash on beer.'

'Oh, yeah?' Maddie said looking at Henry, and when he winked she said, 'Oh. I see. Right.' She was shy suddenly and blushed.

'Anyway, you'll see when you see him.' Henry stopped the car at the Union Street traffic lights. 'How's Tina doing?'

'Well, thanks,' and Maddie smiled the smile of a proud mother. 'I don't get to see her much, but she's doing well. She's on work experience at the hospital. They think she's really bright. She's cleverer than I'll ever be.'

'Nice one,' Henry laughed. 'My Karina thinks the world of her,' and they discussed parenthood and compared worries for their teenage daughters in the not so pleasant world.

Henry wound the Doblo through the one-way system back up to his flat, pulling up smoothly outside. 'Right,' he said and turned towards her. 'I don't want to sound weird or anything, Maddie, but we really appreciate this, you know.'

'It's my job, innit,' Maddie said looking up at the building.

'I mean it.'

'Yeah, I know. Right, so it's like last time, then. Meal and drink and off to bed?'

'That's it.'

'Nothing too... you know. Wild.'

'That's it,' Henry said. 'The basic girlfriend experience.'

'And you'll be here...'

'Yep, if you need me. If he freaks or anything I'll be here. Smoking cigarettes and watching Captain Kangaroo on my laptop.'

'OK,' she nodded.

'And I'll give you a lift home about ten, OK.'

'Right.' Maddie rubbed her hands together and smiled. 'Well, best get into character.' She reached into the back of the car for her bag and winked at Henry. 'Funny old way to make a living, eh?'

Henry eased his seat back so he could look up at the window without moving his head. He had his laptop leant up against the steering wheel and was wandering through Amazon and Yahoo and eBay, picking up the unprotected Wi-Fi signal from one of his neighbour's houses.

'Jeeze, this is boring,' he muttered, wondering how people killed hours surfing the web. He Googled 'Missing Persons Wales' and scanned through the images. He tapped in Girls

Aloud and wondered quietly at just how much the young Maddie had looked like Cheryl Tweedy.

There was no movement up at the window. No sign of either one of them coming to him for help. It was real up there. Real life happening in the safety of his room. Henry looked away from the house, across the road and out to sea. It was too dark to see anything, but it was good to know the sea was there.

Years ago Henry had gone sea kayaking with Dwayne and Gareth and a few others. Maddie's brother Herby was there too. There was a whole gang of them. They'd gone paddling around the coves and ending up on the shore of some beach along the Gower. They'd had a big fire and shared bigger talk with their plans to change the world. Live forever or die trying. There was too much beer, of course, and they woke up with thumping heads as the tide soaked their sleeping bags, but what a night. We were kids then, Henry thought.

Some of the boys were still around, though their lives had changed and their plans hadn't worked out quite the way they'd hoped. Gareth had worked in his dad's pub from school and had never left Wales. Dwayne had been a beacon of optimism before he was knocked off his motorbike by an off-duty policeman. It was a quiet Tuesday afternoon in March and he was waiting at the zebra crossing in the Uplands. The policeman had dozed off behind the wheel of his car after a string of sixteen-hour shifts. Dwayne's dad collapsed when he heard, dying up in Singleton Hospital soon afterwards, and Dwayne's brain was irreparably damaged. A.B.I. – Acquired Brain Injury. A life-changing diagnosis wound up in a three letter acronym.

Henry signed. 'If we'd known then what we know now,' he muttered as he leant back and looked up at the window. Now Dwayne was up there paying for sex with a girl who was saving to get her daughter through nursing college so she wouldn't end up living above a shitty barber on Mansell Street.

They'd all been at school together: Henry, Gareth, Dwayne, Herby and the others, different years some of them, but all part of one big gang. 'Jesus. If we'd known then...'

He looked back at the house just as Maddie opened the door, came down the steps and climbed into the car beside him.

Silently she jammed her bag down into the foot well and reached for the seatbelt.

Henry snapped his laptop shut and slipped it down into the gap between his seat and the door. 'OK?' he asked as he started the car.

'Yeah,' Maddie nodded. 'It was OK,' she said and fell silent.

'There was this story on Yahoo about Jasper Carrot and Condoleezza Rice,' Henry said a bit later to fill the silence. 'I read it just now.' It was all a bit awkward now, sitting there: just the two of them. 'Did you hear about it?' He glanced at Maddie and she shook her head. 'Jasper Carrot's a Brummie, right, and she's from Birmingham, Alabama, and when they were young they met at a youth orchestra exchange thing for the two Birminghams. She plays piano and he's a guitarist. Apparently they went out for a bit, dating, and he wanted to marry her, but it didn't go anywhere.' He slowed along Mansell Street looking for a parking spot. 'Yahoo said the main reason was that she didn't want to be Condoleezza Carrot.'

'Same thing happened to Whoopie Goldberg,' said Maddie, deadpan. 'She had a thing with Gerard Depardieu in the '60s. It went wrong because Whoopie didn't want to be Whoopie DoopieDoo.'

'I had not heard that,' Henry nodded. 'I had not heard that.'

He pulled into the same parking space as before and Maddie lingered before getting out.

He reached for the glove box and took out an envelope. 'Here you go,' he said.

'You know it's funny,' Maddie said. 'I understand all the stuff about how damaged his head is and how he needs this time with me to rebuild his sense of self worth and all that, but...'

'Yeah?'

'Well,' Maddie nodded, 'thanks.' She took the envelope, got out of the car and walked round to Henry's side. He wound down the window and she leant against the door. 'I'm just glad I could help. It's not really about the money with him,' she said. 'It's funny. I really fancied Dwayne, you know, when we were kids. I used to daydream about kissing him before I'd ever kissed anyone.' She looked up as a police car flew past with its siren blaring. 'I never said anything then because he was one of the cool kids with his motorbikes and everything, and me, I never felt there was anything about me. That I was nothing special, you know?' She smiled. 'If I'd known then that I'd be shagging him like this now, well... Real life is a funny thing.' She leant in the car window and kissed Henry's cheek. She no longer smelt of lavender.

'Funny old thing,' Henry smiled. 'Life!'

'I used to fancy you too, mind, Henry. Did you know that?' she winked and turned away. 'Still do.'

'I'll see you, Maddie,' Henry laughed. 'And thanks.'

Maddie raised her arm as she walked away into the darkness.

Chapter Six
7.00pm 5th March 2007

'There's one thing I love about snow,' Karina leant forward in the car, resting her forehead against the cool glass of the windscreen. With narrowed eyes she watched the driving rain sparkle in the streetlights as it fell, puddle surfaces dappled and growing. 'It's proof that God's got a sense of humour.' She glanced at Henry who smiled back at her.

Henry was giving her a lift from somewhere to somewhere else. He couldn't remember where unless he really, really focused. 'It's not actually snowing though, is it,' he said. Playing taxi was about the only time he saw her these days.

'And also,' Karina continued, 'when people write about snow being silent as it falls, it's rubbish. Snow doesn't fall silently.'

'It doesn't?'

'No of course not. Pretty much every single flake loves being snow, yelling "Weeeee" like some overexcited Olga da Polga guinea pig. Some of them are terrified, going "Ahhhhh, I'm falling," but most of them think it's the coolest thing being snow.'

'And what about the rain,' Henry asked. 'What noise does rain make?'

'Well, the rain drops are weeping, obviously. Sobbing. Those drops don't want to be rain. They want to be snow. They want to hang out with the cool kids.'

'Of course.'

'Yes, snow's way cooler than rain.'

Henry laughed. 'I really miss you,' he said.

'Me too,' Karina said.

They were quiet for a while then Henry asked, 'How's it going at the radio station?'

'Good,' Karina said. 'Best work placement there is. Least it should be. Most of the people are great and we're learning loads, but some of the presenters are right knobs,' she laughed, though there was no warmth in it. 'Innuendos all the time, and you know Will Nixon?'

'The lad in your class with Down's Syndrome?'

'Yeah, well he's there with us and a few of the radio people keep taking the piss out of him.'

'Doesn't he have support staff with him?'

'He does, but...'

'Not that good?'

She shook her head. 'Two women and they spend most of the time flirting with the presenters. It's a pretty shitty show really.'

Henry slowed, pulling up against the curb. 'Remind me why we are here,' he said, and she mumbled something he couldn't hear or couldn't focus on.

Karina got out of the car and came round to Henry's window. 'Are you alright, Dad?' she asked.

'I'm fine,' he said.

'Really?

'Ah, well, you know. Things don't always work out quite how you hope. I mean,' he looked past her at a big building that he recognised, but couldn't place. 'When I was young my dad walked out, leaving me and my mum. Mum was a brilliant mum even though she was ill, but I needed a dad. Everyone needs a dad.' He felt his eyes begin to prickle. 'When I was young I said if I was ever a dad then I was going to be a great dad in a great family.' He shook his head. 'It didn't work out like that.'

'You are a great dad, Dad,' Karina held his arm, 'and Mum is a great mum. You two just don't get on, that's all. It's better for everyone that you don't live together.' She leant in and kissed his cheek. 'I don't remember the last time I saw you happy.'

'Happy?' Henry mumbled.

'Man up, Dad. Come to terms with it and move on. OK?'

'Move on?'

'You're no fun when you're moping around.'

'I'll try,' Henry nodded.

'Good. Now, I'm off to see Father Whatsisname. I'll be back in about an hour, OK?'

'OK,' Henry smiled, 'I'll be here,' and he remembered where they were and why they were there and that the big church behind her was the one in which he and Paula were married. They'd both been christened there, and Karina too. 'See you in a bit,' Henry said as he watched her skipping through the puddles and up to join the other youngsters gathered under the overhang outside the presbytery doors for the anger management session.

Chapter Seven

9.30pm March 11th 2007

'I could easily fall in love with you,' Henry said. They were naked in his bed, Henry on his back and Sadie lying on top of him, her cheek against his chest, listening to his heart, playing thoughtlessly with the coarse hairs growing low down on his stomach.

'That's nice,' said Sadie.

'Nice,' Henry laughed. 'Well that's not the word I was hoping for.' They'd spent the day down on the Jersey Marine wandering around, scoping a potential site for the business she planned to start up, Henry taking Dan along for the ride.

'What were you hoping I'd say?'

'Oh, I don't know.' Henry reached for the glass of wine on the chair beside the bed. 'Maybe that you feel the same? Maybe that you can't get enough of me because I'm hung like a bull elephant and sex with me is the best you've ever had?'

Sadie took the glass, looking up at him as she took a sip. 'Well the last bit might be true.' She smiled as she took another mouthful and handed back the glass. 'But bull elephant? Mmm? You've got to remember that size isn't everything.' He laughed as she ran her hand down his belly and away beneath the sheet. 'But then again...?'

'I mean it,' Henry said later. His voice lazy, drugged with sex. 'About falling in love.'

Sadie rested her chin on her hands and looked up at him, her small, soft breasts warm against his stomach. 'What do you want me to say? That I love you too? Or that I might soon?' She shook her head. 'I can't do that, Henry.'

'Don't matter,' Henry shrugged. 'You will.' His head contentedly groggy. 'There's time.'

'Time?'

'Yeah, time. No hurry, is there? You'll fall in love with me, no doubt about it. I'm a legend, me. You'll feel more for me than you've ever felt for anyone. You'll...'

'Ah, Henry,' Sadie sighed. She reached up and brushed his cheek with her finger tips. 'We've spoken about this.'

'This?'

'Yeah. This; feelings and, really, the reason I came back to Wales.'

'Ah,' Henry nodded. 'That.'

'Yeah. That. You've got to remember that I've just left London,' she frowned. 'It's a horrible place where everyone's a stranger, even your friends are strangers. And you've got to remember why I left. A place like that makes you cold.' She nodded towards the window. 'It's not like Swansea, London isn't. It's lush here compared with there.' She curled away from him, sitting up and pulling the sheet around her shoulders. 'On top of that, I did ten years in an industry where everyone's a liar and no one tells you how they feel about anything,' she clenched her fist. 'Not how they really feel. They're so false in the media.' Her face twisted into sneer. 'You become used to it, part of it; the bullshit. It changes people. You have to fit in to survive, or you'll never get anywhere.' She glanced away and then back at Henry with eyes lowered. 'I don't like what it did to me.'

Henry reached up to her. He cupped her elbow and drew her back down on top of him. 'It's alright, love,' he said. 'Tough Swansea girl like you; I'm sure you're still sound inside.'

But Sadie shook her head. 'I'm damaged, Henry.' She rested her cheek against his chest again and closed her eyes. 'There's my marriage too.'

'Robbie,' Henry hissed through clenched teeth.'

'Robbie. I've just left a man who cheated on me I don't know how many times.' Her hand came to her eyes. 'I only found out at all when I read about it in someone else's Mirror over their shoulder in the Underground. There was a picture of him with that whore stumbling out of a tacky club in Slough, and then her exclusive thoughts about the thrill of secret sex with a married man.' She sighed and reached across Henry, stretching for the ashtray on the chair. 'I'm damaged goods, Henry, I told you.' She pressed the joint into his mouth, holding it there as she lit it. 'Damaged, and you've got to see I'm in no position to talk about my feelings. I don't know what they are anymore. I can't talk about anything linked to emotions at all.'

Henry puffed on the joint, the smoke clouding above the bed. He ran his fingers slowly from her slender pale neck down her back, lingering at the base below the paper-panty spray-tan line, where her spine dipped away into the shadows between her buttocks.

'It's not you, it's me, see,' Sadie said, wriggling up onto her elbows to look at him again. 'I'm dead inside. I don't really feel anything about anything.'

'Nothing?' Henry said with a puff of smoke. He held the joint to her lips, watching as she took a few short, shallow breaths. 'You seemed to be feeling quite a lot, you know, just now.'

'It's different in bed with you,' she grinned. 'What's a woman to do but lie back and lose it? It's transcendental.'

'I am one hell of a guy,' Henry nodded.

'Away from bed it's different. I don't know why. I feel indifferent,' she pulled a face. 'It's a shame really,' she said and laughed. 'I just feel numb.'

'And earlier on, out with Dan down at your factory site. We had a laugh didn't we? You must have felt that was fun?'

'I suppose so,' she said, her expression hardening.

'Moody bugger isn't he? I reckon he was jealous of you.'

'Jealous of me?'

'Yeah, you being there when it's usually just the two of us on trips out. He didn't like it to start with. Didn't like sharing me with you.'

'Sharing you? I didn't even know he was coming,' Sadie's tone was serious. 'It was supposed to be our trip; yours and mine. Our trip to look at my site. Dan should have felt like the gooseberry, not me.'

'Don't know about that, but he warmed to you. We had a laugh in the end; the three of us, didn't we?'

'I suppose so,' said Sadie. 'In the end.'

'And are you happy, love? Do you feel happy?'

'Happy?'

Yeah, happy. Right now. This moment. Are you happy?'

'Yeah, I guess so, but...'

'But?

'Alright, I'm happy Henry, OK,' she pulled herself up and kissed his mouth. 'I've warned you about where I am in my head, mind. Please don't push me for definitions. No promises. We'll just see how it goes.' She pulled back away from him, knees against his side and she smiled. 'I'm here naked in your bed with you, aren't I? Isn't that an indication of something?'

Chapter Eight

9.30am 14th March 2007

'WHY YOU GRINNING?'

Henry winked at Dan. He said nothing as he bent low in front of Dan's chair, fumbling with the laces on his shoes.

'THAT GIRL IS IT?' Dan said.

'Could be, big man.' Henry stood up. 'Right. Bag drained, shoes done, hat on, coat on and all gloved up. Ready for off, yeah? Quick in and out at the hossie, yeah?'

'YOU THINK YOU LOVE HER?' Dan's face was still, eyes narrowed, and he made no sound as he typed out the words.

'Nice and polite for the doctor. A routine this and that check up, yeah? You promise, yeah?'

'YOU DO?' Dan repeated, cold and steady.

'I was expecting you to take the piss, not be grumpy, mate,' Henry crouched down beside him. 'What's up?' Dan shrugged, saying nothing, just looking at him. 'OK. We'll talk about it later, OK? Cathy's ready, best get going.'

Cathy closed the door on Sal and walked ahead of them down to the pavement. She'd opened the back of Henry's Fiat Doblo and lowered the ramp ready for Dan. She smiled as she watched Henry leaning on the back of Dan's chair, resting his weight on the handlebars with his feet off the ground as he freewheeled down the path. 'Weeeeee,' Henry said as he swung the chair to a halt beside the car.

'STOP DICKING AROUND,' said Dan.

'Sorry,' Henry laughed.

'SCARED THE SHIT OUT OF ME.'

'Who's been programming this thing,' Henry tapped the type/talk machine. 'Hell of a site more stuff on there now.'

'It's one of the carer girls,' said Cathy. She took Dan's bag as Henry slid Dan up the ramp into the back of the car. 'Marcia, I think.' She reached round Dan to press his keys. 'You don't mind, do you?' she asked and Dan grinned. 'She thought it would be funny to change "HELLO" to "WAZZUP". That sort of thing.'

'So long as Dan's OK with it,' Henry said, exaggerating his accent. 'Dim problem, boys bach.'

'It's a bit annoying actually,' said Cathy, 'especially in public. Dan doesn't seem to mind, though.'

'No, I don't suppose he does,' said Henry.

'She spent a whole evening on it. Nice girl, Marcia. Very funny. She doesn't take any trouble from Dan either.'

'Good lass.'

'She's a pretty girl too,' Cathy said. 'Catholic.' She winked at Henry, glancing down at Dan's hands as he started typing. 'In her thirties, mind. Carlo said she might be a bit old for you.'

Henry smiled. He set back on his haunches. He'd just fixed Dan's restraints and checked the wheelchair for stability. 'Well she sounds dandy,' he said, 'but...'

'LOVES HER,' said Dan.

'I was just about to say that,' said Henry. 'I was just about to...'

'THINKS HES IN LOVE.'

'Oh Henry, I'm so pleased,' said Cathy. She took his arm as he closed the back of the Doblo.

'I'll tell you all about it later,' Henry laughed. 'We've got to get on and there's never any parking at the hospital. I'll tell you all about her over a cuppa after.'

'I park up here, round the back,' Henry said as they neared the hospital. 'Hopefully it won't be too busy.'

Once they'd found a space, Henry crawled into the back of the Doblo, fumbling with Dan's brackets as he released his chair and Cathy eased him out of the car.

Beneath the concrete canopy outside the hospital's main entrance, Henry nodded to a couple of the pyjama-clad, long-term patients he recognised who were huddling by the doorway. Plumbed into drips at one end and catheter bags at the other, they slumped in tatty, brown wheelchairs, sucking on cigarettes, jabbering into mobile phones.

Henry watched Dan's hands clenching the armrests of his chair as they entered the hospital. 'ONLY EVER GET BAD NEWS IN HOSPITAL,' he'd typed earlier. Anxiety tensed his body, his wasted neck muscles taut above his collar.

'Don't be such a pussy, mate,' Henry murmured. 'You'll be in and out in a moment,' but Dan just growled.

The gift shop in the entrance foyer was full of people buying cheap and cheerful stuffed animals and flowers for newly born children and their mothers upstairs. Next door to the gift shop was the subdued office of the bereavement counsellor. Further down the hall, a sign reminded visitors that abuse or threatening behaviour of any kind towards staff would not be tolerated.

'When I started coming to these places they were so different,' Cathy said as they waited for the lift. Her tone was reverential. 'I remember visiting my granny when I was a girl. Hospitals were much more personable then.' She reached to tap the lift call button. 'It wasn't like The Royal on television. Nothing that twee, but at least it felt friendly.'

Henry watched her as she spoke. She seemed so much older than before Helen had died, as she hunched deep into her coat. The last years with Helen had really aged her. The lift doors opened with a creak and a ping.

'SHIT PLACE,' said Dan.

'Alright, fighter,' said Henry. 'Keep your hair on.' He moved round in front of Dan, squatted down to eye level. 'It's hospital, Dan, right. Rules is rules. These are good people; the folk on the wards I mean, nurses and that.' He lowered his voice and frowned. 'Remember - abuse or threatening behaviour of any kind towards staff will not be tolerated. They'll kick you out on your arse.'

Dan laughed. 'ALRIGHT,' he said.

They sat with half a dozen others in the waiting room, looking at the posters and avoiding eye contact. Then Henry's mobile phone rang.

'Oh shit,' he muttered, glancing at Cathy. 'Sorry. Excuse the language. Forgot to turn the bugger off.' He fumbled through his pockets as he left the waiting room. A few minutes later he came back. 'I've got to go, guys,' he said. 'My boss has called me in. Emergency meeting about something.'

'A meeting with the Director?' said Cathy. 'Should we be worried?'

'I'm not,' Henry shrugged. 'Don't see why you should be. He's probably forgotten how to do up his zipper. He's not the brightest.' He threw her his car keys. 'I'll get a bus into town and come by your place to pick it up later on.' He knelt down in front of Dan. 'Alright, big man,' he said. 'You'll be fine, OK? Just some tests, same as ever.' Dan stared at him; frightened, shrunken tiny by his illness. 'You're still on a plateau, right,' Henry took his arm. 'Nothing's changed from last year. You know that. You'd already know if anything had changed. You'd know ahead of anyone; ahead of any of these tests. This is just routine, OK? Don't worry mate,' he said and Dan nodded weakly.

Henry stood up and turned to Cathy. 'Sorry about this,' he said. 'You need anything in town, just phone me, alright?'

He stopped in the doorway and turned back to them, pinching his nose. 'Smell you later, yeah,' he said, and with a wave, he was gone.

Chapter Nine

11.45am 14th March 2007

'Well, look at you. Shiftiness impersonated.' Carlo smiled. He leant against the wall to the left of the County Hall entrance, cup of coffee in one hand and a rolled up copy of the Western Mail under his arm. 'Here you are striding in like you're going to dust some ass.'

Henry stopped and shook his hand. 'I just been with your wife,' he said. 'Taking Dan up to the hozzie. He's got an appointment, you remember?'

'I been watching you;' Carlo said, wincing as Henry squeezed his hand so tight that his knees buckled. 'I saw you getting off the bus, wandering across the car park. Watching you at the Director's car. Sloping up there all sneaky, like.' He blew on his hand, nodding and pointing at Henry. 'You been a bad boy? You done a bad thing?'

'Any evidence, Mr Union Man?'

'There are cameras there, there and there,' Carlo pointed.

'Barney on the gate says they've been out for months. Cutbacks see. Maintenance falls behind senior management salary increases when it comes to priorities. They're going up by 43% from April and have to be paid for somehow. Anyway, you didn't actually see me do anything, did you? Anything more than bending down to tie my shoelaces?'

Carlo shook his head, blowing on his knuckles to cool the pain. 'Well,' he said. 'In the absence of a witness or any photographic evidence, I've got no proof it was you tampering with the Director's Bentley.'

'Shouldn't park in a disabled bay, should he,' said Henry. 'Rules is rules. Same for everyone, prince or pauper.'

'So what d'you do? Key him?' Henry shook his head. 'Let his tyres down?' He laughed to see Henry's grin. 'No way?'

'Anyway, what about you?' Henry asked. 'Why are you up here on a rainy Monday? Defending the rights of some local hero?'

'I'm here in my official union capacity, making sure the deadwood doesn't get taken by the tide.'

'Keeping it real. Great.'

'Only the guy never showed up,' Carlo sighed. 'He's gone on long term sick as of this morning. Bleeding cliché.'

'Aren't we all,' Henry nodded, 'after a while.' He tapped his chest. 'Self confessed dope-head social worker here. You've got to be able to switch off somehow.'

Carlo laughed. 'I'm supposed to be representing your line manager; Dick Brytten. Well, I would be if he was here.'

'Brytten?' said Henry. 'That would explain why I've been called in by the Director.'

'I phoned his wife at work just now and she said he wasn't coming. Great job this. Fighting for other people's rights? Wasting my own life, more like,' he shrugged. 'Brytten's in the poop for double claiming his travel expenses.'

'He was about as much use as the Pope's balls. None of us will be sad to see the back of him.'

'But why should I defend him?' Carlo shook his head. 'He did it, and he admits he did it, but your boss didn't follow the correct protocols when it came to sacking him so he appealed and was suspended on full pay pending investigation, and here I am, four months on, waiting for the twat to turn up.'

'Wow,' Henry murmured.

'Yeah, and the best thing about it is that Brytten's wife is the Chief Executive's goddaughter so he's keeping a close eye on what's happening. I reckon it was him that suggested the sick leave scam anyway and maybe that the Director messed up the procedures on purpose just to help him.'

'What with the stress of the appeal, I bet he'd have a good case for long-term sick leave. Bloody hell! We've got a lot of really good people in here, but we all get tarnished by this crap.'

'And I'll have to hold his hand helping him through it,' Carlo rolled his eyes. 'If he ever gets here. He could be on full pay through sick leave for months, depending how gullible his doctor is.'

'And I bet his doctor plays golf with the Chief Exec, right?'

'And with the Director on Sunday mornings. Clichés, the lot of them. I've seen them up there. Henry, it's like this day after day. Groundhog Day. What was I thinking when I took this job? Don't these idiots see how lucky they are? It's a job for life so long as we don't mess it up too badly. It's nearly impossible to sack a council worker if they're crap. Crapness is acceptable, so long as they don't break the law.'

'Twentieth century Britain, mate,' said Henry. 'New Labour, eh? Though I shouldn't think the Tory's will be much better.'

'You're going in for a meeting with Korkenhasel?'

'The Director. Sure am. Looks like I'm in for an interim promotion type of thing. I've been called into a meeting, but I don't know what for. If Brytten's off on long-term sick, and they've got to keep paying him, it means there's no fresh money in the budget to employ anyone new to do his job. So I guess in the absolute absence of anyone else Korkenhasel is going to tell me how delighted he is to offer me the senior social worker job, with all that it entails.'

'More work, no more money?'

'Same as it ever was.' He reached to open the door. 'How about we go fishing sometime, like we used to, yeah. Just you and me. How d'you fancy it?'

'I'd like it,' Carlo's face broke into a grin. 'Yeah! Just like when we were students. You bring the smokies and we'll forget about all this nonsense. Talk about real life and stuff. I'd like that a lot.'

'And Cathy'd be OK with it?'

'She'd be fine.'

'I got this girl, see, Sadie. I want to tell you all about her,' Henry beamed. 'She's a honey.'

'Oh yeah?' Carlo laughed.

'I think she could be a keeper.'

'Nice one,' Carlo nodded. 'That's brilliant.' Then he took Henry's arm. 'Hang on mate, how old is she?'

'How old? What's her age got to do with anything? She's legal if that's what you're asking?'

Carlo shook his head. 'Just asking. No reason.'

'She's twenty-seven.'

'That would be right.' Carlo said. 'And you're what? Forty?'

'I'm thirty nine, same as you. What of it?'

'Nothing, Henry,' he grinned. 'I didn't mean anything. Just asking, that's all.'

'Tell me, Carlo,' Henry asked. 'Do you still play golf?'

Carlo nodded. 'Yeah. Sometimes. Why? You want to play?'

'Me?' Henry chuckled. 'Shit, no. I whack a ball like Happy Gilmore. They'd never let me on the ground.'

'Ground?' Carlo laughed. 'In golf it's called a course.'

'Whatever,' Henry pointed at Carlo's newspaper. 'Have a look at the jobs section. The Head of Human Resources job just came up. If you're still playing golf and shake the right hands up there, you'd have it in the bag.'

'I saw the advert. Hundred and fourteen plus car. And not just any car. The Director got a Bentley as his "plus car".'

'That's what makes letting his tyres down such fun.'

'I can see that,' Carlo nodded as he opened the paper, 'but you're having a laugh if you think I'm the man for that one.'

'You might not have the boarding-school old-boy bum-chum network to help you, but you've better qualifications than most of them and a truck load more experience. You probably know most of the Executive Committee from the golf club. Funny handshake, round of daisy-chains, call in a few favours, whatever. You'll have it in the bag.'

Carlo peered at him quizzically. 'Yeah?' and then he laughed. 'I'm don't really play that sort of game.'

'The only way to change the system is to get good, courageous people with bollocks the size of cannonballs on the inside. You'd have to dine with the devil to get there, but as long as the devil pays for the drinks, where's the harm, right?'

'Yeah, but me?'

'Someone's got to do it.'

'Someone's got to do it,' Carlo echoed, his nose in the paper. 'I suppose that's true.'

'Well, see you later mate,' said Henry. 'Keep your pecker up, eh. Flowers are expensive. Don't want to see you in a box."

'Yeah. I'll see you later,' said Carlo as he read the advert again.

Chapter Ten

7.30am 7th April 2007

Henry woke as stiff as the chair he'd slept in. He rubbed his eyes with his knuckles knowing it would take more than that to numb the pain. His vision blurred as he peeled his cheek from the window.

'You're the most caring man I've ever met and I wish I'd never met you,' Sadie said. It was her opening the door that had woken him. 'There's something about you. It's either your work, or it's the drugs; but you're addicted to it anyway. There are two people in a relationship, Henry, and I thought I was meant to be one of them.' She stood in the doorway of Henry's flat, red raincoat tight at the waist, bare legs and flat soled shoes. 'It's fucking you up, and I can't stand to be anywhere near you.' She had sunglasses on, and her hair was pulled back, hanging in a ponytail down her back. And she told him she was leaving.

Henry mumbled his way to his feet, a charming stumble-drunk in his head, but a grave disappointment in hers. He held his hands wide as he pleaded, but she turned away.

'Do you know what these last few weeks have been like for me?' she asked. She controlled her voice with effort. 'What it's like living with you? You're never here, and even when you are, you're not really. Your mind is always somewhere else, thinking about someone else. You've no idea what it's like. What you've put me through.'

'I can see it in your eyes. Well, I could if I could see your eyes,' he gestured at her sunglasses.

'And?'

'And?'

'Ah, forget it.' She began to turn away but he took her arm.

'And? What do you want me to say?' he asked as she shook off his grasp. 'I just woke up.'

She ground her teeth and pulled the door closed. He listened to her footsteps as she crossed the landing and then he turned back to the window.

'How long will you be?' Sadie had asked him the night before, just before he went out.

'Six foot three from the top to the bottom.'

'What?'

'You asked, and I answered.' He looked for her smile, but she'd turned her back on him.

'How long,' her voice was colder now.

'Oh, ah, a couple of hours, I guess. Me and the boys, you know, from work. Phil, Winston, Paul, Johnny and the others. Bit of bonding. Now Dick Brytten's gone and I'm the Senior Social Worker, I'm their line manager. Meant to be a team. They're a good gang, and dedicated, most of them, but there ain't much team spirit around. I'll be a couple of hours, might be a bit more. Alright? I'll see you later, crocodile.' As he bent to kiss her, she flinched from his touch, and her skin felt different.

He didn't notice it then; the way she'd moved back from him oh so slightly, but he thought about it later.

Later, much, much later, with his forehead pressed to the window, shot glass in one hand, bottle on the floor between his feet, and a carefully watched joint smoking away between his knuckles, a million thoughts pinged round in his head.

Henry took a drag, watching the paper at the tip flaring away to nothing. He drank, and he smoked and he thought back to the beginning.

'Alright love...' Henry said, and that's how it had started. That was how it usually started.

Sadie had been on a bender the night they met. Newly separated from some TV guy; just back from London and she'd come home rich. She'd spent the day on a retail-high, new dress, new tan, new shoes even, and then a night out with the girls from home, showing them just how well she'd done for herself.

Henry was working. He was a man in a shiny black shirt with a name tag on it. It didn't matter who he was; anyone would have done for her that night. She'd had a flat tyre and he'd helped her change it, and then he drove her home.

She kissed him to thank him right there in her ex-husband's car. Then there was a clumsy fumble that turned into a rumble in the backseat, and all too quickly she'd moved into his small flat on Bryn Road overlooking the sea and St Helen's rugby field. She'd been living with her mum in the Uplands since she came back. Her mum lived on the posh-side of Eaton Crescent; the seaward side. It was quarter of a mile from Bryn Road, but a million miles higher in social status.

And just a few weeks later Sadie knew all there was to know about Henry: that he drank too much, smoked too much, went to work in the same vest he'd slept in, and that he was obsessed by his job.

She knew all of that, and the fact that she was not born to play second fiddle.

Last night Henry had gone for a drink with some of the lads from work. They'd gone to a pub where he knew everyone and everyone knew him. He had a drink and a laugh and a look around. Then they went to a club where he saw this young woman, over there, by the bar, that's the one. She was young looking, too young to get into a place like this unless she'd promised the doorman a favour later. She was pretty too, in an available sort of a way. Her dress could have passed as a nightdress; chiffon or something. It was a look Henry liked, but then he recognised this young woman as Tina, Maddie's daughter: his fifteen-year-old daughter's best friend from school, and he was angry then. With himself for looking, angry with the lads for laughing and angry with her for being there when she was just a young girl and should have been tucked up in bed at home listening to Hannah Montana or, if she'd been anything like Karina, Kiss or Metallica or Lynryd Skynryd on one of Henry's old LPs.

Henry took her arm and she shrugged him off. One of the bouncers came over, a slimy kid; the kind so manicured you want to vomit. 'Fuck off, Granddad,' the kid said. 'Hands off her, right. She's not interested. I'm warning you.' Five foot nothing and more tattoos than brains. A white man with dreadlocks and the smell of a woman's boutique.

Henry smiled. He made a joke about rolling up his sleeves for trouble and found himself flat on his back with fewer teeth than he came in with. Five foot nothing this kid was, but he was quicker on his feet than Shane Williams: a right twinkle toes.

From the ground everyone had looked huge. Henry's vision tarnished as the room span. He'd smiled again as he stood up and tried to explain. Spitting out teeth, he'd looked for his mates, the lads from work, but they'd faded away at the first hint of trouble. One for all and all for one, yeah right! So he'd stood there alone, the karate kid willing him to try something, and Tina and her mates yelling at him, calling him a paedophile, and wanting him locked up.

And all the while Henry was smiling; trying to explain that it was all a mistake as he backed his way to the door and out onto the street. And then someone turned out the lights.

He woke up in the dirty wet alley of romance and broken dreams behind the club, where he found himself lying on his back again, more teeth gone, surrounded by black bin bags, used condoms and dried vomit.

He'd crept home to the wooden chair by the window so he wouldn't disturb Sadie in the bedroom. In the morning he looked such a sight that he'd given her every reason to leave.

As he leant against the window he watched her cross the pavement to the Mercedes. Henry recoiled from the smeared grime on the windowpane from where he'd rested his head. There was a stain on the sill from where he'd dribbled bloody drool in his sleep.

Sadie looked up at him as she unlocked the car. He raised his hand to wave, but she turned away, got in and drove off.

That car was the first place they'd been together, that first night. It was her favourite place for doing it. It was her husband's pride and joy; that Mercedes, and she liked to savour the revenge. Henry's favourite place was in the bath, surrounded by her bubbles and her plastic bottles on the shelf. There was a big bath in the flat; easily big enough for two. Her skin would shine beneath the water. Fine fair hair on her arms, her calves iridescent as they lay there together; he could have looked at her forever. It was great. He loved to lie with her beneath the water and come up a better man.

He watched her car disappear around the corner and down towards the Mumbles Road. He cursed quietly as he eased off his shirt. A hot bath now. With the smellies from her bottles. That was what he needed. She'd feel different later when she came back to collect her stuff. They would talk then and he'd talk her round and all would be fine. And the making up afterwards, that would be great!

But the bathroom was empty. The cold ceramic shelf lay bare. Her towels were gone from the airing cupboard and her clothes from the bedroom too. Everything had gone.

'How long will you be?' she'd asked the night before, her accent even more Swansea than usual.

And when she came into the living room this morning, was it through the bedroom door or the door off the landing?

'How long will you be?' she'd asked. 'Long enough for me to be gone?' she'd meant. He thought she'd smiled, but now it hit him like a sledge hammer.

She'd been leaving already, even before that mess of the night before.

It had taken months for Henry's marriage to Paula to grind to its end. They'd both known it was doomed and they'd found themselves fighting just to fill the silences, neither of them listening to what the other was saying and neither giving a damn anyway. It was a relief when Paula's final explosions brought it to a head.

The abrupt way Sadie had ended it was a shock. Henry never thought she'd just pack up and bolt while he was out having a drink. He found himself sitting on the end of his bed. The duvet had no cover on it. Neither did the pillows. She'd even stripped the pillows. But she'd come back again this morning. She could have stayed away, but she did come back. Perhaps it was guilt that brought her back. Maybe it was just to see how he was handling the fact that she'd gone? Perhaps it was just to check he was ok...

And when she'd opened the door, there he'd been, propped up and drooling like an idiot, avoiding the bedroom so that he didn't wake her.

And he hadn't even noticed that she'd gone.

Henry's shoulders shook as he rested his head in his hands and cried.

Chapter Eleven
1.30pm 8th April 2007

Henry watched silently in the doorway as Tom Atkins laid his hand on his wife's underwear. The old man looked down at it for a long time, the smooth white cotton beneath his sallow liver-spotted skin, and Henry watched him shiver.

'Can I help at all?' Henry asked and Tom shook his head.

Slowly, Tom began taking the pieces of fine material out of the drawer, placing them neatly in the suitcase on the bed beside him. The faded flowery duvet gave silently as it accepted the weight of the old cardboard case. Gradually, Tom emptied the drawer, closing it with a sigh. He opened another and began the same process with his wife's stockings, one by one, laid reverently in the suitcase, and again he sighed.

'Megan always loved her stockings,' Tom said. 'Silk, cotton or nylon, she loved them all. Treasured them as sacred possession. Like bananas and chocolate bars, stockings were always important to her.' He stopped, eased himself upright above the bed. 'During the War they were in demand, and even when she could buy a pack of three tights for a few pounds in Costcutters, they were still special to her. She said they should always be treated with care.'

After the stockings, Tom started on the next drawer down, and when the cardigans were packed, he closed the case. He picked it up, and when Henry went to help him, Tom said, 'Just be there if I fall. I want to do this myself.' Henry stood back and watched as he eased himself downstairs, leaning heavily on the banister. He placed the case with the others on the daybed in the parlour and then carried an empty one upstairs for his wife's cotton shirts which filled two drawers in the cabinet to overflowing.

Tom held a few of the shirts to his nose. All his senses focused on the smell of Megan's perfume. 'It's only slight, but the scent of lavender is there,' he said. 'I remember her wearing these so many times over the last fifty years. She rarely threw things away, even when a shirt was old and frayed,' and Henry watched the pain as Tom smiled. 'It's the small things you miss the most.'

It took Tom much of the afternoon to pack his wife's clothes. The suitcases and cardboard boxes, full of a lifetime's worth of garments, filled up the parlour, and supermarket carrier bags of shoes lined the hallway. They were all she had owned—a record of her whole life contained in a pile of cases and plastic bags. There they sat, ready to go to the charity shop. He'd told Henry that he would go through his own things the following day, but that would be fine: 'There's less emotion attached to one's own kit,' he'd said. 'Won't throw all of mine. I'll still need some clothes, but most will. There's little point in keeping everything.'

Tom's movements were slow, as rheumatism crept around his bones. Henry had to concentrate not to step in and help him with pretty much everything. Megan had told Henry that Tom's doctor had prescribed him various cocktails of Paracetamol, codeine and Tramadol over the years, but they all gave him an irritable bowel, so he'd given up on them, accepting the pain and learning to move more deliberately, more thoughtfully, than he used to.

'He says the pain gives you focus,' Megan had said. She leant towards Henry and whispered, 'He's a tough old bird, that one,' and she'd smiled. 'Brave beyond compare.'

Downstairs, with all the bags and boxes packed up the two men stood in the kitchen. With a trembling hand, Tom filled the kettle and rested it on the grid above the range. He poked the ashes in the grate and added a scoop of coal. He sat down at the kitchen table, resting his arm on the yellow Formica top. Channels of rain ran down the windowpane distorting the lights from the village, and the drumming of the rain on the kitchen's lean-to corrugated tin roof covered the noise of the dual carriageway nearby.

With an effort, Tom picked up the coalscuttle and stepped out of the back door. Automatically he glanced left towards the long-empty kennel. Henry went with him, two steps behind, hanging there silently like a shadow. 'I still expect to see the collie looking up at me,' Tom half turned. 'Eager eyed and hopeful for a walk. I hear the animal's tail beating gently against the kennel's side though I know she's not there.'

There was a short covered alleyway leading to the coal shed, but the wind blew in sideways off the mountain and by the time he was back in the house, Tom's trousers were damp. He threw some more coal onto the fire and leant against the range as the kettle boiled and then as the leaf tea brewed in a small pot. He poured some milk from a bottle into a pair of old chipped mugs and carried them, and the teapot, through to the snug where he turned on the television.

'Are you going to watch the rugby tonight?' Henry asked.

Tom reached forward and flipped the switch on the twin-bar electric heater. 'I am,' he said, stretching his legs and settled down in the chair. 'I find Jonathan Davies' commentary annoying, but I like Gwyn Jones.'

'He usually has sensible things to say,' Henry smiled.

'Megan and I were watching the match in Cardiff when he broke his back. 1997. Club game between Cardiff and Swansea.'

'Two weeks earlier he'd captained Wales against the All Blacks,' Henry said. 'I remember it well. I was watching the game when Mervyn Davies had his injury too. I was a kid, but it's the sort of thing you never forget. A hell of a thing to happen to anyone. Life changes in an instant.'

Tom stirred the teapot. 'Towards the end of 1944 I slipped off the flatbed back of a lorry in the dock at Newhaven,' he said. 'It was raining terribly.' He glanced towards Henry and then back at the teapot. 'Landed heavily on my hip,' he rubbed his cheek with gnarley fingers, 'shattered my pelvis, compacted several vertebrae,' he sighed. 'Five months in a naval hospital in Eastbourne, and then four more convalescing in Nailsworth in Gloucestershire. Then they expected me to report back on duty.'

'There's no chance of a long recovery period when there was a war going on and the country needed every man, I suppose,' Henry said.

'But the war ended while I was in Gloucestershire, and I never went back,' he held up the teapot. 'Would you pour?' he asked. 'I get a bit wobbly sometimes.'

Henry stood up, crossed the room and poured the tea. 'No sugar?' he asked, though he knew the answer.

'I remember when I heard it was over,' Tom said. 'I was with a really pretty WREN. She held my elbow, guided me as I teetered across the lawn outside the hospital. She helped me to a bench and we sat quietly watching the newly arrived swallows floating on the currents below.' His demonstrated the movements of the birds with his hand. 'Then there was shouting and cheering from the hospital, so she left me there on the bench and ran inside to see what the noise was all about. I felt I knew, somehow, but didn't dare to say.' He took a sip of tea. 'There was quite a breeze over the Cotswolds that day and I was shivering away in my flannel pyjamas and dressing gown.' He looked at Henry, but what he saw in his mind's eye was a whole different image. 'There'd been rain the night before, and the last of the cherry blossom hung from the trees in the garden. Beyond, on the bank above the park fields, the first few buds on the rhododendrons had begun to open. Their blowsy flowers were so vivid against the dark green foliage.'

'You remember it well,' Henry smiled, and the old man nodded.

'Like yesterday,' Tom said. 'The spring had been cold, with snow right up to the end of April, but the flowers came, just like they had done every other year, getting on with their life cycle no matter what was happening in the world of men.

'And then the nurse came back. "It was Stuart Hibbard on the radio," she said. The delight in her Welsh accent made my heart sing. She was beaming as she sat down beside me, fingers working madly in her lap. Her cheeks flushed in excitement. She told me the Germans had surrendered.'

'Victory in Europe,' Henry nodded slowly.

'I felt a tear gather in the corner of my eye and I wiped it away with the back of my hand. It was all over. It was funny how the wind made your eyes run.'

'All over,' Henry echoed.

'I hope you don't mind me wittering on,' Tom said.

'It kind of puts a lot of things into perspective,' Henry grinned. 'My girlfriend left me and I got punched in a nightclub. Somehow these things don't seem to matter so much,' he shrugged. 'I enjoy hearing you talk. Please go on.'

'We sat on the bench in silence for a bit then. There was all sorts of noise and shouting in the hospital. The Cotswolds are beautiful in May. The swallows fought the updrafts, and sped back down the valley. England can never have looked so good.' He brought his hand to his forehead, and closed his eyes. 'I'd imagined the end of the war so many times. I never doubted the eventual winner, more where I would be, whom I would be with and, on occasion, whether I would be there to see it at all.' He turned to Henry and shook his head. 'I'd never visualised a scene quite as perfect as this.'

'I'm not surprised you remember it so well.'

'The nurse said that we were going to have tinned pears that night in celebration. She could barely contain herself,' Tom nodded. 'I turned towards her, watching her smile and the way her eyes were never still for a moment and I asked her what her name was.'

'Your Megan?' Henry guessed.

Tom nodded. '"My name's Megan," she giggled. "Megan Evans." And we were married nine weeks later.' He picked up the remote control and switched on the television with the volume down. Colours moved across the screen, but neither of them was watching. 'We moved into the back room here, sharing the house with Megan's parents,' Tom said. 'It was considered a big farm for round here then - nearly fifty acres,' he glanced at Henry who tried to look impressed. 'Fifty acres, yes,' he nodded. 'They had thirty milkers and followers, and the sheep up on the top too. About sixty of them, on the common land. Some people say a place like this doesn't amount to much, but it was Megan's father's life's work and his father's before him.'

'Megan told me,' Henry said. 'She said it had taken them two generations to pay for it, and they owned it outright. They'd worked it all without machines, she said, all by the sweat of the brow.'

'Her father was a tough man. Good heart, but tough. The first time I met him, he told me he planned to get a tractor in a year or two once they'd saved enough. "All being well," he said, and that was him, confident and proud, but finishing most pronouncements with "all being well", or "God willing" - an optimistic caveat typical of a generation that had known the horrors and unpredictability of two World Wars.'

'After that, I guess nothing is ever certain,' said Henry.

Tom smiled. 'He died in 1971. Megan's mother passed seven years before. When her father went, Megan told me that she wanted to die here, in this house, on this land.' His stare was fixed on Henry's face as he spoke, his eyes locked to Henry's. 'We were in our bedroom changing after her father's funeral. "In this house," she said. I remember the words exactly. "I want to be able to look out of the window, down onto the mudflats and the sea. With the lighthouse in the west, and the fires of the refinery in the east. I want to die here like my father did." I'm glad I did that for her.'

'I am glad she was able to,' Henry said.

Tom nodded. He played with the cuffs of his jumper, brushed a fleck of lint off the sleeve. 'This farm was the only place she'd ever called home, and the only place she'd ever wanted to know. In the beginning, I found it hard to understand her attachment to the shabby farm on the windy side of the hill, but by the start of the seventies I'd lived here for over twenty years, the place was in my blood too. I couldn't imagine living anywhere else. I can't imagine the depths of attachment she must have felt for the place.'

'*Hireath*, isn't it?' Henry said. 'The sense of belonging.'

'"You hear me, love?" Megan asked me. "Do you really hear me?" and I nodded as I looked at her sitting at her dressing table. Her fingers never stopped working in her lap. She looked at me in the mirror - staring at me with narrowed eyes. "Not just the words, eh? I mean it. Whatever it takes. Alright? This is where I came in and this is where I go out," And all I could do was nod.'

Henry smiled. There was nothing to say, so he said nothing.

'Now, you must be hungry?' said Tom. 'We have some Maunka honey that Megan won at a church raffle years ago. We'd been saving for a special occasion. May as well eat it,' and he eased himself to his feet.

'I've got to go soon,' Henry said. 'I'm watching Scrum-five with Dan in a bit, but that would be nice.'

Down the mountain and just over the parish line, Megan lay now. Henry stood at the window, looking down on to the lights of the town below. Tom had said that he visited her grave twice a day, making his way down the mountain in the morning and again in the early evening before it got too dark. He also dropped in when he was going somewhere else and just happened to be heading along that road. There was a sign down there that announced the name of the village in bright lettering. Beneath the name was the request -'Please drive carefully', which some joker had defaced painting over the 'r' and the 'v' in the word 'drive'. Tom said that Megan used to laugh every time she saw that sign.

Tom shuffled his way back from the kitchen. 'You wouldn't do me a favour and put the chickens to bed would you?'And he led Henry out through the backdoor to the coal shed where he kept his slip-on rubber shoes. 'It's easy. Just go into their pen and flip down the door to their house.' Henry eased the shoes on as Tom flipped his flat cap onto Henry's head. He held out his moth-eaten duffle coat. 'There's a torch in the pocket,' he said and he stood back as Henry stepped out into the darkness.

Henry felt for the torch, finding first Tom's fingerless gloves which he slipped on, and then worked his way along the cinder path beside the hedge to the chicken run at the top of the garden. The summer before, Henry and Megan had sat here in the sun and she'd told him how the hedge had grown out of some hazel fence posts which had taken root nearly twenty years ago. She'd loved that about nature – to hell with man's intention, nature does its own thing. The hedge now formed a windbreak for the garden itself.

Henry went into the chicken run and shut up the house. Outside again, he walked round the chicken pen. One missed gap in the wire and a fox or a polecat would wipe out the flock in moments. He circled the mesh fence, checking for any holes developing, or any wind-damage caused over the last few hours. The tails of plastic tied to the top of poles to keep the kestrels and goshawks away whipped in the breeze with a sharp crack, and the wind howled through the trees on the distant hillside.

There were only six chickens left, and the birds were so old that they rarely laid more than a couple of eggs a week between them, and most of these eggs had shells so thin that they caved in beneath Tom's pencil as he wrote the date on them. The chickens were company though and Tom had no thoughts of putting them in a pot. They ate his scraps, chatting happily to him as they circled his feet. Megan used to call them her 'feather dust-bins' the way they polished off pretty much all the rubbish she threw them, turning odds and ends into golden yoked, beauties.

Walking back towards the house, Henry relieved himself onto the compost heap. He looked down at the town wondering at all the lights down there, the speeding ones on the dual carriageway and the mournful yellow ones that lined the claustrophobic streets. They were much closer than they used to be. Much closer to each other, as well as to the farm. Creeping up the hill in a never-ending invasion of cement, metal and noisy people. And now the farm would be sold and the development would continue.

The rain had stopped, and the wind had whisked the clouds away, but the clear sky showed no stars. It was hard to see them with all the lights from below. An aeroplane with yellow and red lights flickered silently as it headed westwards, America-bound, and the sound of a police siren whined down in the streets below.

Henry shivered. 'This place will get into anyone's soul,' he murmured. '*Hiraith*? Damn right.'

Henry was pleased that Megan had died here on the farm. She'd been in and out of hospital, but back at home for the end.

He'd worked hard to get her back to the farm. He hadn't realised she was as ill as she was, that she would die so soon afterwards. Still, he was glad he'd been able help Tom keep his word. He was pleased about that, and pleased that she was spared the ordeal that was now to follow - that of selling up the farm and Tom moving out. It was the only logical course of action. A ninety-year-old man couldn't live alone in a place like this. It was madness to even think of it.

The slender beam from the torch lit his way on the damp ground. Yes, Henry was pleased that Megan had been spared all that was to come.

Chapter Twelve
8.00pm 8th April 2007

'Hiya, guys,' said Carlo as he pushed the lounge door open. He prepared himself for the waft of gas-fire warmth. 'All well?'

'Evening, Carlo,' said Henry. He was slumped in an armchair with a mug of coffee on the floor at his side, staring at the Sunday night rugby on the television. He didn't look up. Beside him Dan sat in his wheelchair, also staring at the screen. Henry held a pint glass to Dan's twisted mouth. His crumpled lips were wrapped determinedly around a straw.

'So how's things with you boys?' Carlo asked. He pulled a wooden chair out from the table and sat down. 'Supper alright? Was there enough?'

Henry nodded. 'Yeah, great,' he said. 'He's as full as an egg, this one.' Dan smiled, laughed and squirted a stream of Guinness out of the corner of his mouth. It dribbled down his chin, hanging like dewdrops on his stubble. 'Tell Cathy we loved it.'

'Will do,' said Carlo. 'You guys had a good weekend?'

'Yeah, good,' Henry nodded. 'You finished?' he glanced up at Dan's face, unhitched the straw and moved the glass away. Gently he wiped the older man's chin with a piece of towel. 'OK?' he asked and Dan grinned, strained as if he wanted to speak, but then gave up, sinking back into his wheelchair with a sigh. 'I was up with Tom Atkins this afternoon. I was his wife's social worker. I think I told you about them. She died a little while ago.'

'I'm sorry.'

Henry shrugged. 'Comes to us all.'

'I suppose it does.'

Henry turned to look at Carlo. 'You know, Carlo. I told him all about you when I was up there with him. I didn't mean to. It was just as I was leaving. I hope you don't mind?'

'What about me?'

'About how tough it is on those newly left behind when a loved one dies. Like for you and Cathy since Helen passed away. I wanted to tell him that it does get easier, but then I realised that I hadn't really asked you how you were for a while. I've been caught up in my stuff.' He smiled wearily. 'How are you?' he asked.

'I'm sure it does get easier,' Carlo said. 'In time.'

'In time,' Henry echoed. 'And are you coping?'

'Well, Henry,' Carlo said, and then he stopped and sighed. 'To tell you the truth we don't manage all that well most of the time. Outside we smile, but not inside. I suppose it is easier with two of us together. Being able to talk about her together helps. And believing in God, of course. Knowing there's a heaven and that Helen is there. That makes a difference too.'

'That's good.'

'Some days when I'm down, Cathy is feeling stronger, and it's the same the other way too.'

'It's never easy,' said Henry.

'You don't really know it, until you've been there. But yeah, at least we've got each other.'

'Now, Tom Atkins, he's up there on his own now. No kids. Well, he had one, but he died years ago in the Blitz I think. Tom told me the story, but it seemed a bit confused. It was before he met Megan. There are no grandchildren. Anyway, Megan owned the farm and he's got to sell it now he's on his own. He owes a lot for her care. It's a bit of a mess. He didn't know he could have got help from the Social Services if he'd asked for it. We could have helped, but nobody told him. He's ninety or something. Fought in the war. Got all sorts of medals.'

'Wow,' said Carlo.

'Yeah. He was a Marine or a Para; whichever one that wears a green beret. Megan told me. You wouldn't guess to meet him now though.' Henry felt Dan watching him and worried that he was going on a bit, so he changed the subject. 'Well, anyway, we can talk about that another time.' He held up the Guinness so Dan could drink again. 'On Saturday, what did we do? Went into town, didn't we, Dan. Along the front. Down the shops. I was a bit short on biros so we went to the bookies,' Henry shrugged. 'Dan bought some more DVDs on Dillwyn Street.' He scratched the top of his stubbly head with the tips of his fingers with short, abrupt strokes. 'Not much else really, but it was a good day.'

'More DVDs?' Carlo laughed. He glanced at Dan whose eyes were back on the rugby. 'OK, but be careful.'

'Yeah, yeah. Sure Carlo. No worries.' He waved away Carlo's warning. 'I hear you.'

'Are you still seeing Karina tomorrow?' Carlo asked.

'A week on Friday now,' Henry smiled. 'I'm taking her and some mates up to Cardiff. They want to see the university,' he said. 'She's sixteen. Uni's two years off but she's planning it already.'

'Excellent. Are we still OK to go fishing on Thursday?'

'Sure are,' Henry said, though his mind was still on Karina. 'I wish I saw more of her really, but you know. That's how these things go.'

'Of course,' said Carlo. 'Well, I'll take these plates and be off.' He eased himself to his feet. 'I wanted to say that I'm sorry about Sadie, Henry. We both are, Cathy and me. She sounded nice and...'

'PLENTY MORE FISH,' said Dan. 'BEEN TELLING HIM.'

'He has,' Henry laughed. 'But thanks, I'll be fine.'

'Really?'

'Yeah, really. Been through this before, remember. I've never been the best at picking ones that last. Anyway, I'll be off in a bit now. Marcia's due in at nine and I'll be off to my single man's love-shack. Might have a pint on the way home, though.'

'Sounds delightful,' said Carlo.

'It's the way I paint the picture, Carlo. To tell you the truth, being alone with my thoughts is hell. It's not that long since Paula and I split but it feels like forever.'

'I'm so sorry,' said Carlo.

'Life, isn't it?' Henry shrugged. 'What can I do?'

'GO FISHING,' said Dan. 'CATCH ONE YOUR OWN AGE.'

Henry laughed. 'Alright, mate,' he said. 'I got the message, alright. Lay off, eh?'

Carlo smiled. 'Goodnight boys,' he said and closed the door behind him.

Chapter Thirteen
7.30pm 9th April 2007

'This is it,' Karina said. She held her laptop up in front of her face, peeping over the top of it like Kilroy wos 'ere.

'The Multi-Agency Referral Form?' Henry pulled out a chair and sat down at the table.

'On line. That's it,' said Karina. 'It's all but ready to send off to the Child Care Assessment Team.' She put the computer down in front of him. 'Mum helped me with it.'

Across the kitchen table Paula looked at him. 'Probably should have asked you,' she said.

'Anyone can do it,' Henry nodded. 'Child protection is everyone's business, and for you to have to be handling something like this on work experience is unbelievable. Especially at the radio station. They should know better than that. It's great you took it seriously. It's important everyone does.'

'I'll make you a cuppa,' Paula said. 'Have a look at it with Karina before she sends it off, OK?'

Henry put his arm round Karina's waist as she stood beside him, pointing out the important bits, explaining exactly what had happened.

'You've done the right thing,' Henry said. 'Spot on.'

'I couldn't believe it when she told me,' Paula said. 'I laughed about it first, because it was unbelievable, but I knew it was important. I said she should look on the computer and see what to do.'

'And I did, and here it is,' said Karina. 'The All Wales Child Protection Procedures. There are four categories of abuse - sexual, physical, emotional and neglect. The way I see it, leaving him shitty is neglect and what they said to him has to be emotional abuse, but even if it isn't, it's still wrong. He's not in immediate danger, so there's no need to hurry and call the police. Just fill in the form and away it goes.'

'So you email it off to the Assessment Team so they can decide what's to be done,' Henry nodded. 'It's got to be done, but you're opening a can of worms, you know.' He watched Karina's finger hovering over the button which would send it on its way. 'One click on that mouse. You ready for that?' She grinned at him and he said, 'How about a cuppa tea first, yeah? Ten minutes talking about it isn't going to make any difference.'

'Is there anything you think needs to be changed?' Paula asked as she poured the milk.

'You've split a couple of infinitives, but apart from that nothing,' Henry said. 'I'm really proud of you. Of both of you.'

'It's just mad,' Karina said, sitting down beside him. 'I didn't catch on what was happening to start with, but by the end it was just beyond.'

'And they said all those things?' Henry pointed at the screen. 'You've used quotes - inverted commas. "The Downer". All that? That's exactly what they said?'

'Word for word,' Karina nodded. 'Yeah, and there was more. Those guys working are disgusting. Horrible people. It was the wrong place for Will to go on work experience in the first place. The school made a mistake sending him there. I can handle myself, so can Sally, but not Will. It wasn't fair. Those people are used to getting a cheap laugh by being mean. He was too easy a target. It wasn't fair.'

'But he had his support workers with him to help?'

'They were too busy flirting with the DJs. Didn't concentrate on Will at all. One of them, Francine Morgan, forgot his change bag in the car and she couldn't be bothered to go down to the car park to get it, so when Will had an accident she had nothing to change him into.

'We were in the canteen on lunchtime when it all happened. Will was squirming around like he does when he really needs to go. I had to point it out to Francine. He doesn't always remember and goes by accident. He must have had a turtle's head or something. From what she said, I don't think it was a big mess, stains more than anything, but Francine left him wearing shitty undies anyway.

'And when they came out of the toilet she called him Skid Solo in front of everyone and the other support worker laughed at him and took the piss. That was Marina. She made him sit by the open window saying he stank. She asked if anyone wanted a Brownie, because Will had one on him. She said he could change when he got back to school before the bus home.'

'Unbelievable, isn't it,' said Paula. She opened a pack of biscuits, sliding them over the table.

'And then what happened?' Henry asked as he nibbled on a jammy dodger.

'We went back down to the radio studio after that and they kept on and on about it, Francine and Marina did. Will didn't notice what they were saying to begin with. He didn't know they were having a go at him. Me and Sally, we tried to stop them, but we couldn't. Marina asked the DJ if he could play Skid Row or Working for the Yankee Dollar by the Skids. They went on and on like that.'

'And the DJ?'

'Matty Chalk? He seemed to know what they were on about without needing to be told. He's got a bully's sixth sense. He started talking about how he was having steak and kidney pie for his tea when he got home, only he called it steak and skidney. That sort of thing. And he called Will "the Downer". Never his name. He treated him so differently.'

'Matty Chalk,' Paula spat. 'Karina told me last week that he'd asked her if she'd like him to show her what fellatio was.'

'Forget about that, Mum,' Karina said quickly, resting her hand on Henry's arm as she saw his muscles tense involuntarily. 'There was no one else there, just him and me in the lift at the time. He'd only deny it.'

'Bastard media twats.' Henry took a mouthful of tea and hissed, 'Fuck, that's hot.' He coughed his way to the sink, scooping cold water into his mouth. He turned slowly, water dribbling off his chin. 'You have to do this, you know,' he said.

'I know.'

'But there will be repercussions.'

'I know.'

'Weird repercussions you won't expect. They'll try to turn it back on you if they can.'

'I know.'

'The support workers will say it didn't happen at all, or not like that, or that Will was in on the joke and that you're over reacting to a non-event.'

'That's why I can't go to the school. I want to go higher up to make sure something happens. So they can't hush it up and say they sorted it internally and then they'll get away with it.'

'The radio people will try to cover themselves too. They'll try to make you out to be a liar. They'll say you're seeking fame and attention or something like that probably. All sorts of stuff. It's the way they'll defend themselves.'

'I know.'

'And they'll make it hard on Will. He'll get all sorts of questions from strangers, some of them pretty tough bastards. It'll get in the paper. On the telly, maybe. His privacy will be gone. The media will tell the world he poops himself. A great story that. They'll spin it as a "poor defenceless disabled boy gets a hard time" story, but he'll be the victim twice by the end of it. It won't be much fun for him or his family.'

'I know that too,' Karina said. 'But he's got a lot of friends at school who'll stand by him. He's got good mates. Really he has, Dad. I'll kill anyone that's mean to him,' she laughed. 'He'll be alright. And his family are tough and tight too. I think they'll be pleased we stood up for him.'

'I can go round his house in the morning and tell them,' said Paula.

'And what about you?' Henry turned to her. 'Do you think Karina can handle this thing? There'll be a ton of extra pressure from all angles.'

'We've raised a fighter here, Henry,' Paula said, smiling. 'You know that. She's got my temper and your heart. Can't go wrong with that mix.'

Henry crossed the room and cautiously put his arm around his soon-to-be-ex-wife's shoulders. He closed his eyes, breathed in a lungful of Head and Shoulders as he felt Karina slip her arms around the both of them and he sighed.

'Better click that mouse then,' he said.

Chapter Fourteen
8.30pm 19th April 2007

At the end of Mumbles pier, two men stood side by side, their fishing rods held firmly with lines taut against the wind and tide. Spray rose from the wild sea as it lashed in against the pier's legs and stanchions. The wind sang as it came in from the west around the headland and across the lighthouse. The sun was setting in a murky grey soup and the light from the lighthouse cut weakly through the mist.

'South Wales in springtime,' said Carlo. 'No wonder so many people retire to Spain.'

'You sure you want to be here?' Henry turned his whole body toward his friend, eyes narrowing against the wind which powered in at their backs. He was almost shouting. 'I mean, we could be sitting warm in some pub somewhere.'

Carlo laughed. 'No chance, bud. Not often I get a night out and I want to make the most of it. Anyway, you and me in a pub leads to me in a pub and you off with some girl.' He clenched his fist and gently punched Henry's shoulder. 'Too many times down that road over the years. Here's the place to talk. Like men should. Two men, two rods, battling the elements same as it's been for centuries. Perfect.'

'Perfect,' Henry echoed. He smiled, licked his lips, tasting the salt from the spray. 'I felt quite manly there for a moment. All Hemingway and that...'

'I doubt Hemingway ever fished with a kid's rod bought for a fiver from a toy shop in the Mumbles, mind.'

'But still.' Henry wound in his line and cast again, watching the silver spinner arc and fall into the sea. 'I appreciate it, mate,' he said.

'So tell me about her,' Carlo said, his voice quieter as the wind lulled momentarily. 'This Sadie.' He rested his rod against the railings and reached into his pocket for his tobacco tin.

'Ah man, you should have seen her,' Henry said. He shook his head, sighed and shook his head again.

Carlo snorted. 'The eternal mystery that is woman, right?'

'Something like that.' Henry reeled in his line and cast again. 'She was the kind of girl that...' his voice trailed away. 'She had a smile that reminded you of sunlight on a fish.'

'Yeah, right,' Carlo laughed and passed over the joint.

'I don't know,' said Henry. His face creased into a smile; the kind of smile that's only there to stop yourself from crying. 'This loss,' he laughed. 'I've never felt it before.' He beat himself on the chest. 'It's been, I don't know how long, but it feels like a damp dishcloth, you know, wrung out, in there. It's weird. I've never felt it before.'

'Never? Not when you and Paula...'

'No, not even then,' he held up the joint.

'And you married Paula. You had Karina together.'

'This thing's gone out,' Henry said taking the lighter from Carlo. 'It was a relief in the end when Paula and I caved in.'

'Can't have been easy, mind.'

'Course it wasn't. Especially for Karina.' He watched his exhaled smoke streak away to nothing over the sea. 'We only married because Paula was expecting. You know that.' He felt a gentle stillness sweep over him. 'So different for you and Cathy. You were friends before you even got together. And then you had a life together before Helen came along. It was different for me and Paula. All so sudden.' He clapped his hands. 'Bang! Baby! You remember the mess I was in back then?'

'Yeah I do,' Carlo said. 'How's Karina taking it now?'

'Well. She's brilliant, really. She's the best thing in my life.'

'I'm glad to hear you say it.'

'She's doing so well at school it's amazing, considering.'

'Excellent.

'And more than in school. She's got an amazing heart. Sees right and wrong as clear as day. And she's so grown up. She made a referral to the Child Care Assessment Team a couple of days ago about something that happened when she was on work experience.'

'Shit.'

'Yeah. She got the radio DJ suspended and she's pushing for all the teachers in her school to go on disability awareness training too. She's going at it like a tyrant. She said the school should use it as a pilot scheme that might get rolled out throughout the whole county. When she put it like that the Head agreed. Thinks it will win him some Brownie points with someone somewhere.'

'That's amazing.'

'It is amazing,' Henry nodded. 'She's not perfect, mind.'

'Who is?'

'She's got anger management issues, school says. She sees a counsellor twice a week. One of the deacons from St Josephs.'

'Yeah?'

'She sees right and wrong like black and white; there're no shades of grey with her.'

'Takes after her father.'

'And her mother. Damn, she's got a temper. When she blows, she blows and there's no stopping her,' Henry laughed. 'She'll end up doing someone serious damage.'

'And Sadie?'

'Ah, Sadie. I think about her all the time. It was how she made me feel,' he tapped his chest. 'Like there was hope.'

'Hope?' Carlo took back the joint, eyes narrowing, inhaling deep.

'Yeah, hope,' Henry said. 'She was alive. Dynamic, animated; expressive; her eyes, her fingers, her laughter... When she came back from London it was to build a new life. Her husband, Robbie worked in TV and he really messed her up. He was a presenter on one of the shitty digital channels that no one watches. Anyway, he banged some blinged-up, big-jugged bimbo from Big Brother. Shelly Britty. That was her name. It got in the papers and he left Sadie for her.'

'Shelly Britty?' Carlo said as he mimed a pair of watermelons. 'Helen use to like Big Brother.'

'Grim, eh?' said Henry and Carlo just laughed.

'She's orange,' said Carlo. 'Like she's been Tango-ed.'

'Sadie worked in the media catering for TV films, and that. Then she got an idea about recycling water in kitchen sinks and she designed one that saves gallons of water and thousands of pounds. Hotels pay five quid a cubic meter for water, and they get through so much each year it's unbelievable. Unsinkable Sinks; that's the name of her company. She set it up herself, got meetings with the community development people about some site down on the Jersey Marine where Amazon's going to build a warehouse. And that was before she even got down here.'

'She does sound dynamic.'

'Yeah!' Henry yelled. 'Fuck yeah. That's it,' he laughed. 'That's the word. And she took you along with her. I found myself swept along and the day to day stuff didn't matter. I understand why she left. I'm not easy to live with but I thought we'd do OK.' he cast again. 'Carlo, I see some shitty things in my job. Along with the cops and the nurses, social workers see the worst of twenty-first century Britain.'

'That's true.'

'We do our best, but everyone hates us anyway.'

'That's not so true, Henry. Not everyone.'

'Not everyone, but most,' Henry laid down his rod and took a bottle of Heineken from a plastic carrier bag at his feet. He popped the cap on the railing, passed the bottle to Carlo, and opened one for himself. 'It's hard to remember the good stuff when life is smashing down on you one wave after another, but Sadie, well, she helped me remember the good stuff.' He took a mouthful of beer. 'Social workers see the worst that can happen to people. We do our best to make it better in a system that's shit. It sucks, and we see people suffering because of it. There isn't the money to help, and even when there is, the challenges that people are faced with flattens me. I just don't know how they manage. And not just the sick people, but their families too. They need someone to lash out at and it's usually at us because we can't create miracles. Sometimes we mess up, but even when we don't, we can't create miracles.'

'Jeeze, you go on a bit when you're stoned,' Carlo laughed. 'Even more than usual. Me, I just get sleepy.' He passed Henry the joint. 'It's getting a bit dry down there at the end.'

'I got more,' Henry nodded. He frowned as the smoke burnt his throat. 'It's good to talk,' he hissed and he flipped the last of the rollie out into the dusk.

They were silent for a while, sipping their tins and casting their lines aimlessly, not expecting a bite, just for something to do with their hands. If they'd been in a pub, they'd have played pool or darts or munched on endless bags of pork scratchings, but it was better on the pier. Tighter. Two mates together, one there for the other as they picked over the carcass of what was no more.

'Listen, Henry. I got to say something. I talked to Cathy about it and she said I'm right to say it, so don't get grumpy.'

'OK,' Henry shrugged.

'You remember the girls you used to knock about with at college?'

'Remember? I think about them a lot. Best days of my life.'

'There was Valerie and Katie and Coops and...'

'Coops, yeah,' Henry said. 'She played volleyball for Wales and then went to Canada. I had a thing for a couple of other girls on that team, mind. Remember Sally? The brunette?'

'Yeah, and you loved her until she cut her hair and then you didn't love her anymore.'

'Funny that.'

'And then there was Wendy James,' said Carlo.

'Now she was special. The girl who set the standard. It's her that all the others have been measured up against. And, I'll tell you, Sadie was right up there with her.'

'Well you used to go on about them all in the same way you're talking now about Sadie.'

'I played harmonica for Wendy in that club, you remember? It was the first time I spoke to her.'

'I still cringe about it.' Carlo laughed. 'You idealised those girls, but none of them were real, mate. Not in there.' He reached over and tapped the top of Henry's head. 'You never gave them a chance to be real people in your head.' He looked at Henry, whose jaw was set, staring out to sea. 'You've always been like that, mate. Apart from Paula, you've never given any woman the chance to be a real person.'

'Paula! And look what happened there.'

'You're not listening,' Carlo said and he lit another joint, drawing deeply, letting the silence settle between them.

'She gave me hope, Sadie did,' Henry said eventually. 'Hope that there's beauty in this world despite all the shit.'

Carlo sighed and smiled into the darkness; there's only so much a mate can say...

'You remember Heather Locklear on TJ Hooker when we were kids?' Henry said. 'Officer Stacy Sheridan. Do you remember that feeling you got in your belly at that age when you're old enough to see the inconceivable beauty of woman and still young enough not to have any inkling of all the other stuff?'

'Oh, yeah,' Carlo nodded.

'When I first saw Heather Locklear it literally took my breath away.'

'I had a thing for Phoebe Cates in Gremlins like that. I used to get faint looking at her. The way she stood; there was something about it. I had a poster on my wall. But they're not real, Henry. Poster girls are never real.'

'I don't care about real, Carlo.' Henry turned to face him. 'Why would I care about real? I see real every day at work and it's shit. I've already said that. Even growing up was shit with my mum being ill, my dad going and everything. Who needs real?' He was angry now. 'What I need is someone who will make me feel that life's OK. Can't you understand that?' He reached over, gripped Carlo's shoulder. 'I want to feel the way I felt about Heather Locklear. It made me feel like that just to sit with Sadie. It wasn't just how she looked, but how she was. She had depths, you know.' His arm dropped to his side. 'I think about her all the time. All the time. I know I'm wasted, but you could feel it. She made me know that God's got it right. That there is still goodness here and it's not all shit. At least not all the time. But then,' he shrugged. 'Then she just left me.'

'Yeah?'

'Yeah, I went out one evening with the twats from work and got a beating in some club and when I got home she'd gone. Just like that. She'd just gone.' He knew he was slurring now, but it didn't matter. He didn't care. 'Each time the phone rings, my stomach churns that it might be her. But it never is.'

'There are plenty more fish, Henry. You've got to have faith that...'

'No, don't say that,' Henry urged. 'Everyone says that. Dan just keeps on about it.' He waved away Carlo's offered joint, and then took it anyway. 'Well, shit. You talk about faith, but do you ever think that God just got fed up with us? Like he doesn't care anymore? Like he's heaping more grief just for the sake of it until we drown in it?' Henry put his empty back into the bag, took out another and opened the cap between his teeth. 'He shows us a bit of daylight sometimes, but it's just to take it away again like some sad old sadist? Well, do you? Do you ever think God's forsaken us?'

Slowly Carlo reeled in his line and set the rod down on the pier. He sat down on a bench, reached for another beer and gave it to Henry to open. The wind was in his face now so he turned against it as he re-lit his joint, took a long pull. 'Sit down, mate,' he said, moving slightly along the bench, patting the damp wood beside him. 'Do I ever think God's forsaken us?' He drank deeply, twisting to look at the dim lights of the city across the bay. 'No I don't,' he said and drank again. 'Not for an instant.' He drew again, held the smoke until it burnt, and then exhaled as he spoke. 'The reason why?' he put his arm around Henry's shoulder. 'You are the reason why,' he smiled. 'It's nothing to do with the policy-making fuckwits in the centrally heated ivory towers of County Hall who have no idea what it's like to have the shit of a loved one jammed so high under their fingernails that you can't scrub it out. It's you and people like you. The family carers, social workers, advocates and minimum wage care-workers who never give up. There are shit ones sure; you can find dickheads anywhere, but I mean people like you who care about what you do. People like you with the quiet courage to fight. To do the right thing, no matter what. People who spend each day tending to their incontinent, demented wife who has absolutely no idea who they are. People who knuckle down and get on with it.'

'Wow,' said Henry. 'And you said I was wordy!'

'Shut up,' Carlo said. 'I mean, people whose backs are breaking but fight on because the funding isn't there to get them the hoist they need so they bend and lift them because there simply is no other way. Heroes: the lot of them. They just get on with it, while the fuckwits go on long term sick because they get caught fiddling expenses. I mean the care-workers who report their boss's fuck-ups and the mistreatment of vulnerable people even if it means their own jobs could be threatened. People who believe if they stay silent they're as guilty as the guilty ones.

'Henry, mate,' Carlo said. He leant in close, forehead against Henry's. 'I love you, man. OK? In a totally platonic way. You're a massively flawed human being and you always have been. I know it and you know it, but I love you. It's what makes you human. It's you and people like you that make me know God hasn't forsaken us. You don't flinch at the tough decisions. You try to save us all, simple as that.' Then he laughed, and pulled away. 'God's forsaken us? Don't be daft. You still carry your mum's rosary don't you?'

'It's here in my pocket.'

'I knew it.' Carlo laughed and stood up.

'Twenty-first century Catholic me,' said Henry. 'Rosary in one pocket, three pack of condoms and an eighth of grass in the other. Ready for every eventuality.'

'You don't doubt God,' Carlo said. 'Not for a moment.' He picked up his rod, turned to the sea and cast again, the line wheeling away into the gloom. 'So it went wrong with you and Sadie? So what?' He wound in the line and cast again.

Henry sighed. He closed his eyes and leant back against the seat, concentrating on the full force of the wind on his face. 'You're a good man, Carlo,' he muttered. 'You're full of shit, but you're a good man. Now give me a puff on that spiff and tell me how come you caught a honey like Cathy. I've never understood that?'

'God has been good to me,' Carlo laughed. 'Come on. Let's get back down the pier before the last bus goes, eh? And before I get too wasted to walk.'

'Yeah,' Henry nodded. He slapped his knees and started to pack up their gear. 'Hey,' he said. 'About that job. I'd forgotten to ask. Did you apply or what?'

'Head of Human Resources?' Carlo laughed. He shook his head. 'That was weeks ago. No. Thought it was too big for me.'

'Well they've reopened it. It was in the paper yesterday.'

'Yeah?'

'Yeah. Come on, get up there in County Hall with the policymakers. Someone's got to do it!' He put his arm round Carlo's shoulders, pulling him in tight as they walked along the pier. 'Some bastard's got to do it.'

Chapter Fifteen

5.30am 20th April 2007

'I think about you all the time,' Henry murmured. He sat in the chair by his front window watching the city lights fade as dawn developed across the bay. 'Things we said. Things we did.' His eyes were dry, his tongue felt swollen as it rasped against the roof of his mouth.

He reached for his tea, realised it was cold and put it back down.

'Everything. I analyse everything.' He shook his head. 'I thought we were happy, you know. I was happy. I was really happy. At least, I think I was.' He glanced at Carlo, asleep on the sofa, and he leant forward to rest his forehead against the glass, watching his breath condense. In his mind's eye he watched her in the street getting into her car and driving away around the corner and down onto the Mumbles Road. 'Ah Sadie I really thought you were too. But were you? And if you were, would you have known?'

Leaning back he sighed and scratched the top of his head. 'And was I happy? And if I was would I have known?' Henry muttered as he eased himself to his feet. 'Maybe being with you was the closest we were ever going to get?' He shook his head. 'Happy? What a fucking joke.'

He held his breath as he tiptoed past Carlo on the way to the toilet.

'The existential question,' he said to his reflection in the mirror, and he grinned, not sure if existential was even the right word. 'Probably not.' He washed his hands, turned on the shower and climbed into the bath. The shower curtain was cold as it stuck against his back. 'But what is happy anyway?' he asked and the water said nothing, just laughed at him as it curled away around his feet and down the plughole.

The hot water felt good as it eased away some of his drunken/stoned funk. There were still a few hours before morning, when he'd have to shoehorn Carlo out of the door and down the road so he could get home and wake up before heading off to work.

He wrapped himself in a towel and shuffled back across the room to his chair by the window. His tea was still cold, but he didn't fancy making another one. He looked out across the bay, at the fading lights of Port Talbot as the dawn took control of the day.

'Maybe we were happy, Sadie,' Henry whispered. 'Maybe for a moment.' He shook his head. 'If only you'd noticed.'

Chapter Sixteen
10am 20th April 2007

'Are you sure you don't need me to come in with you?' Henry asked. 'These places can be a bit daunting,' but Karina laughed. She unbuckled her seat belt and turned to him.

'I handled Adult Protection, Dad, I can handle anything,' she said.

'And fantastic you were too,' Henry smiled. 'But this is different. University is a big deal.'

'We got it sorted, Dad,' she said. 'We emailed all the tutors we want to talk to and got appointments fixed.'

'All done?'

'All done,' she nodded. 'And Tina and Sally will be here anytime now.'

'Here?'

'Yeah. We're seeing the first of the tutors in the SU building at eleven. They'd better not be late 'cos we're going to have to get a wriggle on to see them all.'

'You're not nervous or anything? Not even a little bit?'

'Nervous,' she laughed. 'Why'd I be nervous? It's us interviewing them. They've got to want us to choose Cardiff, not the other way round. We could just as easily choose Manchester or Sussex. Can you see me down in Eastbourne wobbling around on the front with all the oldies? Not likely,' she shook her head. 'I know what I'm doing.'

'Of course,' Henry smiled.

'Piece of piss, days like this.'

'Tell me,' Henry said. 'How'd you ever get to be so grown up and self-sufficient? I mean, you can't have got it from me or your mum; we're hopeless.'

'Needs must,' Karina reached over and petted his cheek. 'Perhaps it's 'cos you're so hopeless,' she said, frowning when he flinched. 'I don't mean it like that, Dad. It was a joke, alright?'

'Yeah, I know.' He stroked her hair, cupping the back of her head in his hand and leaning forward to kiss her forehead. 'Still there's a lot of truth in humour, or whatever the saying is.'

'Many a true word is spoken in jest.'

'That's the one!'

'Right,' Karina glanced at the dashboard clock. 'Well, right on time. There's the girls.' She leaned over, beeped the horn and waved. 'I'd better get going. See you later, yeah?'

'I'll be here. And the others want a lift after, too?'

'If it's OK.'

'Fine,' Henry rubbed his eyes. It would be the first time he'd seen Tina since he'd approached her in the nightclub.

'You'll be OK getting the books I asked for? In Waterstone's. Three for two?'

'Yeah, I've got your list,' Henry laughed, patting his pocket. 'Now stop treating me like a child.'

'Day out in the big city. People aren't as friendly up here as they are at home. Capital city mentality, isn't it? Sure you'll be alright?'

'Piece of piss,' he nodded. He reached past her, opening her door. 'Go on, get out,' he said. 'Three o'clock. I'll see you here then. And remember...'

'Yeah, yeah. I know. Don't worry. I won't be another brick in the wall.'

'At least I taught you something.'

'Laters, crocodile.'

And he watched them go, young girls with nerves of steel, off to conquer the world, their futures so bright that all three of them were wearing sunglasses.

Henry drove into the city centre. He parked in the multi-storey on Pellett Street, went to Waterstone's and filled up a carrier bag with nine books, three for two; forty quid. Bargain.

Outside it had started to rain. He smoked a cigarette, loitering in the bookshop entrance and watched a bent old homeless man with a rolled up umbrella wheezing 'Biggieshoe' at no one in particular. Old ladies clad head to toe in shapeless pink plastic cagoules shuffled by like gay ghosts.

She's quite a girl, Karina, Henry smiled. I've no right to have a daughter like her, he thought. She'd brushed off the Tina incident with an 'Ah Dad, you're such a wally!' and they'd had a laugh about it.

'I wasn't trying to pull her!' he'd said, and she'd hugged him tight.

He ground out his cigarette beneath his heel and shook his head. 'How can I ever have said I didn't want to keep her,' he wondered.

When Paula first told him she was pregnant, he'd gone nuts. A weeklong bender and he'd ended up in the cells.

He'd been twenty two, supposedly revising for his final year exams. The college assigned him a mentor to help him cope. 'Call me Tim,' the mentor smiled from across his desk. It was the first time they met; Henry and Tim. 'Not by my surname. I do so dislike formality. Don't you?' He advised Henry that if he didn't love this pregnant girl that he should tell her so and let her make up her own mind what to do with the baby. 'It's not fair on a child to be brought up in a volatile relationship.' He leant back in his chair and pursed his lips. 'Many people become parents without giving it much thought. Is it fair to bring a child into a situation where the parents are at war? Much fairer that the mother, well... you know.'

'Abortion?' Henry whispered as he left the meeting, chilled by the feel of the word on his lips.

And that was what he told Paula. She didn't believe he meant it, and he didn't believe he was saying it. 'You're a Catholic, for fuck sake,' she'd said. 'We both are.' But that was what had happened, and he would always know that he had said he wanted his unborn daughter dead.

Henry crossed the road and bought a copy of the Big Issue. 'We are all of us anonymous,' the old man said as he fumbled for change. He bared a gummy smile. 'Did you know that?' His eyes were tinged with grey like the white in a rotten egg.

'I guess that's true,' said Henry. 'I'm not that sure I really know myself most of the time.'

The old man coughed heavily into his fist and Henry waved away his offer of change. 'When the time comes, we are all anonymous,' and his voice faded into silence.

As Henry walked away he heard an apologetic hissed 'Biggieshoe' start up again.

Henry stepped into a bland, chain-coffeehouse on St Mary's Street. He ordered a pot of tea and sat up on a stool by the window looking out at the shoppers. A pair of young mothers; young girls with sheepskin boots and tight thigh-length denim skirts bent low over their prams as they rushed for cover as the rain became heavier. They looked no older than Karina, though they might have been twenty. Sadie could have passed for twenty, no problem.

Henry opened the carrier bag of books, took out the largest; East of Eden.

Karina had read it before, she'd carried a library copy around for weeks and she'd told Henry all about it.

First off, she'd read The Grapes of Wrath as background reading for a school project on climate change and social displacement. Now she wanted to read everything John Steinbeck had ever written. He flicked through the pages, reading occasional lines and descriptions, like how a woman's rare smile 'flashed and disappeared the way a trout crosses a knife of sunlight in a pool.' He smiled. Karina had quoted that to him and he'd spent weeks misquoting it back to others.

'Fuck, it's a whopper,' he muttered. He turned to the back and found there were seven hundred and seventy two pages. He'd also bought her The Red Pony, even though it wasn't on her list. It was only one hundred and twenty six pages. Might be easier to get through and she'd always liked horses.

Over his shoulder a tight-faced mother and chubby young boy argued at a table. The boy had long wavy hair and a determined chin. He wanted to sit up by the window where

Henry was sitting, and he wouldn't be told otherwise. His mother's whine made Henry's teeth ache.

Henry turned to them. 'I can move if you'd like to sit here,' he said, slipping the book back into the carrier bag. The mother and son looked at him, saying nothing. 'I'll go over there.' He picked up his tea and hopped off his stool. 'It's no problem.'

The woman stood up, silently placing her coffee where Henry's tea had been, her movements urgent, desperate to get the seat before anyone got in ahead of her. She said nothing and the boy looked at him blankly.

'It's alright,' Henry smiled. 'I'm sure he'll give up his seat for me when I'm a wrinkly old boy.'

'Oh, how can you say that,' the woman turned to him. 'How can you say that?'

'Say what?' said Henry.

'How can you say that?' her voice was tremulous as it rose. 'I'm offended now.' People turned to see what Henry had done to upset her. 'You've offended me,' she said and began to cry.

'What?' Henry's voice cracked. 'What did I say?'

'We can't sit here now. That's awful.' She took the boy's arm and dragged him away towards the door. 'You've offended me,' she shouted back at him, fist clenched as Henry stood, shamefaced, with his tray in one hand, Waterstone's bag in the other and everyone looking at him.

'What did I say?' he repeated, looking round. 'Crikey.' He put down the tray, rubbed his blushing cheeks and headed for the door.

'Tell me,' Henry said, as he passed the homeless man outside Waterstone's. 'You don't know a guy called David Kelman living up here, do you?'

'Living rough?'

'Possibly,' Henry nodded. 'I knew him in Swansea. He went missing.'

'Missing?' He eyed Henry cautiously. 'You police?'

'No. I just thought...'

'I went missing,' he said.

'Yeah?'

'Down in Tiger Bay years ago, when it still was Tiger Bay, not what it is now,' he spat heavily. 'There were lights in the sky that came for me. That was the start of it.'

'The start?'

'Tiger Bay. I been missing since then. Taken.'

'Right?' said Henry. 'Taken?'

'Lots of times. Missing.'

'Ooookaaay?' said Henry.

'The lights. They said it was a weather balloon, but I know the truth.'

Henry nodded. 'They?'

'Yeah "they",' said the Big Issue seller. 'I know the names of men they had to hang.'

'Right, OK. I see,' said Henry.

'Yeah. Got to keep it to myself, mind,' he nodded, tapping his nose. 'Can't say more than that.'

'Right. Of course, well, thanks for the magazine.' Henry held up his copy. A shiny-cheeked Charlotte Church beamed at them from the front cover.

'David Kelman,' said the homeless man. 'I'll keep an eye out.'

'Tell him Henry Antrim was asking after him,' said Henry, turning away, trying to remember where he'd parked the Doblo. 'Take care, alright.'

'Cheers,' he smiled. 'And thanks for the talk. Was nice.'

Back in his car as he waited for the girls at the meeting point, Henry reopened East of Eden. Late on in the book John Steinbeck used the German world '*weltschmerz*' Anglicised to 'welshrats' to describe 'the world sadness that rises into the soul like a gas and spreads despair so that you probe for the offending event and you can find none.'

'Welshrats,' Henry nodded. 'Well,' he sighed. 'I didn't even know there was a word for feeling like that.'

Chapter Seventeen

2.30pm 22nd April 2007

Tom Atkins pulled the farmhouse door closed. He edged the letterbox open and slipped his keys inside. He leant his head against the door, listening as the keys landed softly on the doormat. Then he turned, fumbling with the buttons on his overcoat, and walked around the side of the house. A few steps behind, Henry followed him and they headed up the garden, along the cinder path, past the compost pile, the empty chicken run, and out through the gate at the top.

Without speaking, the two men skirted the first field, heading slowly up to the top corner to where the stile would lead him into a field of ewes. The air was good and clear. Puff ball clouds came in quickly off Swansea Bay. There was no rain yet, but it was coming. The gusty wind lifted little whirls of leaves which danced and faded away ahead of him.

A weathered barn owl pellet lay on the top of the stake that they used to lean on as he climbed over the stile. The pellet had broken open, exposing the tiniest broken bones of a vole.

Henry stood on the stile looking out over the field of black faced sheep. They turned and ran from him as his shape became distinct above the hedgerow, but they were heavy with rain so didn't run far and looked back at him with bemused faces.

'I worked my last harvest in September 2001,' Tom said. 'I felt like a child, sitting up there in the Renault's cab, waiting as the younger men loaded my trailer. I had the radio on and the news came on. I was looking up at the high, sand-dune rippled clouds over the sea that day. There were vapour trails heading westwards and the swallows turned tight circles high and low over the field. And the announcer said that an aeroplane had flown into the World Trade Centre in America.'

The ease that Tom said the sentence drew a deep breath from Henry.

Tom sighed as he eased himself over the stile. He glanced down at the ground by his side. 'I always used to walk the fields with a dog. Over the years a whole series of collies. I look down out of habit.' Finding only Henry accompanied him, his chin sank a little further into his coat. 'I think a lot of my first dog when I came here. My best one. A short-legged mongrel. She was more than just an animal. I can looked down now and visualise Nooka waiting respectfully for my instruction.' He brushed away some dampness around his eye with the tip of his finger, and then he walked on.

'Nooka loved tearing the heads off foxgloves as she ran by,' Tom said. 'Burrowing into piles of dry leaves. Chasing the whiff of a mouse or a mole. Her ears were ever twitching, listening for every sound, her nose turning for each new scent.' The remembered dog glanced up at Tom. Her brown eyes had so much depth. Henry watched Tom smiling down at the ground where the visualised dog wagged her tail in acknowledgment and Henry saw a sudden brightness flicker in Tom's eyes.

A group of starlings rested like a slick ahead of them. As the men approached they rose as one, fighting the currents for a moment and then settling smoothly on the earth a little further on.

The steel skeleton of a pig ark sat forgotten in a corner of the field, its tarpaulin cover having ripped and blown away many years ago. There was no money in pigs and no one had been interested in the remains of an arc at the farm clearance sale. The sheep nosed in closely around it.

Two sheep, caught in brambles, pulled themselves out as the men approached. Henry had to bend to help a third whose head was stuck through the fencing. His fingers worked inexpertly as he twisted her head and slipped it back in through the wire. His face remained impassive as the ewe kicked him in the shin as she struggled to get away, then he smiled as he watched her skipping back to join the flock.

The starlings moved on again, flying low, sheltering below the height of the hedgerow, circling the field and settling down again in the same area that they had begun.

At the north side of the field, Tom opened a gate into the small, leafless willow and ash thicket. He bent to pull at the twisted, brittle remains of some bindweed which threatened to smother some saplings as they struggled to grow into something substantial. The woodland smelt of mushrooms.

Looking down, Tom visualised the dog ambling quietly alongside beside them. It was the image of an old dog now he saw, one preferring company of two men to the excitement of flushing clattering pigeons out of the hedgerows or raising a shrike from a neighbour's field of turnips.

A single, silent black crow pecked on the scattered carrion remains of a sheep, killed perhaps by a fox, but more likely by an out of control dog up from the village. The crow wheeled angrily above then, coming to rest in the highest branches of one of the few remaining trees in the heavily flailed hedgerow.

The clouds were longer now and the sky darker, heavy with the rain that would come before night. Higher up, they were touched by the first pink tendrils of a distant sunset.

Turning to the west, they crossed the field that ran alongside the dual carriageway. Walking along the hedgerow, they peered down through the dusky gloom at the headlights of the vehicles. They stopped by a willow growing in the hedge. Silently Tom took out his knife, and cut a branch the right size for a walking stick. The willow had been a fence post, but it had taken root and grown into a tree long ago. Barbed wire ran right through it, cleaving a bulbous scar across its bark. At the top of the field, a slate lined water tank covered the source of the spring that fed the farmhouse. The new owners planned thirteen houses on this field. That meant mains water and they had already blocked the lower end of the feed pipe. The crystal pure water sang cheerfully as it overflowed the tank, slipping away into the undergrowth.

There were no sheep in this bottom field and the grass grew long. A pair of JCB diggers and a monstrous yellow Dooley trailer stood by the gate, waiting for their time to come with the instruction to cut the topsoil and begin the foundations of the new building development. A sign for Samson Construction leant against the trailer ready for erection on the roadside as soon as Tom had packed up and gone. So quickly the farm had changed.

Neither Tom nor Henry looked at the diggers, the trailer or the sign. Their eyes were on the ground.

Stiff limbed but with his weight on his new stick, Tom shuffled back along the lane to the house where Henry's Doblo was waiting, loaded up with the last of his possessions, ready for the half hour ride across town to the sheltered housing unit in the Mumbles.

Without a word, the two men got into the car. Henry switched on the ignition, slipped the vehicle into gear and drove down the hill, away from the farm for good.

Chapter Eighteen

9.30pm 27th April 2007

'Maddie,' said Henry. He looked each way up the street as he drew her in through his door. The rain was pounding on the pavement, but there was no one there.

'What the fuck's happened?' Henry asked.

'I've got nowhere else to go,' she whispered, leaning in against him, hiding, pressing her face deep into his chest. Henry put his arm around her, felt her shivering and led her in and up the steps to his flat.

'Has someone done something to you?' he asked as he toed the door shut behind her, and when she nodded, he said, 'Sit here. I'll get a towel. You're soaking.' He helped her to the sofa and reached for a towel from a pile of laundry on the floor. 'I'll make a cuppa, yeah?' he said. 'You want a cuppa?'

'You got anything stronger?' Maddie's voice was no more than a whisper.

'I'll sort it,' Henry nodded. In the kitchen he flipped on the kettle and opened a cupboard for a bottle of Jack Daniels. Two glasses in one hand, bottle in the other, he was back on the sofa beside her in a moment. 'Here you go, love. I've got no ice, but,' he unscrewed the cap and poured two large measures, 'there's a good couple of noggins in this one.' She held the glass to her lips, threw the drink back in one, and held the glass out to him again. 'Shiiit!' Henry hissed, and he filled it again. Maddie was slower with the second one, and after the third, she put the glass on the table, brought her hands to her face and sobbed.

Henry put his arm around her, drew her in close and kissed the top of her head. She was shaking, shoulders heaving, but shivering too. Not just cold, Henry thought, this is shock, and he regretted giving her the whisky. The kettle flipped in the kitchen, but neither of them moved. It was a good few minutes before either spoke.

'I didn't know who to come to,' Maddie said, peering up at him.

'It's alright,' Henry said. Gently, with his thumb, he wiped away her tears.

'It was just,' and her face crumpled, eyes flooding and she leant in against him again.

'Oh, Maddie,' Henry said. Slowly he eased his way away from her, kneeing in front, resting his hands on her shoulders, looking deep into her eyes. 'Listen, you don't have to tell me anything, OK? I don't need to know a thing. But do I need to call the police? Whatever happened, do you need the police involved?'

Maddie shook her head. 'No police,' she mouthed silently. 'No police,' and Henry nodded.

'I'll get the tea, OK. I'll be two minutes.'

When he came back, Maddie had moved from the sofa. She stood by the window, looking down into the night. She smiled wearily as he passed her the cup. 'This is better,' she said.

'Sorry?' Henry said.

'I mean, better than bourbon. Tea is better.'

'I put a couple of sugars in it. I know you don't normally, but today... I hope that's OK?'

'Today it's good.'

Henry stood beside her, their forearms not quite touching, just close enough to feel the other was there; close enough for comfort. 'There's always something to see from here,' Henry said. 'Especially in the dark at night. The lights, cars, ships in the bay. People walking. It's good,' he nodded. 'All so quiet.'

'So quiet.'

'It's good.'

'When we were kids,' Maddie said. 'Do you remember?'

Henry laughed. 'Lots of it, yeah. I remember lots of it, but I bet I've forgotten a lot more.'

'One time we had a fire in the park, just down there,' she nodded towards the right, down Bryn Road towards Singleton Park. 'A whole bunch of us climbed in over the wall off Sketty Road at the top. You, me, Dwayne and Gareth. Jacob. You remember him? Janey and Caroline. A whole gang. We ran down here to this end. Into the trees.'

'I remember,' Henry shook his head. 'We'd just got back from a cricket tour in Eastbourne. We'd won every game.'

'It was the first time I ever got pissed.'

'Cider?'

'It was cheap,' Maddie nodded, 'After a bit I went off with one of the others away from the group. One of your mates. Your age. Joey Samson. I'd never even kissed anyone before and… '

'That Brummie Bastard.'

'His family had just moved to town and you lot were trying to make him feel welcome.'

'That's right.'

'I was fourteen or something, remember, younger than most of you lot.'

'And sweet as anything you were,' he nudged her arm. 'I remember well.'

'Too young to shave my legs, even. Well this guy, one of the ones in your cricket team, Joey Samson…'

'He's never been a mate of mine.'

'… and he wanted to do more with me than just kissing.' She laughed through her nose. 'It's funny looking back, after all I've done. It's funny to think that I was ever so innocent to really believe he wouldn't want to do more than kiss.'

Henry sighed. 'Joey Samson is a County Counsellor now. He's got his fingers in God knows how many pies. He's always been a twat. He is now, and he was then.'

'I screamed,' said Maddie. 'I screamed when I worked out where his hands were heading. And you came running. You, Henry.' She turned from the window and looked at him. 'No one else did. I could hear them laughing round the fire, but you came.'

'Yeah?'

'You pulled him off me, chucked him on the ground and you kicked him in the bollocks.'

Henry laughed. 'Right in the plumbs. Perfect.'

'He was a big guy, but you really went for him. Jake came up then. You remember?'

'Jake Marley. That's right. I wonder what happened to him.'

'Jake came over and you told him what happened and he picked up a stick and chased Joey out of the park one way and you picked me up and carried me up the hill the other way away from the rest of them.'

'It would have been easy to carry you. You were a tiny thing.'

'You carried me all the way home. In your arms like this, and when we got there you dried my tears on your shirt. It was your Spy vs Spy one. I'll never forget that. It looked good on you. Big strong forearms. I'll never forget any of it. You were so kind. The milkman of human kindness. You tidied me up and you made sure I was OK before you let me go in to my mum.'

'Ah, Maddie,' Henry sighed. He shrugged and put his arm around her, pulling her close.

'We saw two shooting stars that night,' she said.

'Did we wish on them?'

'Yeah, but they were only satellites.'

'It's wrong to wish on space hardware, you know.'

'Yeah I know,' Maddie smiled. 'We always liked the same songs. Do you remember that?'

'I do,' Henry nodded.

'It could have been the perfect evening. The end bit of it anyway. It could have been perfect, if what happened first hadn't happed.'

'I don't know what to say, Maddie. I'm so sorry.'

'You don't need to say anything,' Maddie's voice was muffled against his chest. 'You had a spirit that none of the rest of us had when we were young. I was fourteen, you'd have been eighteen or something, but you were a man already. Not like the others your age.'

'I did my growing up early,' Henry said. 'With my mum dying. I'd much rather it had been different.'

'Your spirit was there in everything you did,' Maddie said, leaning back, her arms round his waist, looking full into his face. 'I've never met anyone like that. So alive and right and full on, 100mph, with no shit or baggage or anything. And you told the best jokes.'

'I did, didn't I?'

'You remember the Chunks joke?'

'That wasn't mine,' Henry laughed. 'It was one of Jake's. Still, it was the best joke ever.'

'Best joke ever,' Maddie repeated. 'And that's what you were like,' Maddie said. 'Pure energy. You still are. Your spirit is amazing.' She took his hand and led him back to the sofa. They sat together sipping their tea, knees touching, saying nothing.

Eventually, haltingly, Maddie said, 'Tonight... this guy... he... he used a ketchup bottle on me.'

'Jesus,' Henry gasped.

'Yeah,' Maddie nodded. Her eyes were dry now; as if she'd had time to process the experience, to start to distance herself from it, trying to stop it feeling so real, like it hadn't really happened to her. 'He told me he wanted to use a ketchup bottle and then take it home afterwards, put it into the kitchen cupboard and think of me each time any of them used it at home. His wife, his son.'

Henry looked at her. He shook his head, grimacing as he found he was chewing his cheek so badly that he could taste blood on his tongue.

'I'd not seen him before; this guy. He booked a room at the Dragon. Just round the corner from my place. He'd told his wife he was away at a conference in Rhyl. He was a bit odd at the start, but no weirder than anyone else. Too much aftershave. I thought it might bring on my asthma.' She stopped, stood up and began pacing the room. 'We were on the bed and...'

'I could do without too much detail if that's OK,' said Henry. 'I mean, well, whatever. Say whatever you want, or need, or, well, whatever you need, OK?'

Maddie laughed. 'You look so uncomfortable, Henry. It's really sweet.' She sat back down beside him. 'Well, what happened is what I said really. He said he didn't want to have sex with me. He said he didn't know where I'd been.'

'That's nice of him.'

'He said he wanted to use the bottle instead. Those were his exact words, or something like them.'

'Shit.'

'And when I said no, he held me down, hand on my throat and,' she sighed, 'and he did it anyway.'

'Maddie, I...'

'I couldn't breathe or scream or,' Henry stood up, looking down at her, sat down again and put his arm around her shoulder, holding her tight, 'Henry it was...'

'Yeah,' he nodded. 'I bet it was.' And then he said, 'I really think you need to call the police, Maddie, really it's...'

'I can't,' Maddie said softly. 'How can I? Where are my witnesses? I get paid for sex. Why would they even take me seriously?' She looked at him. 'Really what's the point?'

'Well maybe it's time to...' his facial expression finished the sentence for him.

'To stop? Well, yeah, but if you really think that, why are you getting me to screw your clients?' She looked away, watching herself in reflection in the window. 'Ah, I don't know.'

'Ah, Maddie, that's different. It's just,' Henry started, 'I can't explain why, but it is.'

'Is it? I hear your words, but your face is saying something else. What your face has just said is that you think I should expect this sort of thing because of what I do.'

'That's not what I think. Not at all.'

Maddie nodded and sighed. 'It was wrong of me to say that,' she said. 'I know you don't think that. Not really.' She looked back up at his face. 'I am going to stop. I've just got one more year doing this. It's part of my plan.'

'Your plan?'

'I've told you about my three year plan, haven't I?' She held up three fingers. 'I've done two years so far, and one more to go.'

'I remember,' Henry said. 'You told me.'

'Yeah. I'm living in a shitty flat, paying seventy quid a week rent, right? Food and bills add up to another ninety. Total weekly expenses one sixty,' she said and Henry nodded. 'Right. I earn three hundred a week doing what I do, tax free, and I save the rest. That's one forty most weeks, often a bit more. That adds up to over eight grand a year. Mostly the work is easy. Like sexual therapy. Simple sex, or sometimes not even that, and nothing happens to me. In three years I'll have saved twenty five thousand. With my history and record nobody in their right mind is going to give me a job that can earn that. It's easy money and it'll pay to get Tina through college. No chance of her ending up like me if she's been to college.' She shook her head. 'One more year to go. It's not like I don't owe it to her; the kind of mum I was when I was using.'

'Maddie,' Henry held her head gently in his hands. 'You were a child yourself when you had her, and you had all that family stuff weighing on you too. You can't carry the guilt for that for the rest of your life. You've got to move on and let all that go. Things happen and...'

'Yeah, I know.'

'And you've got to think of yourself too. You're no good to her if you get messed up by some bastard now.'

She twisted her head in his hands, kissing first one palm and then the other. 'One. More. Year,' she said and smiled.

'She's a lucky kid, your Tina,' Henry said. 'I hope she knows it.'

'She'll never know how I got the money,' Maddie shook her head. 'I'm going to tell her I won the lottery.'

Henry laughed. 'You're nuts, you are,' and he stood up. 'Listen, I haven't got much food in, but I'm Harry Palmer when it comes to omelettes. You hungry?'

'Ravenous.'

Later, as Henry drove home having dropped Maddie back at her flat, he felt hollow. His jaw was set, fingers clenched in fists on the steering wheel as he skirted the roundabout outside the Dragon Hotel. He looked up at the windows, the cold white brightness of soulless hospitality, and he cursed. Anything can happen in a place like that, but anything can happen anywhere. Everywhere. 'Ah, Maddie,' he muttered as he pulled over. 'You've got to take care of yourself.' He stopped the car and got out. No harm in going in and having a look around. Maybe find the ketchup-bottle fucker and kick him in the bollocks.

Chapter Nineteen

3.30am 28th April 2007

Henry sat in the wooden armchair by his window. He was naked except for his jockey shorts. His mother's rosary hung loosely around his neck. He fingered the beads thoughtlessly. The room was dark. He had his feet up on the window sill and his elbows high on the arms of the chair. He drew slowly on a joint, eyes narrowing as he watched the paper crackle and flare, and then he focused on the lights in the street below as he exhaled.

It wasn't a bad place to live. It was warm and safe and the light was good in the morning when the sun was low over the bay and shone in between the plane trees growing through the pavement outside.

'Eighteen months alone.' Henry sighed and shook his head. 'Feels like forever.' He watched a car drift slowly up the street. A boy and girl talked beneath a streetlight as they shivered, sharing a cigarette. Another long night and all's well.

In his bedroom a girl lay sleeping; a blond girl with false breasts and a tattoo of a swan on her inner thigh. A random girl from the Dragon Hotel where the one pint he cradled in the bar as he went looking for a fight turned into three more and the 'Alright, love,' at eleven turned into a 'Come back to mine for a cup of coffee' at ten to two and that turned into a... well, what do you call it when you don't know her name and don't really care what it is anyway?

'And how old is this one?' Henry rubbed his chin with his knuckles, and then his fingers kneaded his forehead. 'Second year at college. No more than twenty.' He groaned as he reached for the glass of wine on the floor. 'Where is sleep?' He shook his head. 'Illusive bastard; sleep.' He finished and refilled the glass without thinking. 'Drink yourself to sleep. Dope yourself to sleep. Shag yourself to sleep.' He wet his lips with his tongue, drew deeply on the joint and watched as the smoke slowly drifted out through his nose as he exhaled. 'What do you do when these just don't work?' The wine tasted good as he drank again. He swirled it round his mouth and swallowed. 'Where the fuck is sleep?' He scratched his chest, his fingers though the hairs sounding like the wind through the long dry grass down on the sand dunes near the pitch and putt. He'd been there with a community nurse on the day the old farmer Tom Atkins' wife, Megan, had died. She'd been the first medic up at the farm after Tom had called 999. Gemma, wasn't it, the nurse's name? He hadn't seen that one coming. He thought she'd only wanted a walk when she suggested going down to the beach, and suddenly there they were tearing into each other, totally lost in the moment, like teenagers hiding in the dunes. Afterwards, as she sat up beside him shaking sand out of her tunic she'd said, 'You seemed so sad when they told you she'd died. I wanted to cheer you up.'

'It was so quick,' Henry said. 'I didn't expect her to go so soon.' He smiled. 'As for cheering me up, well you certainly did that.' Gemma had fine long legs that shone like caramel. He leant up on his elbow watching her dress and then, when she became self-conscious, he looked up at the high clouds and the half moon peeping down shyly, out of place in the daytime sky.

They'd kissed as they parted. The nurse going back up to the hospital and him to the nearest pub he could find. 'Will I see you again?' Henry asked. 'I mean, is this the start of something?'

'I don't think so, Henry,' Gemma smiled, and she took his hand. 'You're a lovely guy, but you've got too much baggage. Take care of yourself for a change, yeah? You've got my number if you want to, need to, well, you know. Take care of yourself Henry.'

So he'd got drunk in the Cricketers on St Helen's Road, and a little later, he and a young social work trainee that he was supposed to be mentoring climbed over the fence into the rugby ground and got chased out the other side by men with torches. They'd got a taxi back to her digs; a small house on Oystermouth Road that she shared with three other students.

Henry relit the joint and pulled again. At least he was here tonight in his own flat, not in some stranger's room lying awake in a bed that smelt of other men's sweat, on a sheet stained orange by cheap fake tan. It was hard to get up and leave like that when the sleep didn't come and the girl was draped across you all clammy and dead to the world.

His fingers found the crucifix on the end of the rosary. He played with it and then slipped it between his lips, the metal tapping gently against his teeth. He sighed. 'God will never give you more than you can handle? Isn't that right, Mum,' he murmured. He took the rosary from his neck, dangled it from his hand, watching as it swayed gently.

He thought of Maddie alone in her flat. Was she sleeping or was the memory still spinning round in her head as she sought sleep? Did that sort of thing happen a lot? Did she sleep in the same sheets she used for work? The same undies? He rubbed his eyes and sighed.

He thought of Dan back there in Carlo's house, surrounded by people that cared. He thought of Tom Atkins, alone, but for sixty years of shared memories and no one to share them with.

One by one Henry thought of the many other people under his charge.

There was Carrie Morgan, the twenty stone Shakin' Stevens fan who lived at home with her uncle and aunt by Cwmdonkin Park; saints the both of them.

Pete and Aly bought a boat and sailed round the world when Aly was diagnosed with MS. 'Are you going to live or are you going to let yourself be dominated by this disability?' Pete had asked her and Aly had smiled and said she wanted to live. The last Henry heard they'd been staying in Malindi after they'd run into trouble in a tropical storm off Kenya's north coast. They'd been rescued by some fishermen in a dhow who'd laughed as they towed them in to safety. 'Better this than knitting club down at the drop in centre,' Aly wrote in an email.

Roland Elliot lived down in the Mumbles. He had mild learning difficulties and should have been living independently, but his mother couldn't bear the thought of not taking care of him. All his life she'd fought for his rights, trying to get him everything she could to ensure he lived a 'normal' life. Now he was thirty-four, and was quite capable, but it was his mother holding him back. Without him to care for, she'd have no one, no income, no home. Henry had found Roland an advocate who was helping him find his voice for the first time in his life. Slowly, bravely, he was becoming more independent and happier in the process. His mother was not happy and accused Henry of being a home-wrecker and breaking up their family.

Henry coiled the rosary, placed it onto the window sill. He took another pull on the joint. 'And I'm a pot-puffing social worker responsible for all of them. A sorry cliché.' He opened the window and blew the smoke towards it. 'A dopey bastard.' The cold felt good on his skin.

Paula had another man now, Ronnie Abercorn. He was from the smarter side of Town Hill, and was an assistant manager in the Monkey Café Bar on Castle Street. He worked eight thirty to five and came home early on a Friday. He paid the bills, mowed the lawn and stayed in at night, happy to watch Simon Cowell and Coronation Street, side by side on the sofa with Paula and a bowl of popcorn. There was no nipping out on an emergency call. No crisis management decision that would change the lives of a family. Nothing like that. It wasn't his fault that he looked a bit like the illustration of the man in The Joy Of Sex books, though having a beard like that didn't really help. He might read the Daily Mail, vote BNP and only laugh at his own jokes, but at least you knew where you were with Ronnie.

Henry smiled as he realised that he envied Ronnie. He was pleased Paula had found someone. She'd always complained that Henry cared more about other people than he did about her. There was no denying that. It was part of the job, and you couldn't switch off, not just like that, not if you really did care.

'A social worker's not a normal job,' Henry told her again and again. 'You can't stop caring and leave it all at work when you come home. You need to commit. No one likes a tourist,' but Paula never did understand. Neither did Sadie, for that matter.

'You're not a God,' Paula had yelled at him. 'Pissing around with people's lives. Who do you think you are to make these decisions,' taking a swing at him, stumbling over the edge of the coffee-table. 'Who the hell do you think you are?'

'I'm just doing my best.'

'And me?' Paula said from where she had fallen. 'Don't I matter to you at all?'

Henry sighed. He stood up, stretched, slid his fingers into the top of his jockey shorts and peered inside. 'Come on then, little fellow,' he said. 'You ready to see if the silicon sister in there is up for round two? Coitus's got to be more fun than sleeping pills.'

He smiled briefly and then frowned. He closed his tobacco pouch and slid it into his desk drawer as he crossed the room.

Chapter Twenty

7.00pm 8th June 2007

It was a rainy Friday evening. It had rained all week. Henry sat in his car watching the rain pattern the puddles which flooded the University car park. He leant forward, resting his chin on the steering-wheel, and released a long frustrated sigh. His mouth tasted stale and he craved a cigarette. He was supposed to be heading out to Killay for a meeting with a woman, Natasha, whose partner, Hugh, had had a stroke. He glanced at the clock on the dashboard. It would be tight, but he might just make it on time.

He nudged Doblo forwards toward the edge of the floodwater, eyeing an Audi in a disabled parking bay. You couldn't tell that the tyres were flat as it sat up to its exhaust in the centre of the lake. Murky bubbles rippled across the shallows. He sat there looking at the water, his wipers drifting to and fro across the windscreen.

He rubbed his forehead with the heel of his hand. His eyes hurt, his head ached and his body felt old. Mostly though, he just felt pointless. He felt weary, sure, but didn't everyone feel weary nowadays. It was the pointlessness that bothered him.

Henry had been invited to the University to talk to some first year students about Social Work from a social worker's perspective. He'd started well, explaining how he'd become a social worker after caring for his mother. He looked out at a sea of expectant faces, keen to hear how theirs was an honourable life choice with a real opportunity to do some good.

But then he went off script and it all went wrong.

'This is real life and there are challenges every day,' Henry said, 'and it's up to us to have the guts to act decently and overcome them.' There was a pretty Asian girl on the third row who nodded and smiled while her neighbour took notes in shorthand.

'One challenge is to get around the red tape.' He'd looked away, up at the lights, searching for the clearest example. 'Our Occupational Therapy department can supply small items of equipment that people need on the say so of a social worker. Generally it's straight away,' he flicked his fingers, 'just like that. But if the disability is worse and the necessity greater; and the individual needs more expensive support and equipment, then there's a lengthy process that has to be gone through. This can take months. The greater the need and the more costly the care needs, the harder it is to access what is needed. The longer the assessments take, the greater the burden the individuals are expected to carry.' The Asian girl's neighbour put down her pen, drawn into a real-life problem faced by a real-life social worker. 'No one is automatically eligible for support and most processes entail means-testing and in-depth, time consuming assessment.' Henry sighed as a thumping began behind his eyes.

'This usually means that people have to have no savings and not own their own home to get maximum support quickest. If people have been wise with their money, saving for their old age, they effectively find themselves penalised for it as they are expected to pay for their care and expenses. This assessment takes a long time. If they have no savings, no house, maybe never ever worked or paid taxes, then the state will take care of them, and that decision happens much more quickly. The AVC scheme is one scheme used to assess an individual's wealth…'

'AVC?' asked the lecturer, grinning. 'I try not to use acronyms in my class.'

'Oh, yeah. Sorry,' said Henry. 'AVC stands for Additional Voluntary Contribution. It's a wealth assessment scheme. Bluntly, through the AVC scheme, the better off people are; the more they pay to cover their own care needs and if they own a house, this is usually the first thing to go to pay for it.'

'But that makes no sense,' one student said. He spoke with the frantic urgency. 'It's illogical and most unfair. If you sell someone's house when they are in care, what incentive do they have to get better when they have no home to go back to? Surely the system can be changed to make it fairer and more sense? One would have thought that they would...'

'"They?"' Henry smiled wistfully. '"They" is "us": the social workers. What you lot are going to be soon. You are going to be a "they". Not an "us."' He smiled. 'You are going to be a "they". But believe me, we're doing the best we can, most of us social workers. There is no logic in this "system" because there's no such thing as a "system" within a Local Authority. The whole thing is chaos. It's the job of the social worker to play whatever game you can to make the best of it for the benefit of the people we support.' He looked around the room.

'I've been in this job for over twenty years and I wish I had a load of positive things to tell you, but these are the realities. Local councils are shambling chaotic dinosaurs and people's lives depend on us to try to make the best of it. We have to follow directives from Cardiff and London, following many instructions that would never have been given if the people who gave them had any memory of what it was like on the front line. Dinosaurs were not known for their intellect, nor for their ability to make swift changes in direction. They had pretty shit turning circles if you remember. Much of what goes on in local and national government is illogical even to us on the inside, and it's up to us to do the best we can in the circumstances.'

The class tutor murmured something about it not being as bad as all that, but Henry cut him dead.

'No!' He slammed his hand down on the lectern. 'We are dealing with people's lives. Vulnerable people,' he hissed, surprised at his own sudden anger. 'If you are going to be a useful social worker you've got to be committed. No one likes a fucking tourist.' Turning to the tutor he wiped spittle from his lips with the back of his hand. 'I apologise for my vocabulary but your students need to hear the realities of their chosen profession. Of the real life they are facing. It's awful sometimes and often the rules make it harder again. The people need us and that's all there is to it. ' He made eye contact with the Asian girl, but she looked away, leaning to her neighbour, whispering something and they both laughed.

'We are the drones that carry the blame when the "system" breaks down,' he said. There was a background murmur around the lecture theatre now as the students began to talk amongst themselves, respect for him gone. 'How we manage, that's what defines us.'

Henry switched off the car. He eased himself back in the seat, sinking down into his coat. 'How we manage is what defines us.' He hadn't planned to say anything nearly as pompous as that, the words just came out. They were a bit melodramatic maybe; he shrugged, but not really. Not when people really did depend on you. Not when... Well, who cares? None of the students were listening by then anyway.

He sat in his car watching his breath-mist thicken on the windscreen. His hands were deep in his coat; his collar turned up high around his ears. He fumbled through his empty pockets looking for the cigarettes that he knew weren't there. His fingers found the rosary, but he left it unused. 'Fuck, I could do with a smoke,' he muttered as he glanced again at the clock. He was going to be late to see Natasha and Hugh.

Natasha was forty seven. Her partner, Hugh, was sixty one.

'I write letters to Hugh,' Natasha had told him at their last meeting. 'I write to him as the man he was before the stroke.' Henry sat quietly beside her at the kitchen table. His hands rested in his lap, files closed on the floor beside him. 'Hugh used to write letters to Karen, his wife, when she died. Father Kelleher suggested he did that. Said it would help him come to terms with his grief.'

'It can help to share what you're going through,' said Henry. 'How you feel about things, even when people are gone.' He smiled. 'They are still with us when we think of them, you know. It helped me when my mum died.'

Natasha looked at Henry blankly. 'Father Kelleher suggested I wrote to Hugh like that even though he's not dead,' she said.

'C.S. Lewis wrote...'

'...A Grief Observed, I know. Father gave me a copy."
'Right.'

'I don't know why he gave it to me, because Hugh isn't dead,' she said. 'I said that to Father, and he just put his arm around me. Hugh's not dead, but the man I knew is dead.' She turned away, her hands to her face, as she cried.

'He's a good man, Father Kelleher,' said Henry. 'And it's true that Hugh isn't dead...'

'I know that. God, how I know that. But it's worse that he's not. That he's still here, when he's not really here. I was Karen's carer, you know. I was here, right beside her and Hugh as she died. Hugh and me, we took care of her together. We became closer as we cared for her. We...'

'People come together in all sorts of ways,' Henry leant towards her sympathetically. 'For all sorts of reasons.'

'Hugh's children say I'm a gold-digger. They say I latched onto him when he was vulnerable, but it wasn't like that. I loved Karen too. I'd known her years. She had Hodgkin's Disease.'

'Ah,' Henry said, his eyebrows arched as if he was hearing that for the first time, though he knew it well having read her file.

'I lived with them here at the end, but I'd known her for years before. We were friends you see. We sang in the same choir, pulled the bells in church. I watched her fade away.' She looked at Henry blankly. 'I saw more of her than her own kids did.'

'Right?'

'They haven't been to see Hugh since she died, you know. They said he and I were together before... but I'd never do that. He'd never do that. I loved her too...'

'Well it's...'

'It's worse that he's not dead. No,' her jaw wobbled as she struggled for control. 'I don't mean that. I can't be saying that I wish Hugh was dead. I don't mean that at all. I just wish he was back as he was.' She turned to Henry, eyes damp but steely, looking for someone to be angry with. 'You didn't know him as he was, did you? He played cricket for Skewen. Captained the club for years. He was on the school's Board of Governors. And he ran his own business. It won a Queens Award for Enterprise.

Did you know that? Well, did you? Prince Charles visited the site. Gave him a cut glass bowl. It's over there on the dresser if you don't believe me. We keep geraniums in it.' Henry shook his head. 'No, you don't know anything about him as he was. As he really was. You just sit there thinking you know all about him from what you've read in your files.'

'I'm so sorry,' Henry said. The shallowness of his sympathy turned his stomach.

'I knew Hugh differently,' Natasha said. Her voice was quieter now; more restrained. 'We climbed Snowdon last summer. We used to sail in the Mumbles. We only had an old Mirror dingy that was hardly big enough for the two of us but it was lovely. A lot of fun.' She rested her head in her hands as she began to cry again. 'It's him I write my letters to. It's him I remember...not...that. Not that in there,' she gestured towards the glass doors of the sitting room where the shadowy shapeless form in an old pair of pyjamas slumped in front of the TV where Dale Winton was whining on about a new product he'd found that had totally revolutionised his whole skin care management regime.

'We have all these memories,' Natasha had said, 'but what good are they when I can't share them with him, when we can't share anything, when...'

Somehow Henry had to drive up there and tell her that her Carer's Assessment had come through and the Authority felt she wasn't coping in her caring role, that Hugh needed serious care support which was best provided in a Home.

Somehow Henry had to tell her that under the AVC scheme she would lose her own home. She and Hugh were not married. The house was in his name and Hugh's children were his official next of kin.

Somehow Henry had to tell her that the only way she might be permitted to continue living in the house was for her to find the energy to fight the Authority's decree and to keep caring for this man who was, but wasn't really, the man she'd loved.

'How we manage is what defines us,' Henry murmured again as he leant his chin on the steering wheel. He eyed the flood water, wondering if, perhaps, it had started to go down. Better to be late than not to turn up at all.

Henry pinched the bridge of his nose so hard that his eyes ran. He sighed, started the car, and edged his way through the water and out of the car park.

Later, after he'd left Natasha ashen and mute at the kitchen table, he drove to the nearest pub and drunk himself horizontal.

He became the bar room bore to beat them all, a Top Gear presenter on an overdose of tedium tablets. 'It's social injustice that defines our age,' he slurred, swayed and staggered as he clung to the bar rail. 'This is the legacy of Blair's Britain. It's one thing to get excited about the Olympics or some fucking golf tournament up in Newport, but wouldn't it be better for a leader to value above all else the welfare of the nation's vulnerable? Wouldn't it, though? Doesn't offer such a good photo-op maybe, but surely it's more worthy? Why can't you have compassion in politics?'

His drinking buddies cheered him along, no idea what he was talking about, and not that interested anyway so long as his hand kept drifting towards his pocket.

Chapter Twenty One

11.30am Friday 31st August 2007

'*Vox Populi...*' the voice said down the telephone.

'There's a misnomer if ever there was one,' Henry muttered, only half concentrating.

'Matty Chalk's morning phone-in show here on Coastal 345. We will be going live at the end of this track.'

'Yes, yes,' Henry said. He stifled a yawn, shifted his mobile to his other ear and looked out of the window. He was in Carlo's lounge room, having just brought Dan back from a trip to the physiotherapist. Carlo was out, and Cathy was in the kitchen, radio on, making a pot of tea. Across the road there was the beach and then the grey blankness of Swansea Bay with the Bristol Channel beyond.

'You will remember this is live radio, Mr Antrim, and also the inappropriate vocabulary you used the last time we spoke. I would ask you to watch your language.'

'Are you still trying to coerce your work experience kids into giving you gob-jobs, Mister Chalk?' Henry asked. 'Or was that just my fifteen year old daughter because she's special?'

'I will ignore that, Mr Antrim,' the presenter said, 'Right, here we go. And welcome back to *Vox Populi*. That was Another Reggae for the Road by the '70s superstar Bill Lovelady. One of my favourites, that. And now we go on to the subject of today's show; Care in the Community.'

A gap in the clouds allowed the watery morning sun to sparkle briefly on the waves. A few lone fishermen stood on the shoreline, wrapped up in big coats and hats. Seagulls gathered and fed on the floating effluent from the sewage pipeline a few hundred yards out.

'...and we have Senior Social Worker, Henry Antrim to discuss...' Henry looked at his watch and he sighed. He put his hand to his forehead and ran his fingertips across the furrows. That was what the aging process did to you. '...we all know about the cutbacks and limited resources for the vulnerable, Mr Antrim,' Matty Chalk said, 'particularly for those who...'

Sal wandered into the room, her wagging tail beating against the door. She slumped down beside Henry, who glanced at her and stroked her head. The dog closed her eyes and sighed with contentment.

'...and Mr Franken, Dan Franken. Now you are his social worker, yes? And you are responsible for his care, board and finances.'

'In a manner of speaking,' Henry said, watching some pied wagtails perched on the path-side handrail that ran from the pavement up the slope to the front door. A buddleia swayed in the wind on one side of the small garden and the scrawny dog rose looked even more pathetic than usual, flopping around against the wall below the window.

'It's true that you are in sole charge of what Mr Franken does with his money?' Matty Chalk asked.

'I'm part of a team, a good and dedicated team of individuals within the CTLD who are supporting an ever increasing number of people, working with increasingly limited resources and a very tight budget.'

'Now is not the time for sound bites, Mr Antrim,' Matty Chalk said. 'You are the one responsible for Mr Franken?'

'Frankly that is none of your business,' said Henry.

The presenter laughed. 'OK, Mr Antrim. I will tell you what is common knowledge and you can be as open or as closed as you like. You will understand, of course, that I would not be calling you, specifically, without good reason.'

'I hope I never understand what goes on in your muddy head, Mr Chalk,' Henry shrugged. He looked back out of the window, reached for his mother's rosary, twiddled it between his fingers, saying a quiet prayer to Our Lady of Lourdes, asking for the patience to keep calm. As he came to the end of the prayer, Sal farted; Henry grinned, tutted, 'Have you no respect?' and massaged the dog's ear.

'Right,' said the presenter. 'We know Mr Franken is on Direct Payments...'

'As are many people. It is a good scheme.'

'Quite, and his account is overseen by the Rowan Organisation with you managing his day to day finances.'

'I am sure you are breaking all sorts of privacy laws here,' said Henry. 'I hear that happens a lot in the media world. You lot have different rules of behaviour to normal people,' but the presenter ignored him.

'Now tell me,' he said. 'I need to get this right for our listeners. I understand that a fair sum of this council money, this taxpayers' money to which Mr Franken is eligible through his benefits via the Direct Payment Scheme, has been spent in the private shop on Dillwyn Street. The sex shop on Dillwyn Street in Swansea. What I'm interested in is who authorised this spending, whether the council has been made aware that one of the vulnerable people they support in an authority-approved premises is a regular visitor to a sex shop? This is taxpayers' money after all. It should be accounted for?'

Henry frowned, and then he laughed out loud. 'Jesus,' he said. The phone felt sweaty suddenly in his hand. 'That, you twat, has nothing to do with you or anyone else.'

'No denial from Henry Antrim. You're here live on the Coastal Radio 345, *Vox Populi* show and I'll remind you. Live on air. We've been talking about care in the community. Whether it really is a good thing, or whether vulnerable people are better off in centrally managed premises? Rather that, than living under the guidance of maverick social workers, particularly ones with lax moral standards. How is it acceptable for a social worker to take so much interest in a client that he becomes a regular frequenter of a sex shop. How does gay pornography sit with...'

'Knob-head,' said Henry. He turned, steadied himself against the wall and switched off his phone. He sat down in the nearest chair and stared at the ceiling. A moment later he heard Cathy walking down the stairs from the kitchen. She came in, smiled wearily and sat down beside him.

'Well?' Cathy said softly, putting her arm around his shoulder. 'That didn't sound good.'

'Ah,' Henry nodded. 'Not a triumph I think, no.'

'Gay pornography?'

'That's the funny thing,' Henry said. He smiled at her. 'Dan was one of my heroes when I was a boy, you know? One of the toughest men I'd ever met.'

Cathy nodded silently.

'You remember I took him to see Brokeback Mountain.'

'A while ago. I remember.'

'I love westerns. 3.10 to Yuma, Butch Cassidy, Gary Cooper movies. That sort of stuff.'

'Everyone likes a good western.'

'I didn't think Dan would like Brokeback Mountain, but he said he wanted to go and he loved it; Dan did. He said he wanted to go again.'

'I remember you both going.'

'A couple of weeks later we were in town, going up Dillwyn Street and Dan said he wanted to go into the sex shop.' Henry shook his head urgently. 'I wasn't my idea Cathy, and I wouldn't let him that first time. I brought him home, but it didn't seem right to stop him if that's what he wanted to do. Human rights and all of that. I asked Carlo what he thought and...'

'Why didn't ask me?' Cathy asked.

'We should have done. I'm sorry.'

'Yes, you should.'

They were quiet for a moment. 'We've always said that Dan should be supported to do whatever he wants,' Henry said. 'You and Carlo have been great like that. Same as you tried to give Helen as full a life as possible, right? Dan's a grown man not a child. He has MS but he knows what he wants. There's nothing wrong with his mind.'

'Nothing at all.'

'Carlo agreed with me. He said he was sure you'd feel the same but we didn't tell you because we were embarrassed.'

'Embarrassed?'

'Yeah, well... I've never talked about anything like that with you Cathy,' he grinned. 'I've never even heard you swear! I wouldn't know where to start.'

'Carlo should have told me.'

'I'm sorry,' Henry looked at his feet. 'I really am.'

'So what did you do?'

'The first time we went into the shop, Dan's eyes went wild. He could hardly control himself and went into spasm. I had to take him out into the street away to calm him down. Later we went back and, well, spent a lot of money on magazines and videos. And it was all gay stuff. You don't want to know what.'

'I certainly don't.'

'Carlo went to see Father Kelleher to ask him what we should do.'

'And did he help?'

'Well, no. Actually, he was away on retreat on Caldey Island, but his stand-in wasn't much help. Father Stephens. Not really much help at all. He said the Catholic Church believes homosexuality is a grievous sin and that pornography is the closest thing to it, and that we were helping the work of the devil by supplying it to the poor man.'

'Wow,' said Cathy.

'Yeah.' Henry nodded. 'He quoted Leviticus. "You shall not lie with a male as with a woman. It is an abomination." Halleluiah,' Henry pulled a face. 'So say the Word of the Lord.'

'Wow.'

'Yeah, but if I remember the Bible, Jesus was more interested in sorting out the bankers and moneylenders than having a go at gays. Isn't that right?'

'He had a good line in fighting social injustice.'

'Jesus was a true social worker, that's for sure.'

'Well,' Cathy said. 'What happens now? What happens now for Dan?'

'Well I don't suppose my performance on the radio will have helped all that much.'

'No,' Cathy shook her head. 'I don't suppose it will.'

Henry felt his mobile phone vibrate in his hands and looked down at the screen. 'Here we go.' He held the phone to his ear.

'Hi Gaye,' he said. 'Yeah, OK. I'll hold.' He cupped the receiver. 'It's Korkenhasel's secretary,' he said to Cathy.

'Your Director?'

'Oh yeah,' Henry nodded. 'I guess this is where we find out what happens next,' he said.

Chapter Twenty Two

6.45pm 3rd September 2007

Maddie turned in Henry's doorway. She smiled as she waved to him and let herself into his house. Dwayne was up there waiting anxiously; curry on the hob, clean sheets on the bed. Monday night and real life was taking place in the form of a cold commercial transaction between two consenting adults.

Henry yawned and pinched the bridge of his nose. He eased himself down in his seat, lit a cigarette and opened the car window. It was still light and the swallows clung to the telephone wires like notes to a clef. He reached for the radio and an old Fleetwood Mac song filled the car—the Peter Green bluesy Fleetwood Mac, not the MOR Californian version.

'Now when I talk to God I knew he'd understand,' sang Peter Green.

'I haven't heard this in years,' Henry murmured.

'He said "Stick by me and I'll be your guiding hand. But don't ask me what I think of you I might not give the answer that you want me to."

Henry smiled, yawned and leant his head against the window. 'Well God,' he said. 'What do you think of me?'

Henry woke to find Maddie tapping on the car window. It was dark and she laughed as he opened the door to let her in.

'Hello sleepy head,' she said. 'Some watchman you'd make.'

'I've been chatting with God,' Henry said as he rubbed his eyes. 'In my dreams, I guess.'

'Oh yeah? And what did he have to say? '

'That I'm a bit of a wally.'

'You are a bit of a wally.'

'He's a good judge of character then. He also said I sleep around too much.'

'He'd be right about that too.'

'Yeah,' Henry said as he slipped the car into gear. 'I guess he would be right about most things, being God.'

Chapter Twenty Three
4th September 2007

'Fuck you very much for seeing me, Mr Korkenhasel,' Henry mumbled in the doorway.

'Of course, it's my pleasure,' Tim Korkenhasel said, shaking his hand briefly. 'I called you in, so I should be thanking you for coming.' His fingers felt cold and clammy as their tips slid in and out of Henry's hand. His nails were white and clipped and the cuffs of his sky blue shirt were buttoned tight against his wrists. 'I hope I didn't hold you up,' he ushered Henry to a chair. 'Got caught in an Exec meeting, you see. These things do go on.'

'No it's fine, Mr Korkenhasel,' Henry smiled. 'Been in the job long enough to be used to hanging around while the important work gets done in the Board Room.'

'Yes of course you have,' Tim looked at him. 'Of course you have,' he nodded studiously, glanced up and saw Henry copying him. 'We've known each other a long time, haven't we, Henry. Since way back when.'

'Since college,' Henry said, sucking on his bottom lip. 'You were my mentor for a time.'

'Was I really? I'd quite forgotten.'

'You were a simple social worker then of course.'

'Of course. I was just starting out.'

'And now you're the big dog.'

'Quite.'

'Big dog with the big plumbs.'

'Yes.'

'You were my mentor until that business with my dissertation about assisted suicide.'

'Oh. Yes. That. Yes of course. I remember that.'

Henry watched his boss's embarrassment with pleasure. 'First there was the one I planned to write about the changes that are needed in the NHS,' he said. 'Too many chiefs and not enough cleaners. You remember? You didn't think much of that idea.'

'Right, yes, I remember.' Mentor and student had had one hell of an argument over that. 'An unfortunate business,' Tim shook his head, remembering how he had lectured young Henry over the dangers of alienating your superiors, making those above feel threatened by your ideas. Somehow even as he had given that advice, Tim knew he was failing Henry as a mentor, and Henry had known it too as he'd laughed and called him a 'dickhead', offering to write about a less controversial subject.

'How about the 'bonus funding clause',' Henry said sharply, grinning as Tim's expression froze and he turned away.

Tim Korkenhasel had been praised in Council circles for the paper he'd written supporting the London Government's Targets for Adoption Strategy that included a 'bonus funding clause' for local authorities meeting adoption targets. This scheme encouraged local authorities to take more children into care and place them with adoptive parents. As the number of new adoptions went up, naturally so did the number of children taken forcefully from their birth-parents. More children taken into care meant there were more children available for adoption and that meant more 'bonus funding' for each Authority.

When Henry questioned him, Tim defended this 'trade in children', pointing out that adoptive parents jump through hoops to get a child to love and care for, while birth-parents were usually 'young girls who found themselves pregnant after one too many bottles of alco-pop and a fumble with a stranger at a bus stop. The children are better off with the new parents who really want them,' he'd emphasised, 'even if it sounds a bit draconian.'

Henry had just been leaving his mentor's office when he turned slightly, peeping back out of the corner of his eye. He had stifled a laugh as he said, 'Actually, I'm thinking about writing about the supporting role a social worker should play when it comes to assisted suicide.' And he left the room before Tim could reply.

'And here we are,' Henry said. 'The years slide by. You're the Director and I, in the absence of anyone more malleable, am a Senior Social Worker in charge of a so-called team of dozens.'

'Yes, quite,' Tim said doubtfully, and he watched Henry grin. 'Well, anyway, surely we've known each other long enough for you to call me Tim. Enough formality! We're both on the same side and I do so dislike formality.'

'Of course, Tim,' Henry nodded. 'Of course.' Henry held his folder of notes tight in his left hand while he clenched his right into a fist.

Tim smiled as he wandered round behind his desk. He had one hand in the pocket of his trousers while he waved his other arm around in an expansive gesture. 'Well, Henry. Do take a pew.'

Henry sank into the easy chair. It was set at right angles to the desk so he had to twist and turn to face Tim, towering high above him across the wide oak desk.

Tim looked down at Henry with amusement. He leant forward, resting his elbows on the table and crossing his fingers in front of his chin. 'I'm sorry about the chair, Henry,' he said. 'It's not the most comfortable is it? I mean to change it, but with budgets the way they are, one has to prioritise.' His lent back in his own chair which gave silently with a lovely smooth action as it rotated. 'It is the bane of my life prioritising,' he said.

'It must be very frustrating for you,' Henry said coolly. Slowly, he opened his file, and rested the papers on his knees. The angle of the seat meant that the top of the papers were way above his head.

Tim's telephone rang and he held up his hand with a flourish. 'Sorry about this, Henry,' as he reached for the handset. 'My phone is supposed to go through to reception. Someone must have unpatched it. Won't be a moment.' His fingers were long and slim and waxen. They reminded Henry of stems of pickled white asparagus just as they came out of a jar slimy, wet and smelling of cheap vinegar. Tim smiled at Henry as he spoke into the phone. He made a face and twirled his hand, indicating the caller was a bore who just wouldn't stop talking, then his brow furrowed and he picked up his pen, twirling it around his index finger.

'Right?' he said. 'Dr Brownender? Right? No, sorry. I don't know the Elizabeth Williams Clinic, I'm afraid. Llanelli? Not sure why I'd have an appointment there either, let alone miss one?' He bent low over his desk as he wrote a note. 'Mmm? Mill Lane, just off Prospect Place. No I don't know it.' He turned to Henry, smiled blankly and shrugged.

'There's a psycho-sexual clinic there; Elizabeth Williams Clinic,' said Henry. 'Amongst other things. Psycho-sexual clinic,' he nodded, smiling eagerly.

'Dr?' Tim said sharply. 'Dr? What did you say your name was?'

'Brownender,' said the voice on the other end. 'Dr Brownender,' and then there was laughter and Tim hung up. He glanced back at Henry.

'Sorry about that,' Tim said, blood rushing to his cheeks. 'A misunderstanding. Some other... You know...' His hands were trembling. 'Anyway... What was it you were saying?'

'I don't think we'd got past the thanking each other for finding the time to meet up, Mr Korkenhasel,' Henry smiled.

'Right. Well, of course, I should be thanking you.'

'We did that bit,' said Henry.

'And please, call me Tim.'

'And that bit too.'

'It's much less formal. More friendly.'

'Of course, Tim.'

'We are on the same side, after all. Just trying to find the right course of action for our good friend,' he glanced down at the papers on his desk, 'our good friend, Mr, erm, Mr Franken. Dan Franken. Yes?'

Henry leant forward as far as he could. He held out a sheet of paper in front of him. 'I thought it would help to write some notes,' he said.

'It's good to come prepared. I am glad you learnt something back there at college.' Tim made Henry stretch as he passed over the notes. 'Of course, I do know a good deal about this case already,' he said. He'd slipped a pair of half-moon spectacles onto his nose and peered down at Henry over the top of them. 'A very unfortunate affair.'

Henry could see Tim's mouth moving. He watched the jaw going up and down, the eyes screwing up to stress the point, but he couldn't hear anything other than a dull drone. There was something about the way Tim spoke that was numbing. Words dribbling out, going nowhere, meaning nothing. Henry knew what he would say, and how he would say it and little room there would be for negotiation.

Tim held Henry's notes up to the light, glanced at them briefly, and set them aside. He took off his glasses, closing the arms carefully and setting them down on the desk. He crossed his fingers and leant back again in his chair. His shoulders were as rounded as its oval backrest. 'It's all rather a pity,' he said and sucked on his bottom lip.

'The thing is,' Henry leant forward earnestly, 'the thing is that this could have been handled better, with more delicacy and dignity. It's been made into a bigger deal than it is really.'

'I agree. The publicity is unfortunate for all involved.'

'Yeah, that's true, and I admit the radio thing could have gone better...'

'Quite. Embarrassment, yes, and not just for him. For the Authority as a whole,' Tim said. 'Social workers facilitating pornography, gay pornography, for people in their charge.' The sudden disappearance of his smile made Henry go cold. 'It's not acceptable,' he said solemnly.

'Well,' Henry said. 'We talk a lot about giving individuals choice in all the Council's strategies, and this is the perfect chance to put those strategies into practice. They cover issues exactly like this. The Fulfilling the Promises strategy, right. It's all about giving service users more freedom of choice, isn't it?' He waited for Tim to nod his agreement. 'Right. It's about empowerment. Empowering people to make their own decisions over how they choose to live their lives in a real life context,' Henry's whole body felt itchy. While Tim smiled and nodded his agreement, his eyes were blank as marbles. 'Surely this is what Direct Payments were set up for,' Henry said with a measured tone. 'It's not a common life choice, but Dan's capable of choosing what he wants to watch or read. I don't see anyone has the right to refuse him his freedom of choice. You must agree?'

'Would you like some tea?' Tim asked; keen to break Henry's flow. 'I'm sorry. I should have offered when you arrived. I could call for some if you fancy a cup? It's not terribly good here, as you know, but a bad cup of tea is better than no cup of tea, isn't that right?' He picked up the telephone and dialled a number.

'No, I'm fine,' Henry said. 'About Dan, you must see that…'

'Hi, Gaye?' Tim said. 'Could I have a cup of tea in here? You sure?' Henry shook his head. 'Just one, Gaye. Yes, thanks. Lady Grey? Yes, that would be excellent.' He hung up the telephone and breathed in, sucking in the air through loose, extended lips, then he lent towards Henry. 'Tell me,' he said, his eyes narrowed and his tone cold. 'The clinic; how would you know that?'

'Know what about what clinic?' said Henry.

'About the clinic in Llanelli? How would you know what it was?'

'Elizabeth Williams?' Henry laughed. 'The sex clinic? I knew a nurse who worked there. She gave me some great tips about pelvic floor exercises. Don't half work well. Lovely girl. She said if you clench pelvic floor muscles, a man's control can…'

'A nurse? Yeah, right. Of course you did,' Tim nodded, his eyes widening. 'Isn't that convenient. And here you are, sitting innocently in a meeting with me when the clinic calls.'

'What? I…?'

'Anyway,' said Tim, smiling thinly. He placed the palms of his hands flat on the desk top. 'Aside from your silly games…'

'I'm sorry, I don't have any idea what you are talking about…?'

'There are three issues I see as the biggest challenge to me in my work.' He drummed his fingers on the desk. 'The first is making sure I have the right information to hand at the moment it is needed. The second is having the support on hand when it is needed. The third is knowing what to do when things have gone pear-shaped. And things have gone pear-shaped in this case with Mr Franken.'

'It's not as bad as...' Henry protested.

'Look,' Tim clapped. 'I don't think we're going to get anywhere here, Henry, to be honest with you.' His tone changed again. 'Your antagonism is misplaced and completely counterproductive.' He wanted this meeting finished before his tea arrived. He placed his hands on the table and resumed his drumming. 'While you are right that our policies are all about freedom of choice and empowerment and so on, and,' he paused, raising his index finger, 'it's your duty as a social worker to do all you can to ensure that everyone in your care is supported to live their life as fully as they are able. Yes?' He waited while Henry nodded. A short, dark-haired woman holding a mug of tea appeared in the doorway. 'Ah, Gaye,' Tim said. He took the tea without looking at her, placing it on the corner of his desk. Henry studied the mug. The World's Best Dad in garish orange lettering. It was cheap and tacky. Tim's son gave it to him on Fathers' Day a few years ago. Tim had wondered if it had been given as a joke, but thought not; surely seven year olds don't get irony.

Gaye smiled at Henry. As she turned towards the door, she said. 'Oh, Mr Korkenhasel. I forgot to say. The chemist just phoned.'

'The chemist?'

'They said your Sildenafil is in and ready for you to pick it up.'

'Sildenafil?'

'That's right.'

'I wonder what that is,' Tim shrugged. 'Must be something for Elizabeth.'

Gaye snorted. 'Sorry,' she said, pulling the door behind her. 'They said for you, by name, but of course it's probably for your wife.'

'Right. Thanks Gaye,' and as she closed the door Tim muttered the word under his breath. He glanced towards the window. Without a word he turned to his computer and adjusted the screen so that Henry could not see it. He moved the mouse and the Google homepage appeared on the screen. Sildenafil citrate. His eyes narrowed and glanced at Henry.

'Mmmm...!' With a yelp he closed the screen and pushed himself back from the desk. 'What the...?' He sprung to his feet. He turned to the window, gripping the radiator, looking down at the steps to County Hall.

'Are you alright,' Henry asked, turning to look at him. 'Mr Korkenhasel? Tim?'

'You'll agree that it's still the moral obligation of the Authority to oversee the overall wellbeing of every individual in our care.' Tim pointed at Henry, his lips trembling as he struggled to control the tone and volume of his voice. He turned, resting his bottom on the radiator. He spoke quickly, coldly. 'I have to say that I'm surprised at you. You're a Catholic, like me, yes?'

Henry sighed. 'Yeah, but...' he said.

'Well, yes, I have to confess I'm surprised that you are not more concerned with the moral wellbeing of those in your care.' Slowly he walked back to his desk, easing himself down in his chair. He leant forward, resting his chin on a clenched fist. 'The Church is not a supporter of pornography, or of homosexuality for that matter. No sex as a recreational activity outside of marriage,' he shook his head. 'Didn't God destroy Sodom and Gomorrah because of the homosexual practices going on there? The Church is not tolerant on these fronts.' He leant back from the table, pursing his lips like he was sucking a lemon.

'Surely the question is over freedom of choice and whether we can help Dan live a life that is as close to the one he would choose to live if he were able.' Henry said firmly. 'It was God that made him gay.' Henry watched Tim's lips stretch into a tight white grin. 'People are having sex all the time whether you like it or not.' His voice rose. 'People are paying for it too. Gay and straight. In real life, Tim, that's what happens. There're health-spars all over the place offering massages with a happy ending. You've got to know that that doesn't mean they're handing out ice creams at the climax.'

'Henry,' Tim started. 'Come on...'

'You can call it sexual healing or a forward thinking complementary therapy. Doesn't really matter what you call it. Dan's a severely disabled man, and his abilities are going to get even more restricted as his MS fucks him up. Surely he's permitted to enjoy what parts of life he still can? Isn't he? What difference does it make if this choice involves pornography? It doesn't harm anyone, does it? It gives him a release. Without a release of some sort we could be talking depression; all sorts of mental health implications. It's not as if he's feeding a crack habit.'

'Henry, Henry,' Tim shrugged, smiled and brought his hands together as if he were giving himself a small round of applause at a game well played. 'I never understand why you're so hostile. We're on the same side. You must remember that.'

'Really?' Henry shook his head.

'Don't be such a cynic, Henry.'

'I'm not a cynic. I'm the opposite; an activist,' Henry said. 'The antidote to cynicism is activism.'

'Sarcasm won't do you any favours. People need us, and here we are.'

'I am really, truly, one hundred percent sorry,' Henry said, 'but we both know the sides we're on. I'm here for the people and,' he laughed, 'your main concern is budgets and covering the Authority's arse.'

'Calm down, Henry,' Tim said. 'We need to focus on Mr...'

'Franken. Dan Franken.'

'Mr Franken. You say you're helping him live a normal life by supplying him with gay pornography, but have you asked yourself what happens next?'

'What happens next? I'm not a fortune teller. I don't have crystal balls.'

'You say you should help him with whatever he wants, yes? I want to ask what you plan to do when he decides he wants to have sex? Gay sex? Are you prepared for a string of prostitutes to come visiting him? Male prostitutes?'

'Now you're being ridiculous,' said Henry. 'It's not television. Not Jeremy Kyle. Don't make a mockery of this.'

Tim leant forward above him. 'Do you really think I am making a mockery?'

Tim's voice carried an added edge that Henry recognised and he groaned. 'Maybe you are right and that is where it will end up. But at the moment we are nowhere near there and it's mad to make the jump from magazines and videos to rent-boys,' he said. 'You might know more about this sort of thing than I do, but to my mind they're worlds apart; magazines and butt plugs and...'

'Worlds apart? Well, maybe,' Tim said. 'But from what you say, you should be helping people with whatever they want, no matter what. Butt plugs? I don't even know what one is...'

'They showed a George Bush shaped model of one on Have I Got News For You.'

'Anyway, what you're saying is that if they choose to break the law, you'd be doing the wrong thing if you stopped them. Isn't that so?' He was silent for a moment, his index finger and his thumb kneading his lower lip, and then he shook his head and continued. 'No. I don't think I'm being silly. Another scenario. How would you feel if he started going on the Internet. Gay chat rooms.' He patted the top of his computer monitor. 'How would you feel about helping him with that?'

'Computers?' said Henry. 'I'll suggest it to Dan, see what he thinks.'

'That's not what I meant.'

'What difference does it make,' Henry mumbled. 'It's choice. We couldn't stop some bloke in the street doing that. It's just that Dan needs us to help, that's all.'

'What difference?' Tim scoffed. 'A whole world of difference.'

'You might not like it, but it is Dan's choice and if that's what he wants to do, so be it.'

'You really expect me to believe you think it's as simple as that?' Tim said. 'I've known you a long time, Henry. Long enough to know when you are trying to push my buttons.' He nodded slowly. 'Butt plugs!' He shook his head. 'I don't believe you think this situation it is as easily managed as you imply it this. Not for an instant.'

'Dan knows exactly what he wants. Why don't you go and talk to him?'

Tim held up his hand. 'Enough,' he said at something approaching a shout. 'You can't really expect the Authority to tolerate this situation?' His exasperation was so sudden that

Henry felt he was putting it on for effect. 'We would be telling the world that the Authority sympathises and encourages and, in fact, actively encourages such debauched behaviour.' He shrugged, snorted and shook his head.

'But' Henry started. 'Oh for fuck sake...' There was no way to argue the point. 'Dan was very happy,' he said softly. 'For perhaps the first time, very briefly, he was very happy. That must count for something.'

'Certainly...'

'I'm sure you've read his file and will know what a tough life he's had?'

'Yes, yes of course I have.' Tim gestured towards his computer. 'His case is all on file, all in there.' He looked at Henry and then back at the computer. 'I used to think a hard drive was something you parked your car on,' Tim said, realising as he said it how lame a joke it was and that there was no way Henry was going to laugh. It was much funnier when the Leader of the Council had said it during the Board meeting. Everyone had laughed then. 'Anyway,' he sighed.

Henry pulled himself to his feet. 'I just hope this won't affect Dan's living arrangements.' He put the folder down on the desk and lent on it.

'These things take time to resolve themselves.' Tim looked up at Henry. He didn't like people talking down to him, so he stood up, held out his hand and guided Henry towards the door. 'To be frank, this situation has made me question your judgment.' He shrugged as he opened the door. 'You're Senior Social Worker now.'

'Temporarily.'

'I'm not one to make decisions hastily,' Tim said, 'but I will take into account what you said.'

'I'm grateful for that,' Henry nodded.

Tim's eyes widened. 'Well, Henry, I think that's perhaps the first honest thing you've said today.'

Tim held up his hand as Henry opened his mouth. 'I'd like you to bring me the files for all your charges.'

'What? All the files?'

'Yes. You have how many cases on your desk?'

'I'm supporting just over fifty people.'

'Right. Well if you'd send them along when you have a moment. Backdate them for, say, the last six months. Pop them on a dongle and bring them up.'

'A dongle?'

'A George Bush shaped one if you like.' Tim glanced at Henry hoping to see a smile, but Henry's face was blank. 'It's just a routine assessment, you understand, but essential too.' Tim shook his head emphatically the way he'd practised in the mirror so many times.

'One of the hardest things about my job is telling people things they don't want to hear,' Tim said. He reached up and rested his hand briefly on Henry's shoulder then he withdrew it with spider-like delicacy.

Tim's asparagus fingers slid gently into Henry's hand. They tightened for an instant but were quickly removed and Henry found himself wiping his hand on his trousers as if he'd accidentally touched something odious.

He called to Gaye from the doorway. 'Could you go with Henry down to his desk? He has some files for me. Wait while he sorts out the dongle.' And he gently toed the door closed behind them.

On the way down in the lift, Henry felt his teeth grinding. 'Man, I could do with a cigarette,' he said. He clenched his jaws so tightly that his cheek muscles bulged.

'You alright, love?' asked Gaye. She looked at him with motherly eyes.

'You know,' Henry whispered, 'I don't much care for our boss.'

Gaye giggled girlishly. 'Not many people do,' she shook her head. 'Not many people do.'

A little while later, back at her desk, Gaye raised her eyes from her computer as Tim Korkenhasel breezed past, not a care in the world. 'Won't be in tomorrow,' he said. 'Going up to London to take Julian up to the school train. Start of term already.' He shook his head. 'Where does the time go?' He winked at her. 'Where does the time go?' He grinned the grin of a man who believed himself untouchable. 'If anyone wants me, tell them I'm on a course.'

Chapter Twenty Four

17th September 2007

'So, the decision makers have done their review and they reckon this is the best place for you. You're staying here then, Dan,' Henry said as he slumped down onto the sofa, but Dan wouldn't look at him. He reached for the buttons on his talk/type device.

'THANKS,' he said and the two of them sat there in silence. Dan's eyes drifted listlessly. He accepted food and drink without relish and watched the television with little interest. When Henry said something, Dan lifted his eyebrows in acknowledgment, but said nothing, and when Henry got up to go, Dan nodded at him and that was it.

'It's like he's died inside,' Cathy said a few weeks later. 'He's broken. It's like he's so embarrassed that he's given up.'

'He's always been a man's man, with the rugby and that,' said Henry. 'You know there are gay rugby players. Rumours about Gareth Thomas and one of the Magners' League referees. Can't remember his name. None of them have hopped out of the closet yet though. Maybe one day. It would help a lot of folk if they did.' He stood with the Fideis outside their house. 'Hell, I wish we could've kept it secret.'

'We ran into Ruby, his wife, when we were out in town,' Cathy said. 'She just stood there laughing at him. Didn't say anything. She just laughed. I thought she was going to laugh her head off.'

'The carers say he's trying less physically. His body's stiffening because of it,' said Carlo. 'It's been weeks now and it's like this whole thing has frozen him.'

'He doesn't look anyone in the eye anymore,' Cathy said.

'I really think he's frightened we're going to send him away,' said Carlo.

'Desperate times, eh?' Henry nodded slowly. 'I wish we could find something, someone, for him, you know,' he shook his head. 'Wouldn't that be amazing? But before we can sort that one out, the big question is what're we going to do to help him now?'

'Perhaps it's harming him being here if he thinks we blame him...' said Cathy.

'Don't be daft,' Henry laughed. 'None of us are judging him. I don't think he thinks we are either. The whole thing's a joke. Dan's got to know that,' he sighed. 'Desperate times.' He sucked on his lip. 'Well how about we go away, me and Dan; just the two of us? No one need know. Just for a couple of days. Just the weekend. Give him a break, you know?'

'A change of scenery?'

'Exactly. Get some fresh air in his lungs. There's this guy I know who has an organic farm in north Pembrokeshire with cottages. We used to go there when Karina was little. It's up near Cenarth. She loved it; feeding the pigs, walking in the woods, seeing the badgers; that sort of thing.'

'Might work,' said Carlo doubtfully.

'The cottages are all set up for disabilities though they take anyone,' Henry said. He was smiling now, warming to the idea. 'I'll give him a ring. See if he's got any space for the weekend. It's out of season now so shouldn't cost too much. Just me and Dan. I think it would do him good.'

And the following Friday evening, as Henry opened the back of the Doblo and said 'Right then, sunshine, here we are,' Dan laughed, looked up at him and growled 'Thank you,' though it might have been 'Fuck you,' Henry wasn't sure.

The next morning Henry knelt down in front of Dan. They were on the decking outside the cottage. The early morning sun warmed their faces. They'd had breakfast watching rabbits chewing pennywort from a dry stonewall nearby and an elderly bow-backed palomino pony grazing in a distant field.

'Listen mate,' Henry said. 'I've no preamble about this but I've got some grass here,' he held up a little bag of what looked like oregano. 'I know you're not a smoker, so what do you say about us making some hash cakes?' Dan looked at the bag, twisted in his chair to look at Henry. 'We could make a weekend of it? Get smashed, sink a few beers. Watch crap on the telly? What d'you say?'

'GRASS?' said Dan.

'Yep, the sacred weed. Ganja! It's good stuff.' Henry licked his lips in anticipation. 'I've got an old mate in Ipswich who grows it hydroponically in his garage. I don't get it locally because people talk, you know, and my job... Anyway, my mate grows it for a friend of his who has MS. He says it helps him with his balance and stuff. He posts me a baggie in an empty toothpaste tube now and then just for the hell of it. It's good shit.'

Dan shrugged, his eyes gleaming. He struggled with his keyboard and wrote. 'NEVER DONE IT.' Dan's hand travelled so slowly now over the keys.

'Don't worry,' said Henry. 'If you want to, we can; no worries. I reckon it'll do you good. And if you don't, then that's fine too. You can just sit and watch me get wasted. But if you'd like to...'

'SURE?'

'Sure. If you like it I could make more cakes and bring them in for you at the Fideis.'

'SURE?' Dan said again.

'It might actually do you good. The MS people; the MS Society, they say cannabis can help reduce pain,' he shrugged. 'My mate says it's cut his mate's muscle spasms and tremors. He's got better balance and bladder control now. His speech is better than it's been in years.'

'YEAH?'

'He still talks shit, mind, but then that's my mate's mate for you. Anyway, listen; I had a smoke with one of the doctors in Singleton who reckons his patients on herbal cannabis are better at controlling their symptoms than those popping prescribed pills. He hasn't run clinical trials to prove it, of course, I'm just telling you what he said, and that's all.'

131

'RIGHT?'

'So we could make some cakes and see how it goes?'

'OK.'

'No, Dan. I don't want to hear an "OK" from you,' said Henry. 'That sounds like I am coercing you into it. I need a "YES" or "NO" answer from you on this one. Either one is fine, but it's totally your choice. I'm simply providing the option.'

'YES,' Dan hammered into the keyboard, gurgling into a laugh. 'FUCK YES.'

'OK,' Henry smiled. 'Don't shout. Don't have a cow.' He stood up and wheeled Dan back into the cottage. 'The only thing is that if I don't cook it enough it might make you a bit loose, you know, in the bowels.'

'WELL YOU'RE CLEANING IT,' Dan said and Henry laughed.

'I'd better get it right, hadn't I, eh?'

'I'M BIT GUMMED ANYWAY.'

'Too much information, mate,' Henry said. 'That's way too much information.'

Chapter Twenty Five
11th October 2007

Henry opened the door and Maddie giggled as she bounced past him into the room. 'Make yourself at home,' he said, and she bent into a deep bow before him. She wore a bobble-hat pulled down low to just above her eyes and her coat was done up tight to her chin. 'Hang on, what's happened?' Henry looked at his watch. 'Why aren't you with Dwayne? You're supposed to be with him tonight, right?'

'Yeah I am,' she said, 'but the thing is that he's got a girl with him.'

'He's what?'

'Yeah. My jobs done. He's got his confidence back. His mojo,' she laughed. She took off her coat, laying it over the back of the sofa, and pulled up the sleeves of her red woolly jumper. 'I went round, banged on the door, and this girl opened it. She only had her knickers on. Then Dwayne came up behind her and he only had his undies on too. It was a bit awkward really.' She put her hands in her pockets, and quickly took them out again. 'He told the girl that I was a friend of his brother's, of Gareth, and he told me that Gareth was out.'

'Right.'

'Yeah, and then he told me that the girl was his girlfriend and he'd see me later. He said to say thanks to you.'

'Simple as that,' Henry laughed. 'Well, job done. Nice one.'

'Yeah, I guess so, only its Friday night and,' she shrugged and scratched her arm, 'well, what's a girl to do? Blown out on a Friday night when I was on a sure thing, and I thought, well, I thought I'd come round and bother you,' she laughed. 'Thought it would make a change from last time I came by. You know, I'm a bit more jolly this time. You doing anything?' she twisted awkwardly on her heel and looked him up and down. 'Or maybe you've got a date. You don't wear a suit that often.'

'Been at a funeral,' Henry said. 'Tom Atkins. I was his wife's social worker. She died in back in the spring.'

'I'm sorry.'

'Yeah, well,' Henry nodded. 'He was a nice guy. Quiet. A gentleman. I went to see him a few times. He wasn't the same since Megan died. They'd been married since the war. Sixty two years.'

'Let's go out, Henry,' Maddie said. 'Go for a drink or something? You could tell me about them. We could drink a toast to the two of them'

'Could do,' Henry said. He nodded towards his laptop. 'I've been working on that thing. Joey Samson's construction company bought Tom's farm. They're building some massive estate up there. I don't know how they got planning permission because it doesn't seem to be within the Unitary Development Plan.'

'Wow,' Maddie said. 'You really do know how to have a good time.'

'Samson is a county councillor mind, so I guess different rules apply.' Henry looked at his watch. 'I've got to go to a shitty works event in a bit.' He shook his head. 'Some old guys retired. He was a church minister with links to the social services. I don't really understand the link. Anyway, I've got to make a speech. I've got to go along and say what a great guy he was. Thing is, he was one of the old school. Never liked him, silly old git, and there'll be loads more just like him there.' Henry had meant to have a shower when he came in and to change into something tidier, but then he got drawn into the computer and he hadn't done either. 'I've got to tell you, Maddie, you really don't want to come along to that.'

'Yes I do!' She took off her bobble hat and her hair fell across her face. 'Sounds a riot.' She peered at him coyly though her fringe. 'Unless you'd be embarrassed to be seen there with me?'

'Let's do it,' Henry smiled. He looked at his watch. 'Right, well, if you're coming with me I really need a shower and then we'll go. I'm honking.'

'Charming.'

'Ten minutes, OK? You want a cuppa tea...? You know where the kettle is.'

*

'I'll just be another couple of minutes,' Henry said. He felt better now, freshly showered and shaven. He glanced at his watch as he leant over his laptop. 'I'll just turn this thing off.' He glanced over at Maddie who was curled up on the sofa staring out of the window. 'We've got plenty of time and we do not want to get there early.' Henry really did not want to go and get lectured by one old bugger after another. Why are there always people who think they could do your job better than you, especially when they've never tried? No matter the situation, there always seemed to be egos at play. He sighed. With Father Kelleher gone back to see his family in Cork, the only priest that Henry would have called a mate wouldn't be there. Shame it couldn't snow and have the whole thing abandoned.

Henry rested his chin on his hands. He leant in towards the laptop. His eyes narrowed as he re-read what he had written. The intricacies of local planning law made it a work of magnificent bureaucratic genius, as near perfection as anything he had ever seen. He shook his head in awe. Congratulations were due to all the mandarins who had compiled this devious pile of nonsense. Few government departments could have written anything quite as garbled and open to interpretation. It was almost poetic in parts, and included so many contradicting edicts that it made your head spin. No wonder each local authority was able to play with it in a different way to justify any result they'd intended.

He saved and closed his file with a sigh. You can know all this stuff, but what difference would it make in the end? There would be some snitch somewhere whose job it was to find some other loophole to slip through, and Joey Samson was a slippery bastard.

It was early evening, he felt cold and he shivered. Evenings like these were such a drag. Last week he'd had to go out all formal to support Father Kelleher at the church. He'd been asked to go along and explain the importance of Criminal Record Bureau checks because the diocese wanted everyone who had 'access to children' to have one done. The parish flower arrangers had refused, saying it was an intrusion and an insult to suggest they needed them. There had been no flowers at church for the last three weeks as a standoff had ensued. Henry had yelled to himself in frustration as he drove home afterwards.

He was just about to close down the website when a picture popped up in front of him.

'Ah!' His hands froze above the keyboard as a picture of two naked men sitting together on some steps filled the screen. 'What the hell's this,' he muttered as he closed the box and found another springing up in its place. This one had three men soaping each other in the shower. The next had three sailors joined together in a daisy chain. With brow furrowed, he'd closed that picture as fast as he could and then a film started up, the thumping soundtrack making him jump and yelp involuntarily. He reached for the laptop's off-button and found he was shaking as the machine fell silent and the screen went blank.

'Shit!' he said.

'Are you ok, Henry?' Maddie asked. Her voice sounded floaty and far away. 'Henry?' she murmured. 'Is everything alright?'

'It's nothing,' Henry sighed. 'I think maybe I've got another virus on this damn thing, that's all. I'll have to get Karina over to clean it up again.' He pushed the chair back from the table, stood up and stretched his back. 'It seems to have been invaded by a load of naked men.'

'Oh.'

'Yeah, and they're not that shy with each other,' he nodded, turned round and sat back down again. 'I'm afraid I just panicked and turned it off. Not sure if that was the best thing to do.'

'Oh,' said Maddie. 'You didn't lose anything important?'

'Lose anything? No I saved all that matters, but now I've got a whole bunch of images in my head that won't go away!' he started to laugh. 'Bit of a shock, really.' He turned to Maddie and smiled. 'I wonder how they got there. I was looking for something for one of the guys I support earlier. It was probably something to do with that. I've been so careful about viruses after the last time, and I'm pretty sure the virus checker's up to date. I know it is on my work computer. The guys there are sharp, but I forget on my own one.'

'Ah,' Maddie nodded. She chewed her lip.

'Ah?' Henry looked at her. 'I know that tone.'

'Ah,' Maddie crossed the room and sat down on a chair beside him. 'See, the thing is,' she said.

'Yes?'

'The thing is....' Her tone was gentle; a little dreamy. 'I had a peep on the computer when you were in the shower...'

'OK?'

'...and I'm not sure how it happened but I ended up there. I don't think I did it. You had a thing open. An icon. And I clicked on that. I tried to close it and it got worse and worse.'

'It couldn't get much worse than what I saw.'

'I think it was there already.' She turned to him. 'Henry? Why was that icon there?' she asked and Henry laughed.

'My boss gave me the idea,' said Henry. 'Korkenhasel. It was his idea.'

'Why would he do that?'

'Well, in a roundabout kind of a way he said we should help the people we support to watch porn as a sex-therapy type of thing.'

'Well, there's progress.'

'Maybe he didn't put it quite like that, but that's what gave me the idea,' Henry said. 'And then I got the idea that it would be good to help him find someone, so I had a look and, he held his hands in his lap, palms together, 'and found the gay club site and,' rubbing them slowly back and forward he looked up at her sheepishly, 'and then you knocked on the door and I thought I'd closed it.' At the sound of the dry skin on his hands he looked down and studied them.

'Oh,' Maddie brought her hands to her face to hide her smile. 'I was a bit worried that I'd misjudged you and that you were more into boys than girls.' She could feel her face reddening as she struggled to hold back her laughter. 'Henry, you don't know how relieved I am,' and she giggled.

'It's a bit embarrassing,' Henry said. 'And no, it's women for me. No question.'

She turned to him and kissed his cheek. 'I'm so pleased,' she said, and she stood up. 'So do you think he'll like them; these pictures?'

'I can't see myself actually suggesting it.'

'No?'

'Not really. The internet scares the shit out of me,' he said. He stood up and crossed the room, picking up his mobile and keys from the bookcase. 'We should get ready to get going. Don't want to be too late.'

'Did you find a club,' Maddie watched him as he moved around the room.

'Well, I found the Gay Wales website. They have club nights all over the place.' He chewed his finger, glancing at her. 'Then I went somewhere else and all the pictures started turning up and I couldn't think of a way to ask Dan if he'd like to see them.' He sat down again at the table and pulled a face at her. He shook his head. 'I just can't think of a way of starting the conversation.'

Maddie stretched and yawned. 'Sorry,' she said. 'I don't know what's the matter with me? I almost fell asleep on the sofa over there when you were in the shower. I don't know why. I wasn't really that tired.'

'You've always been a night owl,' said Henry pulling on his trainers.

'I know. I made a cup of tea and had one of the cakes you've got in there, then I got really, really tired. And then I nearly fell asleep. It was you coming in that woke me.'

Henry laughed. He fumbled with his coat as he crossed the room and sat beside her. 'How are you feeling now?' he said.

'Why are you laughing?' Maddie asked. 'Why?' She looked at him as he wiped tears from his cheeks. 'Well, I'm fine now. Still sleepy, but I'm OK. Really relaxed.'

'Dan's cakes. Did you have a whole one?' he choked as he spoke and began to cough. 'They were supposed to be cut much smaller.'

'I don't normally eat cakes at all, but they smelt really lovely so I had two.' She smiled as she ran her fingers through her hair.

'Two? And then you felt sleepy?'

'Yes, kind of stoned.'

'I'm not surprised.' Henry stood up. 'Oh, Maddie. It was a hash cake, love. The cake was a hash cake.'

'What?'

'I make them for him. It's why he's been so much happier; so much more chilled out since we had our weekend away.' He kissed the top of her head. 'How do you feel now?'

'I feel very well,' she nodded and then she started to laugh.

'I'm sorry. I should have warned you they were there.'

'I should be angrier than I am. I've been clean for ages'

'Mmm.' Henry said. 'Is it going to be a problem?'

'Hope not,' she shook her head. 'I feel pretty OK about it at the moment.'

'I suppose that's the hash cake for you.'

'Mmm.' Maddie looked up at him. 'Should we take some of the cakes along with us tonight do you think?'

'What?'

'It might cheer things up a bit?'

Henry laughed again. 'Do you think Dan would mind?'

'We could save him a few. They taste nice, those cakes do. You're a good cook. You'll make someone a wonderful wife one day.'

'We could cut them into tiny pieces and just have enough for one each so no one gets too much.'

'You're serious?'

'Mostly they all drink too much anyway so will be getting taxis home, so that won't be a problem.'

'Well, if you've got it all planned out...'

Maddie nodded as if it was all agreed.

'Oh, Maddie,' said Henry, turning to her. 'But then again, I don't know.'

'What difference would it make? What difference does anything make, eh? Anything? If we all fall asleep down in County Hall does it matter? Does it really matter? I shouldn't think we'd be the first to do that.'

'They're nice cakes, you say?' Henry shrugged, and slapped his knees. 'Well, alright then,' he stood up.

Maddie nodded. 'And they are tasty,' she said.

'I'll go and box them up.' Henry looked at her watch. 'Crickey,' he said. 'We'd better get a wriggle on. Don't want to be late.'

*

'Maddie, there you are. Where'd you go to?' When Henry found her, Maddie was sitting on the wooden bench outside of County Hall. Her elbows were on her knees, fingertips to her eyes, and she sobbed as the rain and sea spray soaked her.

Henry was out of breath and panted as he swung her coat around her shoulders, eased her bobble-hat onto her head. 'I told you it would be a shit do, Maddie, but I didn't expect you to do a runner like that.' He crouched down in front of her. 'It's not the dope, is it? Are you ok?'

The lights of County Hall reflected against the damp promenade and the wind sent ripples across the puddles. The waves crashed behind the low mound above the sea and the wind whistled through the conifers. 'This is crazy, love,' said Henry. 'Come on, Maddie. Let's go.' Gently he tried to help her to her feet, his hand cupping her elbow, but she resisted, wouldn't move. Henry sat back on his heels. He looked along the empty promenade, west towards the Mumbles, and then back up at the building. Two thirds of the lights were on, though the offices had been empty of office-jockeys for hours.

Henry rocked back on his heels. He hadn't wanted to go to this thing in the first place, hadn't wanted to take her along either. One drink, say a few lies and bugger off home. Simple as that, but then the director got hold of him, sent him upstairs to search out some pointless report that could easily have waited till Monday. And when he came back down again, Maddie was in tears and running for the door. Absolutely no part of the evening was supposed to include sorting out a stoned hooker weeping in the rain. But as soon as he recognised the thought, he was ashamed of himself and felt himself shrinking within his coat. 'Come on, love,' he said. 'Let's go,' his voice had softened, like he was speaking to a sick child. 'Whatever it is, it's not doing us any good staying out here.'

Wearily Maddie allowed him to help her to her feet. With his arm round her, she walked in a daze as he led her round the building to the car park and his Doblo. Silently she sat beside him as he drove through the town back to her house, but when they got there, she leant across and took his arm. 'No, please,' she said. 'Not here, Henry. Not now.' And he eased the car back into the traffic, heading towards his own flat.

Upstairs, on the sofa, in one of Henry's T-shirts and with a blanket round her, she sucked in the steam from her tea. 'One of them knew me tonight,' she said. 'They knew who I was. What I do.'

'Who did?' Henry asked. He was standing by his stereo, fumbling with the wrapping on a new CD he'd bought, Mermaid Avenue, and he wasn't really concentrating on what she was saying.

'One of them knew I'm a whore,' she said, and Henry's hand froze above the play button. He'd never heard her use that word, or any other like it before. 'He said he was involved in the case when they took Tina away from me. Child protection or something. He said I was a junky whore and always would be. Then he said I should go up to the toilets with him. He said I could do him in there. He said he'd tell everyone he knew what I was if I didn't.'

'So you ran?'

'So I ran.'

'Right,' he said, and he turned to face her. 'Who was he?'

Maddie shook her head. 'Just some bloke. I don't know his name.' She watched his face, his eyes narrowing, and the way he looked at her. 'I don't even remember him. I just want to forget about it,' she said and she began to cry again.

Henry crossed the room and knelt in front of her. 'Maddie, you can just stop, you know. Really, you can.' He gestured back over his shoulder, vaguely seawards towards County Hall. 'That lot. They all work in social care in there. Every one of them. They're meant to be compassionate. They all work with vulnerable people. They know how complicated life is. How fucking challenging. If one of them would say that to you, fuck knows how they are treating other people. People more vulnerable than you.' He rubbed his eyes, looked out at the blackness of the night, and then back at her. 'You need to tell me who it was.'

'I just want to forget,' she said.

'He could treat other people like that. Or worse.'

'You're going to say that it would be my fault for not telling you now?'

'You could stop it.'

'That's not fair,' she shook her head. 'I'd never keep it from Tina if I went to the police. She'd know where I get the money from. She'd never take it from me then. She'd never get to college. She'd never talk to me again. It's just not fair of you, Henry, to say that.'

'What he said to you isn't fair either,' Henry said. 'Life's not fair. Let's just finish this. Come on, Maddie. Let me help you finish this. It's your chance to really make a difference.'

'I think I want to go back to my flat now,' Maddie said. 'I'm going to go now.' She started to get up.

'Ah, Maddie, come on,' Henry started.

'Have you talked with God lately?' she asked and Henry shook his head. 'Next time you do, you can ask him "What the fuck?"'

'Oh Maddie...'

'I'll get a taxi on King Edward's Road.' She dropped the blanket on the sofa and reached for her jumper and her coat. They were both soaking wet. In the doorway she turned back to him. 'What you've just said to me is so unfair.' She closed the door and was gone.

Chapter Twenty Six
8.30am 15th November 2007

Henry woke with a jolt and rolled off his sofa onto the floor. 'Oh fuck,' he mumbled as he stumbled to the bathroom and made it to the toilet just in time.

In the kitchen, he peered into the fridge but found nothing appealing. He spotted the remains of one of last night's beers on the worktop, finished it off for breakfast and then he headed for the door. Expressionless, he looked back at his room. Then he shook his head. He felt for the rosary in his pocket, opened the door and stepped out onto the landing.

Sitting hunched over his desk, Henry's earplugs jammed into his ear, his eyes glazed as he stared at the computer screen.

He'd tried to wrap his head so deeply in paperwork that he wouldn't be able to see or think of anything else, but it wasn't working. It was the twenty-third anniversary of his mother's death, and he couldn't concentrate. He tried to forget, to think only of his work, but the memory of her as she died was in his head and there was no way of getting it out again.

Karina had rung him the night before. She'd told him he should pull a sickie. 'We'll go down Pembrokeshire for the day,' she'd said. 'Get ice creams in Cenarth like we used to, yeah?' and he'd laughed and asked what sort of example would he be setting if he did that sort of thing? She said she was worried about him, so he thanked her and told her not to worry.

And when she hung up, he'd started to cry. No daughter should have to worry about their dad like that.

Here in the office, with the thrash-metal band Slayer pounding in his ears, all he could hear was his mother's laboured breathing; 'the death rattle' some nurse had helpfully called it, just before the end. He squeezed his eyes tightly shut; leant forward and opened them again, hoping that he would see something other than her hollowed cheeks. 'Complications,' the nurse had said. 'There're always complications. It's them that kill them, see?' and he'd looked at her blankly, wondering if her words were supposed to console him.

He felt for the rosary in his pocket, his fingers flicking along the decades, not praying; just feeling it there. They'd bought it together the last time they'd gone to Lourdes. They'd taken a trip up to Gavarnie, a small village high in the Pyrenees. They'd drunk chocolat chaud looking up at the snowline and laughing as the children rode donkeys up and down the road.

Henry carried the rosary when he felt vulnerable; not every day, just, well, on days when the world felt shitter than usual. Pretty much every day actually.

'God will never throw more at you than he knows you can handle, Henry,' his mother had said, and Henry had laughed. He'd been sleeping on a mattress on the floor of her room, fitting his O Level homework in around taking care of her 24/7, doing all he could to keep her comfortable, and he was knackered. He'd laughed when she'd said that. And because he'd laughed, she'd wept. 'You must take your faith seriously, love. Really you must. It will help you be a better man. Without faith there isn't anything,' and every year he ripped himself to pieces that he could have been so callous as to have laughed at her when she said it.

'If you are listening in now God,' Henry whispered, 'make something happen today, OK? Make it different, special. If not, it's going to be a hell of a long day.'

Henry's phone rang. He thought of pretending he couldn't hear it because of Slayer, but he noticed a work-placement student looking over, so he switched off the music, reached for the phone and swung the receiver to his ear.

'Hello,' he said wearily. 'Henry Antrim.' The woman's voice on the other end was quiet and tentative, but he knew it instantly. 'Sadie?' His mouth felt dry and dirty; like he'd licked an ashtray, and the dish-cloth tightened in his chest. 'How are you?'

'I'm downstairs,' she said, 'with my uncle.'

'Thank you, God,' Henry mumbled, his hand covering the mouthpiece. 'I'm on my way.'

Henry bounded down the stairs to the reception, a smile aching his cheeks. He threw a quick wave in the direction of Adele, the pretty young receptionist who was always so friendly, and knocked gently on the door of Meeting Room Nine. Inside, Evan Griffiths sat beneath a blanket in a tatty brown wheelchair. Sadie sat bolt upright on a chair beside him. Just seeing her shortened Henry's breath and made him feel sick.

'Hello,' Henry said. Panting and out of breath, he pulled up a chair beside them. He picked up a file from the table and sat with it closed on his lap. 'Sorry if you've had to wait a long time.' He smiled at Sadie, noticing her taut mouth and anxious eyes. 'So,' he leant forward, his fingers scratching at an imaginary itch on his forehead. 'I'm Henry. I've heard a little about you, Mr Griffiths, from one of my colleagues but it would be good to get to know you better, OK? So, how are you?'

'Fair enough, Mr Antrim,' the old man rasped. He cleared his throat with a coarse cough. 'Fine, fine.'

'And you?' Henry asked Sadie who shrugged and looked away. She sat with her hands in her lap, fingers crossed and nails unpainted. She was clasping them together so tightly that the skin had rucked up around her knuckles. 'Listen,' Henry said softly. 'This could take a while with me and your uncle. How about you take a break? I'd really like a chat with you later to see if I can help you, as the carer, but there are a few things I should discuss with Evan that you don't really need to be in on. Alright?' He knew he could have said that better, clearer, and he cursed silently as he felt himself blushing.

'I'm fine here,' Sadie's lips quivered. She glanced at her uncle, chin high, eyes bright but anxious. She had her hair tied back, just like she'd worn it on the day she left him. 'Best know what's what, isn't it,' she said. 'If that's ok with you, Evan?' and her uncle nodded.

'If you're sure?' Henry hoped his smile was reassuring. 'There's this book I want to give you,' he said. 'I'll get it before you go. I've got loads of copies upstairs. It's called The Selfish Pig's Guide to Caring. Have you heard of it?' Sadie shook her head. 'It's by a guy whose wife's got Huntingdon's Disease. It's the best thing I've ever read to help new carers know what to expect.'

'It is daunting,' Sadie said. The shadow of a few lines deepened around her eyes. 'I've never had much to do with helping people in this way before,' she glanced at her uncle. 'Tell the truth, I've tried to avoid it most of the time. Bit scary not knowing if I'll cope.'

'I'll get it for you later.'

'Course you'll cope,' Evan said. He patted her knee. 'She's a good girl, this one. Her and her mum; taking me in. It's good of them and they'll cope. Her mother's the same: tough as boots.'

'Do you have a big family, Mr Griffiths?'

'Just these two now. But they have lots of friends in church.'

'Right.' Henry frowned, remembering the words of a speaker from the MS Society at a conference who'd said; 'You might get lucky and stumble on a friend prepared to provide a bit of respite, but it's more usual for them to be busy or away when you need them most.' Without a large, immediate family to call on, a carer is easily isolated. It is harder for family to turn their back.

Henry opened Evan's file. He looked at the top page then shut it again. Friends tell you to give them a call if there's anything they can do, but they don't really expect you to take them up on it, especially not when it's 3am, the urine bag has burst and you haven't had a full night's sleep in weeks. With family it's different. It's easy for friends to say the words, drift away and forget.

'Right,' Henry said again. 'So. You've just moved house. Change of town. Change of social worker. Change of pretty much everything.' Henry smiled. He glanced at Sadie, but she was looking down at her hands, pushing at the quicks of the nails. 'So, here we are. How can I help?'

'Listen now,' Evan said. 'I've been through this a million times.' He spoke English slowly and awkwardly, Welsh being his mother-tongue. 'You are where you are with me, right. I don't bullshit.'

'OK?'

'Don't give a shit about my care, anyway,' Evan shrugged. 'Got all the kit I need from before, equipment, like. And these two can help when I need it. Know I'm dying, I do. Obvious isn't it. Look at me. I've made my peace with God so where and how don't much matter to me, see?' Henry's eyes drifted from Evan's face to Sadie, who sat, barely moving, staring at her hands. 'What I want is for these two to be safe after, like.'

'Safe?'

'Right,' Evan nodded. 'You've my file there, isn't it?' Evan's face remained impassive as he studied Henry's face, and then he smiled. 'It's all there.'

'You've not read it, have you?' Sadie asked; her tone chilly. 'Evan's file?'

'I've only just seen it. You uncle was the responsibility of one of my colleagues.'

'Funny, see,' said Evan. 'Never did imagine having a "file," see. Not me. Had lots of things, but never a file before.'

Henry smiled. 'I give my word I'll never treat you like a file, a case or anything else like that.'

Evan nodded. 'Right.' He rubbed his chin with the back of his gnarled hand. 'Sadie's mum's my sister, right. Married a teacher, moved here. I stayed on the farm. Took over from my dad.'

'OK,' said Henry. 'With you so far.'

'Had to sell the farm to pay for my care up in Cardiff.' He looked at Henry, searching for understanding, but Henry shook his head. 'All the money went for my care, they said.'

'Right?'

'But it wasn't my farm. Not really,' he shook his head. 'Was hers too. Sadie's mother's. Social Services had no right to make me sell it, to use all the money when she owned half, right?'

Henry waited for him to continue, but then he said 'Right, well legally that's an easy one to sort. You get a good lawyer and they'll have a crack at it.'

Henry watched as Evan steeled himself. 'I never had nothing to do with lawyers and don't want to start now.' He sighed with head bent and then he turned in his wheelchair until he faced Henry full on. 'Bastards,' he said.

'I have a cousin works in Iscoed Chambers,' Henry grinned. 'I can put you in touch if you like?'

'We want nothing to do with lawyers if we can help it,' said Sadie. She glanced at him with a quick anxious movement like a rabbit. 'It's them thirty years ago that messed this up when my grandfather, Evan's father, died.'

'Right,' Henry nodded.

'Yeah, if the lawyers had done it properly then the farm would've been safe now,' said Evan. 'Capital gains or inheritance tax or death duties or something,' he shook his head, 'that's why my dad wanted it split. When I got ill, social workers sold the farm, like, from under me.'

'Fuck me,' said Henry. 'Sorry. Wow. Really?'

'And when the money ran out they shipped Evan on us,' Sadie said. She caught Henry's eyes.

'I'm a farmer,' Evan said. 'The farm was my life. Don't know nothing about legal stuff, but I know when I been conned.' Henry sat back in his chair, one hand to his chin, while his other hand slipped into his pocket, reaching for his mother's rosary. 'I was ill when it happened, see. When I got well enough to know, it was too late.'

Henry glanced at Sadie who was watching his hand in his pocket. Henry froze, realising she thought he was playing with his testicles. He started to take his hand out, but then stopped again; fearing it would be an admission of guilt. 'Right,' he said, louder than he needed to. 'Now, where did I put my pen,' and he flipped open the file to look pointlessly in there.

'There must be something on record somewhere,' Sadie said. She leant towards her uncle, resting her hand on his forearm. 'I read about the AVC scheme on the internet, taking people's homes to pay for care.'

'Ah,' Henry nodded.

'Not right, that,' Evan said bluntly. He stared at Henry. 'Bastard social worker up in Cardiff did the paperwork to sort it,' he said. 'Donnie Something, his name was. Said it was the only option. I don't want to go to court about it. No one wins in courts, except the lawyers.'

'You'd find few to argue with that,' said Henry. 'You can go to the Local Authority Ombudsman over complaints like this. I can do it for you as your social worker, but I'm compromised. You would be much better served through someone independent like a lawyer. Or I can get you an advocate, though you'd be better off with a specialist in this sort of thing. They'd know better what they were doing.'

'He just wants someone to accept responsibility and give the money back,' said Sadie. 'It wasn't Evan's farm.' She turned to Henry quickly, looking at him full on. 'It was my mum's too, or it should have been.' The clouds cleared and a sudden streak of sunlight through the window caught her across her face. She squinted in the brightness. Then the shadows came back, she turned away and her face showed true exhaustion.

Henry wanted to go to her; to hold her, to tell her that it would all be alright, that he would help and it would be OK in the end, but he didn't say any of that, because none of it was true. Forrest Gump was right when he said, 'Shit happens,' sometimes life is as simple as that. Shit just happens.

Sadie shook her head. She reached around her uncle to support him as he closed his eyes and bent forward as he fought off a wave of nausea. She looked at Henry, mouthing 'Please help us' at him.

'Do you want a drink?' Henry asked, standing up. 'I can get you a drink,' but Evan held up his hand to stop him. Henry hovered above his chair, and then sat down again.

'It's not right,' Evan said eventually. 'Taking your home like that. If I didn't own nothing they would have paid for my care anyway.' He thumped the arm of his wheelchair. 'That's right, isn't it? That's how it works?' Evan looked at Henry. His tongue flicked out of his mouth, bringing dampness to his chapped lips. 'So,' he said. 'You're my new social worker,' he nodded towards his niece. 'She said she heard you were different to the other ones; that people say you're the kind of man who puts things right.'

Sadie smiled weakly, distantly. 'That's why we came to see you,' she said. 'I would have come before, but...' and Henry nodded.

The hint of a smile found its way to the creases around Evan's mouth. 'So will you help me?' he asked.

Henry groaned. 'I won't lie to you,' he said, hoping his words wouldn't sound too pathetic. 'The AVC is a bastard of a thing to break once it's rolling,' he said, realising his voice had risen. 'Cross-county stuff makes it harder. Councils don't like being criticized by other authorities. Especially if it impacts on how they spend their money.' He stood up, crossed the room to the window and glanced down at the Director's Bentley. He felt his brow tightening. He glanced at Evan and then Sadie, whose stare hadn't wavered. 'Councils have an army of lawyers.' He went back to his chair and sat down again. 'My boss?' he laughed. 'He'll have kittens when this one ends up on his desk.' He turned back to them. 'He plays golf up in Cardiff with their Chief Executive.'

As he watched, Henry saw the fight drain out of Evan. 'The little people always lose,' Evan said, slumping deeper into his wheelchair.

'We just want what's right,' Sadie shook her head. 'That's all.'

'Who doesn't,' Henry said. His face softened as his anxiety faded into defeat. 'I just want you to know it's a tough one, this one, if you want to fight it from within, that's all.'

'But it is worth trying?' Evan asked blankly.

'My cousin,' Henry repeated. He bent down, crouching in front of Evan, taking hold of the wheelchair's arms. 'He's the way to go. Really he is. Last time I saw him he talked about the British Institute of Human Rights and how the Human Rights Act is being used to protect people when the Authorities misuse power. He warned me to get my house in order. I Googled it afterwards. Article Eight is about people having a right to a home. I don't know, but maybe it could be argued that they've infringed your human rights? I can ask him about mates-rates if it helps. The local authorities will close ranks to keep you out. It would be impossible if we tried to do this from within. But human rights stuff, they're scared shitless of that.' He looked at Sadie; his stomach turning circles. 'I really want to help both of you, but...' lamely he shook his head. 'You could see your Assembly Member, maybe, I don't know. They are pretty ineffective, most of them.'

'Evan's been failed by enough politicians already,' Sadie said; her voice and her face expressionless. 'AMs, MPs, MEPs, local councillors, everyone. It's a shame there's no Rebeccas anymore. Go up there and sort it ourselves.'

'Politicians!' Evan spat. 'Waste of time.' His eyes were steady as he looked first at Sadie, then at Henry, then he whispered. 'Tell me, Mister Antrim, would a social worker be allowed to help me with my obituary? Perhaps we could put in there about how the local council shafted me?'

Chapter Twenty Seven
28th November 2007

POVA.

'Oh, God,' Henry murmured, and he waited for a moment for God to reply. When no reply came, he held the mouthpiece to his chin looking down at the letters he'd just written. 'Oh, bollocks,' he said and he rubbed his eyes.

'At the risk of breaking the confidentiality of the confessional,' Father Kelleher had said, 'I think you'd do well by paying Natasha and Hugh a visit.' The old priest spoke so softy. 'I can't say more, Henry, you'll understand.'

'Yes of course, Father.'

'You will visit them. I'm a little bit worried, you see.'

'Later today. No problem,' and as he heard the line go dead he wrote the four letters on his note pad.

POVA. The safety procedure for the Protection Of Vulnerable Adults.

Henry thought of the last time he'd been to see Natasha and Hugh just a few days before. He'd been so pleased that Natasha seemed to have come to terms with their situation. She'd dug deep and found an extra inner strength to carry on taking care of Hugh.

'Don't worry Henry. I will do the right thing,' she'd said as she'd shaken his hand goodbye.

And now, in his car, as he headed out towards Killay, he shook his head. 'Do the right thing,' he muttered. He slowed at some traffic lights. 'For who? The right thing for who?'

Ten minutes later he sat in his car in the street outside their house, looking up at the building, unwilling to go up for the fear of starting a chain of events.

'Please let me go,' Henry's mum had wept towards the end. 'Why won't you let me go?'

'Because I've got faith that they'll find a cure and that you'll get better,' Henry had said, and he'd leant forward to kiss her cheek. He reached for the TV remote control and turned the volume up on Neighbours.

As an adult, he couldn't remember the number of times he'd stood with a family beside a hospital bed watching as they'd pleaded with the doctor to do something to end their loved one's pain? He'd watched the doctor slowly increase the morphine drip way beyond the recommended rates, knowing full well that it would hasten the death of their patient as the muscles relaxed, the pain fell away and the heart... slowly... stopped.

And now Natasha, up there alone, saying that she planned to 'do the right thing' just before she headed off to confession to scare the holy crap out of Father Kelleher.

'What the fuck does anyone make of that?' Henry popped a stick of nicotine gum into his mouth, grimacing at the taste. 'The right thing. For who? Oh, God!'

He sighed as he took his mobile phone out of his pocket, scrolled through the directory, looking for the name of a girl, any girl, someone he could bank on for a drink later. He smiled as he visualised the girl's face - the nurse from the beach when Megan Atkins died. He dialled her number, held the phone to his ear.

'Hi Gemma?' he said. 'It's Henry Antrim.' He paused. 'Yeah, I was wondering... tonight...Yeah... Today? Yeah, well since you ask, it is being a pretty shitty day today. I'm having a serious case of real life today.' He swapped the phone to his other ear. 'Yeah, I suppose this could be described as a booty-call,' he chuckled as he heard her laugh. 'So...You're not working tonight? Good girl. Thanks, Gemma. I'll see you later.' And he hung up.

'They didn't find a cure for Hodgkin's, did they Mum.' He spat out the gum into his hand, wrapped it in tissue paper and jammed it into the ashtray. 'I'm so sorry I made it so hard for you.' He took out his rosary, held it up to his mouth and kissed it. 'I was an idiot; a fucking bell-end. I'm sorry it took me so long to hear you.'

He reached for the file on the passenger seat, fumbling for the page marked POVA. He read the words. The protocol had to be followed to the letter.

'They'll find a cure for everything in the end,' Henry repeated. 'Will they bollocks!' He opened the car door and stepped out into the street.

He slammed the door and turned towards the house. 'What the fuck is the right thing?' he said.

Chapter Twenty Eight
2.30pm 9th January 2008

Henry yawned. His fingers played at the nicotine patch on his bicep, picking away at the corner till the stickiness had gone and the skin beneath was red sore. The stuffiness of the meeting room made his eyes itch. The woman beside him had been snoring softly for some time.

It was the middle of the afternoon, at a Community Carers Support Group meeting. Henry sat with a group of social workers at one side listening to the Director's annual pep talk.

Tim Korkenhasel glanced briefly at the drowsy audience and ploughed into his talk. 'In the past five years the Authority has implemented over seventy new initiatives,' he said proudly. Behind him a large, colourful pie chart lit up the wall. With a quiet click on the remote control he changed the pictures of his PowerPoint presentation. 'Alongside the Welsh Assembly Government's latest ten year strategy, we are developing a new focus of person-centred planning, which we will call "citizen centred," to be more in line with the work in other Local Authorities.' He watched how the colours reflected on the faces of the listeners. 'Our goal is to ensure that the customer receives the right service from the right person in the right place at the right time and at the right price.' The Director smiled as he watched the eyes of the audience blank out. One by one their attention drifted away as he spoke many words, but said very little.

Henry was looking at the visuals but all he could see was Sadie's face. He saw her outside the Odyssey that first night, illuminated by the neon lights, and he saw her grin as she lay in the bath wearing only a thin layer of bubbles. He saw her in the back of her ex-husband's car, sweaty and out of breath, and he saw her standing in his kitchen, in one of his old Billy Bragg T-shirts as he made her breakfast, laughing at something he'd said. He saw her as she looked at him and smiled one rainy Sunday when they walked arm in arm down to the arcade in the Mumbles and sat close together eating Joe's ice-creams, cosy beneath the bus stop near the crazy golf. And then he saw her from his window as she got into her car and drove away.

Henry rubbed his eyes, shook his head and zoned in on what good old Tim was saying. The picture of a smiling child sitting in a wheelchair with ice-cream all over her face beamed up on the wall. Summer really did feel a long time ago. 'The intention is to make the customer's voice a reality…' It was amazing how he could remove any variance of tone. It was almost as if he wanted people to doze off.

'Using the multitude of strategies and complex funding streams, I am proud to say that my team is amongst the most effective, efficient units within the Principality.' Theatrically, the Director furrowed his brow, brought his hand to his chin and lowered his voice as he continued. 'Of course there is still so much more to do.'

Henry drifted off again. He remembered how Sadie had been sitting with her uncle; grey and drawn, a little like his own mother when she'd first become ill. He thought of his mother, many years earlier, walking beside his father on Swansea beach when his father bought ice-creams from a man with a trolley. His dad had smiled as he heaved young Henry up onto his shoulders and laughed as he'd reached out to hold his wife's hand, his chest out, proud of the glances his wife got from other men as she walked along quite happily in her bathers. He must have loved her once, even if he'd been so gutless that he left her when she got ill.

'Care for the elderly is one area that needs constant reflection, analysis and redeployment of funds,' Tim said, catching Henry's eye. Slowly, he ran his eyes along the row, quickly establishing a connection with as many people as he could in the briefest moment possible. 'There is a growing need for us to provide a more flexible and responsive service for palliative care. New plans; strategies and policies to best suit ever changing individual needs.

'The Assembly has approached me to manage a project looking at how we can improve choice options and flexibility in replacement care for carers and those they care for,' said Tim. 'I have spoken to Mrs Berwick,' he glanced at the Cabinet Member in charge of Health and Well-being, who grinned drowsily at the end of the front row, 'about finding volunteers from all spheres of the care world as we develop the new Strategic Vision for Community Care. The more input and involvement we get from those of you working on the coal face, as it were, the more chance we have to improve the provision.'

Tim turned to look as the last slide shone up on the wall. It was a picture of an elderly lady grinning as she pushed the wheelchair of a child along the seafront. Holidaymakers in the background waved from the tourist tram as it rounded the Bay.

'By listening to everyone and by working together, with closer, more coordinated links between the voluntary and private sector, we plan to roll out an all-encompassing service to meet the needs of our ailing elderly and often alienated population.'

The Director clapped his hands and Mrs Berwick opened the floor for a quickly curtailed Q+A session.

A few minutes later the social workers and carers huddled in groups at the back, queuing for tea and passing round biscuits. The Director had just left the hall. 'Such a tight schedule,' he'd explained.

'It's an awful thing to say, but I wish he had a disabled child,' the woman standing next to Henry whispered. 'Then he'd see how terrible the services that make him so proud really are.' Henry nodded sympathetically, trying to focus on what she had said. Mrs Khalid was a Lebanese asylum seeker. She was a devout Muslim who wore a hajib. She worked at a support centre for parents with disabled children in one of the most deprived areas of town.

'Even if he did have a disabled child, he still wouldn't understand,' another woman scoffed. 'No way,' she wriggled with indignation. 'Gordon Brown had a disabled child who died. Did that make any difference to how he treats the disabled? Did it hell.'

'Cameron, the Conservative one,' said Mrs Khalid. 'His son is disabled, but we've seen no sign of understanding of carers issues in any of his Tory propaganda.'

'Caring Conservatism,' Henry smiled. 'I hate party politics. I'm not sure how it's possible for a committed capitalist agenda to have anything to do with compassion. Anyway, we have to hope Cameron will be better. He's probably going to be our next leader, unless there's a miracle.' He felt a hand rest gently on his shoulder and turned to find Mrs Berwick smiling cautiously, gesturing him away from the group.

'Henry, could I have a word,' she asked and he followed her to two empty seats. 'Sit down won't you? This won't take a moment.' She sat and adjusted her skirt. 'I want you to join the Reference Group the Director mentioned,' she said. 'I need social worker input. Someone who will listen, keep focused on the key points but speak up when there is something that needs to be said.'

'Wow,' Henry watched Mrs Berwick's face closely, 'that's very flattering.'

'Take this paperwork.' She handed Henry a slim sheaf of paper. 'I know you're stretched as it is, but have a think.' She frowned. 'I know it's hard sometimes, especially when there's negativity around, but you have to keep positive.' She turned back to Henry and sighed. 'There're a lot of good people in positions of power, really there are. People who have the power to make changes for the better.' She took his arm. 'Please be brave and strong and help us.'

Henry smiled. 'I'm chuffed you asked me to join,' he said. 'That's great.'

'Excellent,' Mrs Berwick clapped her hands against her knees. 'Thank you.' She heaved herself to her feet. 'I know you're busy, but if you want something done you should ask a busy person. Isn't that right?' She shook his hand with a firm shake.

'I'll get in touch later in the month to arrange a meeting. I've already asked Carlo Fidei. You know him: Helen's dad? He's had years of experience as a parent-carer.'

Henry nodded. 'He's a great man.'

'Thank you,' she said, taking his hands in hers. 'Thank you.'

As Henry walked home along the seafront a little later, he felt his eyes itching again. His backpack was full of papers and his coat pulled tight against the wind. With his tight, black Ospreys beanie on his head, he grinned to think he must look a little like a spent match.

The amber glow of the streetlamps of Uplands and Townhill shone through the early evening mist, and further away, fading up into the valleys, a twisting serpent of light marked out the roads and pathways home. The car headlights on Mumbles Road below him made him slit his eyes, forcing moisture into their corners. The gentle breeze coming in off the sea blew a tear across his cheek. He dabbed at it with his finger, the dampness disappearing into his woolly glove.

Soon he would be home; enjoying the company of the television, the view from the window, the six-pack in the fridge, paperwork to do and people to think about; home. He couldn't even stop in with the Fideis to talk about the rugby with Dan because Marcia the carer had taken him off to some wheelchair-friendly gay club up in Rosolven that Maddie had found out about from a friend of hers who went there. Oh, well, Henry sighed; maybe a pint on the way home instead.

Henry looked down at his shoes. He nodded along to the metronomic pat of his feet. The floodlights of St Helen's Rugby Ground flickered in the wide puddles Henry skirted. He pulled his coat tight and blinked again and his mobile phone rang.

He looked at the screen, eyebrows rising as he read the name Gaye Jones - the Director's secretary.

'High Gaye,' he said. 'How's it going? Bit late at night for a work call isn't it?' He heard her laugh, and then her tone was serious. 'OK? Right. OK. Tramadol?' His hand tightened on the phone. 'OK, thanks. It's good of you to let me know.' A dull ache began behind his eyes. 'He's quite a guy, our boss.' He swapped the phone to his left had and reached for the rosary in his pocket. 'I'll give Carlo a ring. Best get the Union onto it right away. Thanks Gaye. I really appreciate the heads up.'

He slipped the phone back into his pocket and whistled a long low single note. 'Right,' he said. 'The end game. And so it begins.'

Chapter Twenty Nine

10.00pm 14th February 2008

Maddie stopped and turned to look at Henry. She smiled, reached up on her tiptoes and she kissed his cheek. Then she giggled, took his arm, pulled him close and walked on. 'I love going to the movies,' she said. 'Thanks for taking me.'

They walked together, their steps soft and synchronised on the pavement. Passing beneath the streetlights, their shadows reached out far ahead and then drifted back beneath them fading, away to nothing. The puddles on the pavement were lit up by the car lights, flickering like real diamonds in Maddie's imagination, and cheap fairground imitations in Henry's.

Henry sucked his teeth, longing for a cigarette, and his eyes narrowed as he peered down the street. He couldn't see her face, but he knew Maddie was smiling.

'When did you last have a date?' he'd asked her earlier as they waited to pay for their popcorn in the Multiplex.

'You mean a real one? Well, that's years ago,' she took a slurp from her coke. 'It was before, you know.' Henry took his change and they turned from the counter. 'I couldn't believe it when you asked me out,' she said.

Henry had smiled. 'I've heard good things about the film and didn't want to go alone. Not on Valentine's Day.'

'Really?' the doubt came quickly to her eyes. 'That's why you asked me? Just as company? Didn't have anyone else to go with?'

Henry laughed. '27 Dresses is hardly the title of any film I'd choose to go to alone. Sounds like a film that... what's the name of the woman with the horsey face? Jessica Parker. That's it. The one from Sex in the City. That's it. Terrible toss.' Maddie looked at him confused. 'No Maddie. Seriously,' Henry took her arm. 'I asked you because I wanted to take you out on a date. An old fashioned thing. Going to the movies on a date. Popcorn and fizzy pop. This one sounds like a date movie. A chick flick. What we see doesn't really matter, does it?'

And now, walking home in the dark afterwards, Henry's thoughts were following the 'that's two hours of my life I'll never get back' train of thought rather than anything else. And then when she turned and kissed him, his heart felt heavy.

As they passed the Unitarian Church on the High Street, Maddie stopped again, stepping in front of him. She put her hands up to his face, cupping his chin and she smiled the weariest, most pitiful smile Henry had ever seen. Weary, yes, but so honest, and her eyes were alive. 'Thank you, Henry,' she said.

'What for?'

'For everything,' Maddie shrugged. 'It's just been lovely. A lovely evening. You've made me feel more special than I have in so long.'

'It's alright,' Henry nodded, uncomfortably. 'I had a good time too. Thanks for coming.'

'It's like a dream come true.'

'Well you know,' Henry looked away, her gaze too heavy to hold for long. 'Anyway, the night's young. Wait 'til later.' His words felt awkward, unnatural. 'Later you'll really have something to thank me for.'

'What do you mean?' Maddie's hands dropped as she turned to see where he was looking.

'Well, you know. We'll get back to your flat and then you'll really have something to thank me for.'

'Henry, It was a lovely first date,' Maddie said, her voice hardening. 'But it was a first date.'

'Yeah,' Henry said, though his tone showed he didn't care either way.

'Did you enjoy the film?' Maddie asked.

'I enjoyed the event of going there with you, I guess.'

'You guess?'

'Yeah, I guess.'

'But the film?'

'Yeah, it was OK. Cheesy chick flick. Did what it said on the tin, I guess. It was fun. What about you?'

'It was a crock of shit,' Maddie said. She was angry now. 'It was insipid, formulaic, predictable, blah, blah, blah.... Whatever. I just wanted to go to something, anything, with you, on a real first date.'

'Wow, Maddie. Alright,' Henry laughed, surprised by her venom.

'But life isn't like it is in the films and it's fucking irresponsible to set people up to think that it ever can be,' she said.

'It was a just a film, and it wasn't so bad.' Henry reached to put his hand on her shoulder. 'Wow, Maddie, you've got me defending it.'

Maddie shook his hand from her shoulder and walked away. 'To me it was a first date, but to you it's just a step towards getting shagged, isn't it?'

'Well...'

'Yeah, right. It's always the Katherine Heigles who get the James Marsdens,' Maddie said. 'Katherine Heigle is really annoying and I don't even like James Marsen, but why don't I ever get someone who appreciates me for me? Maybe I get what I deserve.'

'You deserve a lot, Maddie.'

'Really? I don't give a shit about the hot hate-sex with random strangers or whatever the fuck she says in the film. I just want a few Kodak moments of my own.'

'Come on, Maddie,' Henry said. 'We've both been around the block enough times to know that all the happy-ending talk in films is bollocks. It's like...? Fuck, what did they say? It's like we want to believe in Santa Claus, but you can't because we all know he's not real. I don't know what your favourite song is, but it's true that it probably was written about a sandwich.'

'Really? It's New England, Henry. Kirsty MacColl's version. A sandwich?'

'You like Kirsty's more than Billy Bragg's?'

'Yeah. It's got good memories for me.'

'OK, well, I've always been a Billy Bragg fan.'

'I know.'

'Yeah, OK, so that one's probably not written about a sandwich, but still...'

'I want to be the girl that Billy was looking for.' She looked at him coldly. 'I want someone to feel like that for me. I want my la, la, la, la means I love you.'

'Oh come on, Maddie. I'm not going to trade Billy Bragg lyrics with you, this is ridiculous.'

'Is it?' Maddie started off again up De La Beche Street, arms pumping, almost running, anything to be away from Henry as fast as possible. 'I used to think you were the milkman of human kindness, Henry,' she said as she fumbled with her key outside her flat. 'Nowadays I have no idea what to think of you.'

Henry tried to calm her, to coax a smile, but when this failed he said 'So I guess Valentine Day's over, right?'

'Wowzers,' Maddie said. 'Like I care anymore.' And she closed the door in his face.

Chapter Thirty

9.30pm 25th February 2008

Senior Heath Care Solution:

Question: 'So, you're a sick senior citizen and the government says there's no nursing home available for you. You've got to sell your own home and you'd hoped to leave that to your kids. So what do you do?

Answer: 'Take one gun and shoot a local council official in the legs. You don't have to kill them. A serious injury will do fine.

'This will get you sent to prison where you will get a roof over your head, three meals a day, your heating, electricity and television paid for and all the health care and support you need from trained professionals. New glasses? No problem. New hip, knees, kidney, lungs, heart? All covered, and your kids can come and visit you as often as they do now anyway.

'And who will be paying for all of this? The very same government that told you they couldn't afford for you to go into a nursing home in the first place.

'Oh, and one more thing, while you are a prisoner, you don't have to pay any taxes.

'IS THIS A GREAT COUNTRY OR WHAT?'

'Very funny Carlo,' Henry typed. He moved the arrow so it rested above the send icon. 'Very funny indeed,' he said aloud as he tapped the mouse. Seconds later a new message flashed up in his in box.

'You at home, Henry?'

Henry smiled. 'Sure am,' he typed, and as he did; his telephone rang. 'Hi Carlo,' he said 'Did you get it?'

'The Head of HR job? Did I fuck!' said Carlo. 'It went to a guy from north Wales. He was Head of Communications up there. Retired six months ago with a two year pay golden hand shake. He came out of retirement especially to do the same gig down here.'

'Wow?' said Henry, changing hands with the phone and closing down his computer.

'Yeah. His assistant got his job, and Dic Brytten got the other guy's assistant job. It was a right old game of musical chairs.'

'No way.' Henry frowned.

'Oh, yeah. Your old line manager hopped up a couple of steps on the ladder. That twat I was supposed to be defending on a double claims charge is moving to Colwyn Bay as assistant head of Human Resources because his wife's got a Godfather who's Chief Exec, or something like that. Nepotistic sons of bitches.'

'I'm sorry, mate. Should have been yours.' As the computer screen faded to black, Henry felt himself relax.

'I looked into your thing,' said Carlo.

'What Gaye told me?'

'Yeah. She's a good lass, that one. Knows the difference between right and wrong and doesn't want to see you get burnt.'

'It's good of her.'

'I'd say. Anyway, about this Tramadol. I got my mate Iain in the IT department to hack into Tim's computer to have a look.'

'No way!' Henry laughed. The half-chewed gum flew out of his mouth, bouncing once on his desk before it ended up on the floor. He coughed, picked it up and flicked it into the bin.

'They've got a Central Server down in County Hall so it's a piece of cake for the techie guys. Don't worry. You've got nothing much to worry about. Tim wrote himself a memo and called it Henry Antrim—evidence of assisted suicide.'

'Fuck me.' Henry smiled to hear Carlo chuckling away down the line

'Don't worry. It's no biggie. He's got a folder with "evidence" on all sorts of people. Not on me though. I was a bit gutted about that. Seems I'm not as important as I hoped I was. Anyway, yours wasn't hard to find.'

'Still, you've got to know where to look. Thanks, mate.'

'Happy to help. And so were the IT crowd. They've got a lot of time for you, Henry. A lot of people have, and the thought of us drones getting one over on the management helped.'

'Excellent.'

'Anyway; the Tramadol,' said Carlo. 'Tom was on it.'

'What? Tom Atkins?'

'Yeah, for his arthritis. His wife wasn't though, was she?'

'Megan? I don't think so.'

'Megan? That's it. She wasn't on it, but the autopsy found it in her system. Maybe Tom gave it to her to help her at the end, I don't know.'

'She always said she wanted to die up on their farm.'

'Maybe he just helped her at the end. But as far as I can see, the Director can't pin anything on you. He might try to suggest you should've known she was suicidal, but that won't count for much.'

'I never knew.' Henry grimaced.

'And since Tom has passed away now too they can't chase him for it.'

'I wish I had known. It's a lonely road, that one.'

'Yeah, I thought of you when they told me.'

'Well,' Henry sighed.

'Still, I'm sorry mate.'

'I wish I'd know about Tom and Megan.'

'You'd better thank Gaye for letting you know.'

'Yeah I will, and I'll tell Tim to piss off or he'll have more than flat tyres to worry about.'

'Nice one!' Carlo laughed.

'Karma. Always evens things out in the end,' said Henry.

'That's true.'

'Whoever is unjust, let him be unjust still. Whoever is righteous, let him be righteous still.'

'I know you're on first name terms with God, mate,' said Carlo, 'but don't go getting all biblical on me, Henry.'

'It's not biblical. It's Johnny Cash.'

'Johnny Cash? Well, that's got to be biblical surely.'

'Yeah, probably, in the first place,' Henry waited a moment. 'So this Tramadol thing. I don't really want it hanging over me. What's the plan here? How do I make it go away?'

Carlo laughed. 'Well, now here's the thing. And you're going to love this one. You've got to stride into Tim's office tomorrow morning, like you're Alan Ladd or Gary Cooper or someone. Tell him you want the Senior Social Worker job permanently with a pay rise, all benefits, the lot.'

'Just like that?' The telephone shook in Henry's hand as he laughed. 'There's not a hope in hell he's...'

'But first you tell him that that Konnie from Cardiff sends her love.'

'Who the...?'

'She's a Polish hooker who lives in Cardiff.'

'What...?'

'Do you use your work computer at home?' Carlo asked.

'I've got my own laptop at home. I use that when I have to. My work one stays at work.'

'Not Tim. He takes his work computer home with him and he uses it for all sorts of stuff in his off time. You're not going to believe it. Evidence of every website that he has ever been on is all stored in the council's central archives. The IT guys were killing themselves about it. I've never seen anything like it. See, Tim cleans up his browser big time, he scans it every night, but his complete surfing history; it's all there like a nasty shadow on the hard drive. It's really hard to get rid of it. It's all there, if you know where to look.'

'You can prove he's been visiting Cardiff Konnie?'

'No. No actual evidence of that. Just that most nights he goes onto some pretty freaky websites and he seems to like Konnie more than a little bit. Why would he be checking her out if he wasn't planning...'

'I don't really give a shit what he does in his own time, Carlo. I'm no saint.'

'I know that Henry, but he's not going to want anyone else to know. You don't have to do anything more than tell him you know and he'll be shitting it. Just ruffle his feathers a bit.'

'So, I go into his office, tell him Konnie says hello, oh and by the way, can I have a promotion?'

'Yep, that's the way to play it. And you could send him the Senior Health Care Solution joke I just emailed you. Say you've got a whole bunch of OAPs lining up to pull the trigger if you don't get the job.'

'Just like that?

'"Buenos días dickhead" and just walk out? As a plan it works for me. And when you get the job you pay for our tickets at the Wales/France game. The Grand Slam decider.'

'Yeah, but when I get sacked, and we are watching it at home, you get the pizzas Carlo, alright?'

'There's no way he's going to sack you.'

'So, tomorrow?'

'Strike whilst the iron's hot, Henry. Make this Tramadol thing go away for good.'

'Tomorrow?'

'Listen Henry. You remember what your mother used to say? About God and never giving you more challenges than you can handle.'

'Sure I do.'

'Well you've got to keep faith in that.'

'You take care of yourself, Carlo.'

'You too.'

Henry rested his forefingers against the bridge of his nose, his hands forming a church and steeple.

'Tomorrow's the day,' he murmured. 'You're a good man, Carlo Fidei. You always have been,' and he thought of Carlo holding Karina for the first time all those years ago - a tiny creature with black fuzzy hair and huge eyes.

'How far do you think a baby can see?' Carlo had whispered as he peered down at the tiny form snuggled into the crook of his arm.

'How far? I don't know,' said Henry.

'Reckon this one can see right into your soul.'

'Yeah?'

'Yeah.'

'I wonder how I'll do,' Henry said.

'As a dad? You'll do fine.' Carlo smiled as Henry reached to take the baby from him.

'My mum used to say that if you have faith you can do anything,' said Henry.

'Belief in yourself has to help.'

'She also said that God never throws at you more than you can handle.'

'Well, I don't know about that, Henry. But faith's got to help.'

'Hope so,' Henry whispered as he laid Karina back in her Moses basket. 'Fucking hope so.'

'My mum used to say, "Never trust a man whose haircut cost more than your shoes,"' Carlo said. 'I'm not sure how much that one's helped me!'

Henry's face creased into a smile. The window rattled in its frame, water crawling down it as the rain came in off the sea. His eyes flicked from the window to the blank computer screen and then back up to the window. Behind the screen, the deeper blackness of night made him feel tiny. He pursed his lips, the tip of his tongue flicking out to touch an area of soreness. His fingers felt for the nicotine patch on his shoulder.

'I couldn't give a shit what you do, nor who you do it with, Tim, you twat, but I'm guessing you won't want everyone else knowing,' he sighed, stretched and crossed the room to flick on the kettle in the kitchen. 'I think Carlo'll be right about that one. But blackmail? I don't think so. I think I'll hold onto my aces for now.'

Chapter Thirty One
5.30am 9th March

Henry found his clothes beneath the kitchen table, his shoes by the front door of the house he didn't recognise. He had a glass of water and let himself out into the dawn.

It was early Sunday morning and his mouth, again, tasted like a dog basket, only this time it was as if the dog had died in it.

He coughed up something horrible and hoiked a chewy great glob of phlegm into the gutter. He peered at it closely. His lungs were full of gloop from too many cigarettes and dairy products, but it was clear, so wasn't a chest infection. Could have been worse.

He looked up at the sky. There was no sign of the dawn. He had no idea what street he was on as he walked along it. As for the girl in the strange bed; her name, even her face were a mystery.

He turned left – downhill. Hands thrust deep into pockets he shrugged. I'll recognise something or get to the sea sooner or later, and he spat again. The taste of cheese and garlic filled his mouth and he remembered the visit to Pizza Hut the night before; the lager and the way those sneaky little shits had tried to stitch him up. He smiled then, nodded his head and began to feel better about himself.

He'd been drinking in the pub by the railway station. Watching the rugby as Wales beat Ireland over there in Croke Park, when one of the students he was mentoring called him over. She was blond, well of course she was, and big chested, and... Well, anyway, she'd smiled, licked her lips and ran her hand through her hair, making all the cliché signs that she fancied him. Even at the time Henry thought it was all a bit obvious, but then as he wasn't doing anything much and Wales had won, and when she suggested going for a pizza he'd said yes, and off they'd gone. He was all set for a good night; fifty quid in one pocket, a three pack of condoms in the other and he'd carefully left his mother's rosary at home.

The meal started well, she looked great, sat so close that she warmed him and she smelt like a florist. She wore a white cotton shirt with a lacy white bra beneath and her areola were such a magnet for Henry's gaze that concentrating on a conversation was a nightmare. But then her friends started to arrive and all of a sudden there were six, eight, twelve of them around the ever expanding table and the date had become a party.

Henry didn't mind. He struggled to focus as his mind drifted to Maddie, to Sadie, even to Paula and what they'd all be up to on a Saturday night like this. Karina was out in Cardiff with her mates, watching the game on some big screen somewhere. Before long she'd be a university student like one of this bunch. He hoped she wouldn't end up like this one, cosying up to her middle aged mentor, as he sat there awkwardly like someone's dad while the students went on about stuff he'd never heard of and couldn't give two hoots about anyway.

Still, the blond girl sat thigh to thigh and didn't seem to mind that he could see right down her top, so all was well.

Then, when he went for a pee, one of the waiters followed him, leant against the wall beside him and said; 'You do know what's going on, don't you?'

'I'm trying to having a wiz, mate. Not sure what your game is.'

'Your Karina is a friend of mine,' the waiter said. 'I know her from anger management at St Josephs. You gave me a lift home after one of them once.'

'That's nice,' said Henry.

'And I don't mean what's going on in here.' The waiter nodded towards the door. 'Out there. You do know that you'll end up with the bill for the whole lot of them?' Henry laughed.

'I mean it,' the waiter grinned. 'She's done this a whole load of times.' He patted Henry on the back. 'Tell Karina that Marcus said hello, OK?' and he left Henry to finish his wee.

'Pay for the lot?' Henry said. He looked at himself in the mirror above the urinal. 'Not a chance in hell.' He pulled up his zipper and left without washing his hands. He went back, ordered more beer and wine for everyone, a round of garlic bread too, and the biggest ice cream on the menu.

A bit later he got up, blamed his age for his weak bladder, and then he walked out into the night.

'And that's why you don't wear a coat,' he muttered as he stumbled up Wind Street. 'Aids the quick getaway.' He had his hands thrust deep into the pockets of his jeans and he grumbled to himself about all sorts as he headed home.

He was going home; really he was, only on the way he stopped in for a quick short and a chat with Gareth at the Odyssey. It was in there that he'd met Sadie all those short months ago. Sweet firecracker Sadie. The girl who'd rocked his world. The girl who was... well... who was probably up at her mum's house helping her uncle go to the toilet or watching Ant and Dec on the telly.

And then in the Odyssey... one of the bar staff smiled at him longer than she might have... and he woke up in a strange house in a strange street that he didn't recognise.

And then he was walking home, alone, bored to death of the whole damn cycle.

He came to a bridge over a wide river, and he stopped again. Slowly his mind ticked over. Where in Swansea is there a river like this? 'It's the Tawe,' he muttered. 'I've been in Neath!' It was miles home.

He sighed, unzipped his fly, and turned to face the wall. He looked down at the steaming stream of urine as it powered between his feet, but then a gust of wind caught it and he peed right down his leg.

Hopping, he cursed silently and did up his trousers. Feeling the warm dampness against his skin, he looked up at the sky to see if it was lightening, then he crossed the bridge and headed onwards home.

An hour later he stepped into the all-night cafe outside the station. They were playing Buddy Holly, and the girl there had a nice smile. Henry ordered a massive mug of tea and a mountain of toast, and he peered at a Sunday paper that someone else had left behind.

He was going to turn to the back pages, to the rugby section, but the headline on the front page caught his eye. Revolution for home care for old people. He held his clenched fist to his mouth, gulping back a rancid belch and he folded the Observer awkwardly over his knee.

Cash deal gives choice over services read the by-line. One of the most radical welfare reforms in a generation... also for younger disabled people frustrated by their lack of choice. The proposals wouldn't come in for six months, said Alan Johnson, the Health Secretary, but it represents a radical transfer of power from the state to the public.

Without taking his eyes off the paper, Henry reached for his tea and began to feel better. He took a sip, yawned and turned to the second page. This is the end of a paternalistic and controlling culture, said the Social Care Minister, Ivan Lewis. A quote from the chair of the Local Government Association finished the report. It should provide the foundation to give people independence, choice and dignity over their lives.

Henry looked out of the window. It had started to rain and thumping great seaside raindrops smashed against the glass. The shower wouldn't last long, but there was no point in hurrying breakfast.

He grinned as he imagined his boss reading this article. He'd be having kittens. The thought of offering choice and any form of power to the people would really piss him off.

Henry leant his forehead against the glass.

When the rain stopped, and the pee on his leg had dried, he paid his bill and left the cafe.

He walked along Alexandra Road humming softly. His head still hurt, but the toast was soaking up the alcohol and he didn't feel quite so sick. His mouth was still furry, but at least the dog basket felt clean.

He spat again as he crossed Orchard Street. A lump of wallpaper paste flopped onto the pavement and as he looked up he came face to face with Maddie who fell into step with him.

'That's beautiful,' she said. 'A happy Sunday morning to you too.'

'Sorry,' Henry frowned. 'Been a bit of a night.'

'Walk of shame now then, yeah?' she asked and he nodded. 'Bet you don't even know her name?' Henry rolled his eyes. 'Not a thing about her, I bet? Not even what she looked like?'

'I know where she worked,' Henry said and Maddie tutted. 'What about you?'

Maddie shrugged. 'I know his name. It's Peter. Short, fat, Cardiff Blues fan.'

'A Cardiff B'loser. Sounds a dreamboat.'

'He was balding too. Bit of a BO issue. But, I'm a hundred and fifty quid better off than this time yesterday and I didn't even have to take my knickers off.' She shook her head. 'No, I wouldn't say I'm on a walk of shame.'

'Some bloke pays you a hundred and fifty and he didn't do anything?' Henry's mouth was dry; his cheeks ached as he tried to grin. He felt guilty as he walked beside her; shameful of how he'd been the last time they'd met.

'Not everyone wants a fuck, Henry. There's more to comfort than that.'

'Great sex!' Henry said a little too loud. 'That's every man's dream. Anyone who tells you different is a liar.'

She stopped and looked at him. 'Hell, you've got a one - dimensional view of life.'

'I mean, he can't be much of a man if he just wants to cuddle.'

'I go round to see Peter once a month,' Maddie said. 'The second Saturday night of each month. He makes us supper, a lovely curry yesterday. Naan bread, poppadums, Kingfisher lager; the works. Then we sit on the sofa and watch whatever movie he's got from LoveFilm. Bridget Jones last night. The second one. Not as good as the first, though better than 27 Dresses. He drank too much. I helped him up to bed. I lay next to him, spooning, and held him as he passed out. Then this morning I told him what a nice guy he was. A real gentleman. I made him coffee, few bits of toast. He gave me the money and I went home.'

'Sounds a riot.'

'You're a prick, Henry. You know that?'

'And you?' Henry stuttered. The skin across his nose felt tight as if he held back tears. 'If you're casting stones remember you're not exactly been an angel.' His voice failed him as he saw how she was looking at him. 'I mean, why don't you...'

'Why don't I...? What? Stop whoring?' She started to cry. 'I'm going to. You know I'm going to. I've got my plan. And then I'll have achieved something. I'll have made it right for Tina. Then I'll stop. I'll be really, truly clean and I'll find someone I can love. Who I can be proud of. Someone I can take care of, who'll take care of me. Who'll be proud of me too.' Her voice was soft, pained; honest. 'Someone who will love me who I can love back? Like a normal person?'

Henry felt his knees going, bucking beneath him. He crouched down, forehead against them, breathing deeply. 'Jesus,' he sighed. He felt hot, far hotter than a walk in the dawn should make anyone.

'Are you alright?' Maddie crouched down beside him. Her anger gone, concern filled her voice.

'I'm sorry,' Henry said. He glanced up at her, reached over, and wiped a tear from her cheek with the tips of his thumb. 'I'm so sorry Maddie, really I am. I didn't mean to talk like that. It's not fair of me. It's...' He was all tenderness now too. 'I don't know what it is... Something about you... I don't know why I speak to you like I do. You do something to me and... You make me feel vulnerable. I... I just need to push you away. I just don't know.'

They looked at each other for a long, silent moment and then Maddie said, 'The truth is that I have found someone to love, Henry. I just don't deserve to be loved back yet. I know it.' Her voice was softer still. 'I have someone that I can't stop thinking about, worrying about. Someone who is wasting himself and his life on beer and pointless women. Someone who is killing his own spirit.' Henry held his breath. 'The only thing is, that he's a prick.' She looked at him evenly, stronger now that she'd come out and said it. Her eyes were red-rimmed and burning. Her nose ran and she pinched it away; wiping her fingers on her trousers.

'Oh,' said Henry. His hand dropped from her cheek.

'I might be a whore,' Maddie said, 'but I'm not a prick. You know my plan, Henry, and my spirit is doing just fine. In fact it's growing. It's glowing.' She stood up, looked along the street. 'I want to achieve something with my life. It's not much, but my plan is that thing. After all I did before; I want to set Tina up safe and sorted. That would be an achievement to be proud of. I would be proud of myself then.' She looked back at Henry. 'I don't really give a shit about sex. I never have. There's more to life, and much more to love than sex, no matter how great the fleeting instant is.' She reached down, took his hand in hers, pulled him to his feet and then held his hand up to his chest, pushing it tight against his heart, so hard that he took a step backwards. She smiled wearily. 'Sex is a brief passing thing. I want someone who'll look at me the way that I know I look at you. Someone who will be happy to make me pancakes for breakfast. That's the only other thing. Not every day, mind,' she said. 'I wouldn't want them every day.' She put her hand to his face, cupping his cheek. 'Come on. Let's go.'

They walked together up De La Beche Street hand in hand and when they stopped outside the Skin and Ink Tattoo Parlour Henry said; 'What you said back there. I am a prick, and I know it and I'm sorry, but... What you said...'

'I meant it, Henry. What you do with that bit of information is up to you. I love you, Henry, and I want to be with you, but I don't need you. I can survive on my own.' She touched his cheek with her lips. 'Take care of your spirit, Henry. That's more important than anything,' and she turned and let herself into her flat.

Chapter Thirty Two
11am 10th March

'Cheers, love,' Henry said. He folded his papers under his arm, took the teacup and wandered away from the counter to sit by the cafe window.

He looked out at the puddles as the rain came down. He watched two little girls, sisters probably, struggling to jam an awkward package into a letterbox. The paper ripped, one started to cry as their mother came over and told them off. The mother put the package into her shoulder bag, grabbed each child by the hand and dragged them away toward the newsagents.

Running the tips of his fingers across the stubble on the top of his head, Henry sighed. In the bag he had a pile of papers, notes and documents that had come to him following an Authority-wide review of all Council Staff Level Assessments. As Senior Social worker, it was up to him to go through them, though really it was the Director's task, had he not seen it as a hot potato and delegated the task to Henry.

Henry had tried to read the turgid nonsense up at his desk in County Hall, but there was no way he could work up there. The place was like a morgue. The living dead shuffled around, pale and drawn with hunched shoulders and grunted conversations. They were good people, most of them, or at least they wanted to be. The system was failing, and everyone knew it. It couldn't cope, and the cuts would only make it worse. All eyes were on Henry as his eyes swam.

As he went through each review he found that every single member of his team was due to be downgraded. They kept the same workload, the same responsibility points and credit for years accrued. All these things which still, in theory, carried the same point weighting, only the new assessment method meant these points were worth less in the overall scoring rational.

Henry had groaned audibly as he'd read the covering document. He leant back in his chair, hands behind his head and he stared at the ceiling. He looked round, saw all the faces peering his way, gathered his papers, got up and left.

'I'm off,' he said to everyone but no one in particular. 'I can't fight your corner with you chumps looking over my shoulder.'

'I can't afford to lose points, Henry,' said Walter, who'd been a social worker even longer than Henry had. 'I got a daughter just started Uni. I just can't afford a cut.'

There was a murmur, as everyone else pleaded their case. Henry shrugged. 'I'll do what I can, though you know it's a foregone conclusion,' he said. 'You lot know who should be doing this, don't you?' He nodded towards the Director's closed door. 'That chocolate teapot, but he's off playing golf on the Gower.'

'I thought he said he was on a course,' someone said.

'He is,' said Henry. 'A golf course.'

'Senior management are not being reassessed,' Gaye, the Director's secretary shook her head. 'You should know that there are seven of us ready to hand in our notice, Henry.'

'No pressure then,' Henry said. 'Thanks for the warning.'

And as Henry sipped his tea in the cafe he muttered, 'Chocolate teapot. Not even as much use as that.' The Director was a stumbling block in so many ways. He was the one that killed the spirit that should be driving this team, not sapping it of energy. If there were life in the team they could have provided a united front against the changes in the system and the cuts in pay that would follow. As it was, there was no heart and no inspiration and if there were seven people already threatening to quit, God knows how many more would follow.

Henry knew that many of the best ones would quit. They'd done their time, served their country, but enough is enough.

Those who stayed would include the ones who knew they wouldn't survive in the dog-eat-dog private sector. It was safe in the Authority. You got treated like shit sometimes, but you didn't get sacked for being shit.

'And the shittiest of you all,' Henry murmured, 'is Whining Walter.'

Henry spread the papers out across the table. There was a folder relating to each member of the team, and he had a folder of his own so he could comment.

'I'm the hangman,' he nodded. 'No wonder Korkenhasel delegated it.'

He'd just opened the first folder when a woman's voice behind him made him stop and turn.

'Hello Henry.'

There she was with her wet raincoat, hair tied back, and an anxious half-smile.

'Sadie,' Henry sighed. 'I didn't hear you come in.' He stumbled to his feet, leaning towards her awkwardly, his cheek leading the way, and then checked himself. He held out his hand, and checked himself again. To shake her hand formally or kiss her cheek like an ex-lover? He just wasn't sure.

She looked around doubtfully. 'I saw you though the window and just didn't know.' She pulled a face.

Henry laughed. He looked down at his hands, spread his arms wide and said, 'Come here,' and he enveloped her in a hug as though she were a long-lost friend.

'So how are you?' Henry asked after he'd bought her a coffee and they were sitting safely opposite each other. He looked at her cautiously as he stuffed the reports back into his bag, and he sensed her tension.

'How am I, as in you're a social worker and I'm a carer, or how am I as in I'm your friend?' Her tone was sharp.

'It's all the same isn't it?' Henry said gently. 'But friend, really.'

'The same? I suppose it is,' she shrugged.

'And your uncle? Evan? How's he doing? Has he made any progress with the farm?'

'He's been arguing with the solicitors about their fees.' She looked out of the window. 'Knew it wouldn't get anywhere, but...' She shrugged. 'We're going to go to the Council Ombudsman ourselves. Easier that way and we don't want to compromise you.'

She glanced quickly at Henry, her eyes cold and Henry looked away, out of the window. The mother and children were back with a repacked package which the mother slid into the letterbox. The rain was heavier now; the cars spraying the road. The wind shifted the leaves on the plane trees. The mother had a scarf pulled tight around her face. She bent down, smiling as she talked to the little girls and then she took their hands and the three of them walked away, the children skipping and the mother laughing with them.

Sadie sighed and shook her head. Her fingers worked at each other, pushing into her cuticles. 'Mothers and kids. Mothers work so hard, nappies, food, bathing: all that. I've never done it, mind, but it gets easier, doesn't it, as the kids grow up and get more capable?'

She didn't look at Henry as she spoke, just out the window at the passing cars.

'And they make their choices, parents, mostly, about if they want kids at all. It's hard work, but it's not for ever. Children grow up and get more capable.'

'That's true,' said Henry, nodding his thanks as the waitress brought over the coffee.

'This morning...' Her fingers pressed the cup until it became too hot, only to bring them back moments later. 'This morning I wanted to push Evan down stairs.' She bent to smell the coffee, inhaling the steam and leaning back. 'He started calling for me at six so I took him a urine bottle. When he'd finished he spilt it all over himself so I had to change his sheets and bed-bath him.' In the grey light her face was drawn, her eyes dull. 'I dressed him, shaved him, took him to the toilet, and he had chilli nachos at the multiplex last night so wiping his bum wasn't pleasant.' Henry laughed as she scrunched up her face. 'Mum made him breakfast and I went round the corner to get his paper.' She glanced at Henry.

'Right.'

'Tuesday, see. The Western Mail has a farming supplement. He always likes that, Evan does, so I got him the paper and Mum was crying when I got back. She's done her wrist lifting him and can't take weight anymore.'

'What happened?' Henry asked.

'She fell last week and it's all strapped up now. Says she's fine, but she dropped the kettle this morning and burnt herself. Didn't have the strength in her wrists to hold it. I've told her not to take chances, but she does it anyway. Didn't want Evan to see what she'd done so she hid until I got back and I finished making his breakfast while he sat there reading the paper. Mum was in the bathroom running her hand under a tap.'

'Best thing for a burn; cold water,' said Henry inanely.

'Yeah, I suppose. When I'd done his breakfast I had a cup of tea, and made Mum one and we sat side by side on the bath drinking it.' She took a sip of her coffee.

'You want a biscuit or a cake or something?' Henry asked. 'They're good here. Homemade.'

She shook her head. 'Evan called out when he'd finished, said he wanted to be pushed back to his room. I asked if his breakfast was alright, and he said the tea was a bit weak. He didn't say thanks or anything, just that the tea was a bit weak.' She shook her head. 'He's lucky there were no stairs nearby because he would have been down them,' she looked at Henry. 'I could have said it was an accident, easy.'

'I'm sure he didn't mean it,' Henry repeated. 'We all say silly things.'

'Yeah, I know,' she turned away again. 'And he'd be gutted if he knew how upset he'd made me and that Mum was hiding from him in the bathroom.' She leant forward, eyes narrow, staring at Henry. 'I never signed up for this, you know. To be a carer. I'm not that kind of person.'

'Few people think they are,' Henry said. 'Not until they have to be.'

'I came home to live with my mum for a bit to get my life back after London. You know all about that,' she shook her head. 'And then suddenly he's there with us. If I wasn't there, Mum couldn't cope and Evan would be in a home somewhere, but I am here and you hear the stories about some of those places; those homes. There was that guy who fell out of bed and boiled his brain against a hot water pipe for hours before anyone found him. He couldn't move. Still alive, but...'

'That does happen, but it's very rare,' Henry said. 'They check all the places and most are great. Really they are.'

'He's her brother,' Sadie said, 'and she had to take him in.' She started to cry. 'God I hate families.'

Henry moved round the table. He sat beside her and passed her a serviette for her eyes. 'It's OK, love,' he said. He put his arm round her, kissed the top of her head, his chest tightening as her scent filled his lungs, his cheeks pulled into an aching smile, rather that than cry with her. He held her close and she didn't push him away.

'I didn't meant to do this, Henry,' she whispered, her eyes red and nose streaming. Her cheek was damp against his chest. 'I didn't mean to come in and cry on you as a way of getting closer.'

'I never thought you did,' Henry said. He moved back away from her, resting his hands flat on the table. He looked down at them; the bulge on his left knuckle from when he broke it one time, and the horrible yellowy nicotine stain on his right middle and index fingers which just wouldn't scrub away. 'I want to help. I just want to help.'

'I know,' Sadie said her voice lower. She put her hand on his. Then she raised her hands to her face as the tears came again, slim fingers covering her eyes; hiding her tears. 'I'm sorry. I don't know what's the matter with me. It's just...I'm so tired. My mum, she begged me... He's her brother and she couldn't do it alone. I couldn't say no to my mum, could I?'

Henry grimaced. 'I'm so sorry.'

'I don't want pity either. It's about Evan not me. He's the one that's dying,' her shoulders rose and fell in heaving sobs. The cafe manager came over to see if she was alright, but Henry smiled and he moved away again. 'I feel like the victim, but it's Evan that's dying, not me. I've only been caring for him two minutes and here I am, crying in a cafe with you.'

'Oh, Sadie,' Henry mumbled.

'How do people cope with their body packing up around them? How do parents cope with a disabled child knowing it's always going to be like this, only it's going to get harder? I thought I was tough, that I could handle anything. Robbie's affair, the divorce, the humiliation, coming back here and starting again. Anything... But how do other people cope with all this stuff?'

'Sadie you're looking at me like I should know the answers, but there are no answers. We come and go in the hands of a nurse. That's all I know. There are no happy endings.' She looked at him and snuffled into the paper towel. 'Real life is shit and the truth is that often people don't cope. Good people. It's just not in them to be a carer and there's no shame in that. Some people can run marathons and others just can't. It's OK. Some can, oh I don't know, juggle or yodel. And others can't.' Gently he reached out and rested his hand on her shoulder. 'It's OK to be angry.'

'Evan's last social worker told me it won't be forever. She said I won't have to care for him forever. She said Evan would last that long.'

'Cold comfort,' Henry groaned.

Sadie smiled weakly. 'I am angry,' she said. 'But not at Evan. Not really.'

'No?'

'Last night we went to the pictures down in the multiplex. It was Mum and Evan and me. That's where he had the nachos. People didn't give us room or anything. Going through doorways and stuff. It was like we were invisible.'

'Yeah, I see that a lot.'

'Before, you know, when I was out on my own people always saw me,' she said; her eyes wide. 'Like you did that first night we met.'

'I remember,' Henry laughed. 'Nuclear Pussy. You were hard to miss.'

'Yeah. It was a lot of effort, but I dressed for it, you know. I'm not proud of it, especially not now, but it mattered to me to be looked at like you did. It's always mattered to me, but especially after Robbie. I needed men to look at me. Like I was worth something. Like I still had *it*.' She brought her hands to her head, covering her face. 'Fuck, I'm so shallow.'

'Don't be daft, love,' Henry smiled.

Sadie looked at her watch. 'I got to go in a minute,' she said. She finished her coffee. 'He'll need a pee and Mum can't take him, not with her wrist.'

'I'll give you a lift home if you want?'

'Thanks, but I'd rather walk. It's not far and the air will do me good.'

'OK.'

'Thanks, though.'

'You don't get much time for Unsinkable Sinks, I guess?' Henry said.

'I put off four meetings with the business development people before they stopped returning my calls,' Sadie shrugged. 'Don't blame them. The plot I was looking at has gone now. They gave it to someone recycling carpet tiles.'

'And your mum? How's she doing?'

'She's as bad as he is...' Sadie's hand came to her eyes again. 'I don't want to be disloyal but she gets so flustered it's like I'm caring for two of them most of the time.'

'I could try to get you some support so you can get time to do your sinks or...'

'I've tried that,' she said, 'but Mum and Evan won't even talk about it. Mum thinks she does more caring than I do, and Evan doesn't think caring for him is all that hard. He's used to life at his pace, but I'm not.' She slid up her sleeve to show him her watch. 'The minutes go by so slowly, everything takes forever but we get nothing done.' She pulled herself to her feet. 'Better go.'

In the street, Sadie said; 'That book you gave me, the selfish pig one...'

'Yeah?'

'The guy said something about how carers are like lovers. They're convinced they're the only people in the world, in the whole of time, who's ever felt the way they do.'

'Yeah?'

'Well, it helps to read that; to be told that there're others like me, who feel like I do. It's a good book.'

'It is,' Henry laughed. 'I wish more people had it.'

'But how about you, Henry? I'm so absorbed I never asked how you are.'

'Me? Oh, I'm fine.' Henry shrugged. 'No worries here.'

'No, really? There must be something going on with you?'

'Well I've stopped smoking.'

'Excellent!'

'For good this time. Even the pot. I stopped yesterday.'

'Oh, yeah,' Sadie laughed.

'For real,' Henry said. 'Totally. I had a bit of an epiphany.' He fingered his shoulder. 'I'm on patches, but they make me sick, and I'm chewing the most disgusting gum,' he laughed. 'And I'm still gagging for a fag most of the time.'

'It'll pass. Twenty-one days, they say.'

'Hope so,' he smiled. 'Apart from that life's pretty peachy. My boss is out to get me, of course, I hardly see Karina, and apparently I'm a bit of a prick. But it could be worse.'

Sadie took his arm. 'When we were, you know, together.'

'It's OK,' Henry said. 'We don't have to talk about that stuff...'

She cut him off. 'When I left, I didn't tell you why.' She looked down at her feet. 'Robbie phoned me a few days before. I think I was going to leave anyway, but Robbie called and...'

'Robbie?' Henry felt the hairs on the back of his neck rise.

'And he told me that he was going to be a dad. Shitty Britty was pregnant and Robbie was going to be a dad.' She looked up at Henry, her eyes filling. 'He said he wanted to ring to tell me so I didn't read it in the papers like before.'

'That was big of him,' Henry laughed. He reached into his pocket and handed her a crumpled piece of tissue. 'If you'd given me fifty guesses for why you left me, I'd never have got that one.'

'When we were together he told me he never wanted kids,' Sadie dabbed her eyes. 'I got used to not wanting them because I wanted to be with him.'

'Right?'

'I guess he just didn't want to have them with me.'

'I'm so sorry,' said Henry.

'Still,' she sighed. 'If I ever do have kids, with all this taking care of Evan, least I'll know what to expect.'

'You'd be a great mum,' Henry smiled. 'One day.'

'I'm sorry I left how I did,' Sadie said. 'I panicked. Had to get out, needed space, but I shouldn't have just gone; not just like that. It wasn't fair to you. We should have talked.'

'I thought it was because of my job. I can be a bit obsessed.'

'A bit?' Sadie laughed, she shook her head and took his arm. 'I wanted to explain, that's all. I just had to get out, you know. Get away. And now I've been away and things are a bit different and...' her voice faded.

'I'm not easy to be with,' Henry looked away, up the street, to the changing traffic lights and an ambulance pulling up on the pavement. Fleetingly, he wondered what sort of emergency had happened and whether he knew the person who needed help. 'I am a bit obsessed.' He shook his head and looked back at her. 'You've got nothing to be sorry for.'

She let go of his arm and looked at her watch. 'Gotta go.'

'OK,' Henry nodded. She reached up, kissed his cheek and smiled. He felt a prickling behind his eyes, and he stared at his feet like a shy adolescent.

'Listen,' Sadie said, her cheeks reddening. 'I know what I did and I'm sorry.'

'It's alright.'

'No, what I mean is... there's no reason why you should, but...'

'But?'

She looked at him cautiously. 'I'm not promising anything, Henry. It's like my life's on hold at the moment, and I can't think of anything serious at the moment, but... I think I need someone like you in my life. To be a support and a shoulder and...'

'Oh,' Henry blushed as he smiled. He reached for her hand and held it gently.

'Do you think maybe you'd give me another chance?' Her voice rose as she tried to sound confident. 'I'm getting myself sorted bit by bit and it would really help me to think about it if we could, maybe, give it another try?'

'Well,' Henry said. 'I never thought you'd ask me that.'

'I've grown up, you know, and with Evan I understand more about what you do. More about you. Isn't it good to feel needed?'

'OK,' Henry said. We'll see, yeah.' He smiled, took her arm and kissed her cheek. 'We'll see.'

'Excellent,' Sadie said and Henry nodded as he watched her walk away.

Chapter Thirty Three
10.30pm 10th March

Monday night and Henry stood alone on the sea shore. He'd been to Cardiff on the train to see David Kelman who'd just checked into a homeless hostel. Now Henry was back in Swansea, taking a massive detour to walk the last bit home along the sea. He found that he'd been thinking about Maddie. He didn't know where she was or if she was working, but he hoped not and imagined her *cwtched* up at home all snug in a pair of blue and white flannel jimjams.

'Thinking of Maddie, not Sadie,' he said. 'Well?' Sucking on his teeth, he looked out into the darkness.

He drew the sea spray deep into his chest, coughing as the cold bit into his lungs. He laughed as he turned his back on the sea, his eyes scanning the shoreline from the Mumbles Pier in the west, round the bay and to the refineries in the east. He wondered at the number of times he had scanned the same shoreline over the years. More lights in town now than there had been forty years ago, and far fewer at the top of the towers over there in Port Talbot. He sighed as he thought back to his childhood, to the days before his mum got ill and his dad left. He'd worked there then, his dad, in the refineries. Long shifts and little money, but it was a good job, a real job, a manly job, and the pride in his dad's voice when he spoke of the place had never left him.

'I wonder what you'd have thought of social work, eh, Dad?' he mumbled. 'Not much, probably,' and he wondered what he would do next if the Director got his way and Henry got the push. 'Get a job in an old people's home probably. Some shit like that.'

Henry shook his head. His eyes narrowed as he looked up above the city, up into the valleys to one of those twinkly lights high above which belonged to Tim Korkenhasel. 'I wonder what you're up to, you old fucker,' Henry said, and the image of a lonely man at a window appeared in his minds-eye.

Henry chuckled as he walked back across the sand towards St Helen's Rugby ground. 'Let's see who's got the biggest balls for this battle, yeah. You try to do me for assisted suicide, and I'll have Polish Konnie down here on the first bus possible.'

As the lights of the Cricketers came into view, he fingered the nicotine patch on his shoulder and nodded to himself. Perhaps just a quick one before home.

Chapter Thirty Four

9.35pm Tuesday 11th March

Henry looked up at the lurid florescent lights above the door. He took a deep breath, sucked his teeth and sighed. The sign said Scarlet's. Swansea's most flamboyant gay nightclub. He looked at his watch. He was already over half an hour late. Dan would really have the shits if he was much later.

He pushed the door open and stooped inside, standing awkwardly at the top of a sleep flight of stairs. Kylie boomed out at him from speakers above his head. The walls were uneven, shaped and moulded to look like the entrance to a tunnel, and the light, bright red, cast disorientating shadows.

'How'd they ever get Dan down here,' he muttered as he gripped the handrail and eased himself downward towards the sound of a very busy Tuesday night. 'We'll be doomed in a fire.'

At the bottom, the club opened out with a brightly lit bar at one side and a small, crowded dance floor at another. In the middle there were tables, chairs and Dan at the heart of it all, relaxed, laughing as someone played games with his communication device. Sitting beside him, Marcia, leant close and whispered in his ear, and Dan turned towards Henry. He smiled and nodded him over.

'He knew you'd be late,' one of the men said. 'Reckoned about an hour.'

'He said you'd be here, but you'd be too chicken to be on time,' said Marcia. 'Too scared of Dan not to bottle it completely.'

'You know me as well as I do,' Henry, all bashful, scratched the top of his head and grinned. 'Nothing to be scared of, right?'

Marcia took his arm. 'That's right,' she said. She stood up. 'You sit here by Dan. I'll get you a beer. Back in a minute. Dan wants a word.'

'Am I in the doghouse?' Henry asked.

'Don't worry,' Marcia shook her head. 'I helped him earlier. Got a speech sorted.' She clipped the communication device back onto Dan's chair. 'Alright Dan? Can you reach from there?' she asked and Dan nodded. 'Come on, you lot,' she said to the men in Dan's group. 'Give them a bit of space.'

Dan grinned as his finger rose and shook over the button. Henry smiled as the others left them.

Henry wanted to laugh and point out the irony of Nails sitting here amongst them. No longer the miserably bitter outsider, he'd found fraternity in a group of the least likely band of brothers imaginable. Back in the day, Dan's fists would have swinging, knuckles bloodied at the very suggestion that he'd ever be in a place like this, least of all be one of the regular crew. Henry wanted to laugh, but said nothing. He shook his head, kneaded the nicotine patch on his arm and enjoyed the moment.

'I KNOW I'M A BIT OF A BASTARD,' Dan said. 'BUT YOU BEEN GOOD TO ME.'

'Nothing more than I'd have done for...' Henry started, but Dan's machine spoke again so he stopped.

'YOU BEEN BETTER THAN ANYONE OVER THE YEARS. YOU MAY BE A WOMBLE,' he winked at Henry, 'BUT YOU'VE TREATED ME FAIR. FAIRER THAN I DESERVED, THE WAY I'VE BEEN; GRUMPY AND THAT. I GOT THESE TICKETS. SIX TICKETS TO THE GAME ON SATURDAY. CARDIFF.'

'Wow,' Henry nodded. 'How'd you get six? It's the Grand Slam match. Tickets are like gold dust.'

Dan grinned. 'KNEW YOU'D ASK THAT,' he said. 'FROM A FRIEND OF ONE OF THE LADS HERE. NIGEL OWENS GOT THEM.'

'Nigel Owens the referee?' Henry said. 'So it's true about him being a...?'

'BEING A WHAT?'

'You know.'

'WHAT?'

'Well...' Henry shrugged. 'I don't know what. I'm sorry. You were saying?'

Dan shrugged and turned back to the keyboard. 'I WANT TO TAKE A GANG. YOU, ME, CARLO, CATHY AND YOUR KARINA.'

'Karina'd love it.'

'YOU DON'T SEE ENOUGH OF HER.'

'That's true.'

'AND ONE SPARE TICKET.'

'Right?

'YOU TWO TOOK ME TO WOODEN SPOON DECIDER, YOU REMEMBER?'

'All those years ago. I remember. It was a shocker. You said it would be a long time before there was a new dawn for Welsh rugby.'

'AND HERE WE ARE.'

'And here we are. Chance to win the Slam twice in three seasons.'

'AND I GOT A SPARE TICKET TO GRAND SLAM DECIDER. WHO COMES WITH US IS UP TO YOU.'

'To me?'

Dan grinned. 'DON'T WASTE IT. THE GAME WILL BE LEGENDARY. BRING SOMEONE WHO MATTERS,' he typed. 'BUT FIRST. I WANT TO TALK TO YOU.'

'Are we not talking now?'

'CALL PIERS AT THE BAR.'

'OK.' Henry signaled over to the bar and the barman came over, sitting beside them. 'You Piers?' Henry asked, and the young man with bouncy hair nodded. 'What's this all about?'

'Well, Henry,' Piers said. 'Dan's worried about you. Says you're on the slide. You drink, womanize, drugs. The lot.' He looked at Dan who nodded. 'He says that doesn't bother him, but he says you've lost your mojo.'

'My mojo?'

'Your heart. You hardly come to see him, and when you do it's like you're one hundred miles an hour all the time.'

'There is so much paperwork,' Henry said weakly. 'I got a lot on.'

'YOU ALWAYS GOT A LOT ON. BUT YOU USED TO HAVE TIME FOR ME.'

'And not just time for Dan. He says you never go see anyone unless you have to now. Whatever happened to the old Henry? He's vanished.'

'Shit,' said Henry.

'Yeah,' said Piers. 'There was a thing on the radio a while ago about people working in a women's refuge in London who were suffering from vicarious trauma. Dan thinks you've got that and that you're suffering from some sort of traumatic stress disorder. Says it's messed up your priorities and whatnot. The radio said that psychological and physical stress can damage the integrity of decisions. Dan says you carry everything.'

'NO ONE LIKES A TOURIST,' said Dan. 'YOU SAID THAT. A STUPID THING TO SAY.'

'Basically he says you need help.'

They both looked at Dan, sitting there grinning.

'This is your intervention, Henry,' Piers said. 'Like for addicts, but your sickness is something else. Dan's wanted to tell you for a long time, but...'

'But I never came round?'

'Something like that.'

'Shit, mate,' Henry said. 'I never knew.'

'AND NOW YOU DO. I GOT SIX TICKETS AND YOU CAN COME WITH KARINA AND ONE OTHER. BUT YOU'VE GOT TO CHANGE.'

'OK,' Henry nodded. 'I will. I stopped smoking, you know. And kicked the dope.'

'THAT'S A START.'

'I can change.' Henry shook Piers' hand as the barman stood and turned to go. 'Thanks mate,' he said. 'It's good of you.'

'Glad to help,' Piers said. He ran his fingers through his hair and turned on his heel. 'You've done well for Dan over the years, he says. It's him you should be thanking now. He doesn't fancy you, but he loves you. He really cares about you.'

Dan's eyes were damp as Henry turned to face him. 'You're crying,' Henry laughed. 'You big poof,' and he shook his head. 'Fuck! Shit! I'm sorry. I didn't mean to say poof. That's offensive. Sorry.'

Dan nodded. 'IT'S IN HERE WHERE STRENGTH IS,' he typed, and then he tapped his own chest with his gnarled fist. 'DONT LOSE IT IN THERE, HENRY.'

'I get it, mate. I really do. For a chance to see the game on Saturday I promise I've heard you.'

'I'M WILLY WONKA AND THIS IS YOUR MAGIC TICKET. WHO ARE YOU GOING TO TAKE?'

'Dan, mate,' Henry laughed. 'I have absolutely no idea.'

Chapter Thirty Five
3.30pm 12th March

'It is good news, Sister,' Henry said. 'David just walked into the hostel in Ely, straight off the street. No one knew where he was, and then he just turned up. I don't know when he'll be down, but he's fine, which is the most important thing.'

'It's a miracle,' said Sister Georgina. 'Mrs Kelman will be so pleased.' She handed Henry some plates and a knife. 'We don't see you as much as we did, Henry,' she frowned. 'It has been mentioned.'

'Been busy,' Henry said sheepishly.

'Well, you are always welcome at the Sancta Maria. You know that.'

'Thank you,' said Henry. 'I'll try to remember.'

The nun led Henry up the stairs. 'Mrs Kelman is in the second room on the left.' She rested her hand gently on his arm as he passed her.

'That's it,' said Henry. 'Thank you.'

'Hi Molly,' Henry said as he stood in her open doorway. She turned from the window and smiled at him.

'Hello, dear,' she said. 'It's lovely to see you.' She pointed to the chair beside her bed. 'Come and sit down and tell me all about it.' She looked back at the window, and in the time it took Henry to cross the room and sit down, she'd forgotten about him.

'I've brought you something,' Henry said.

'Hello Dear,' Molly said. 'I didn't hear you come in.'

Henry smiled. 'It's good to see you looking so well,' he said. 'I've brought you something.'

'How lovely,' said Molly. 'Is it a box full of aliens from Mars?'

'No, I'm sorry,' Henry laughed. 'It's not a box of aliens from Mars.'

'Are they from Jupiter?'

Henry shook his head. 'Not from Jupiter either.'

'What aren't?' asked Molly, worried.

'The aliens.'

'What aliens?' Her voice trembled, eyes deepening as she frowned.

'The aliens that I haven't got for you.'

'You've brought me some aliens?'

'No I haven't,' Henry said softly. 'That's the thing. I brought you a cake. It's a strawberry jam sponge.'

'Is it my birthday?' Molly clapped, delighted. 'Oh how lovely.'

'I don't know,' Henry shook his head. 'But, you know, I really think it might be.' He opened the box and Molly peeped in. 'I have no candles, I'm afraid.'

'I do love candles,' said Molly. 'But I don't suppose you're allowed them anymore.'

'You see, I didn't know how old you were and wasn't sure I'd get them all on the cake.'

Molly giggled. 'You are cheeky, David. Really you are.'

'Sister Georgina got me a knife and some plates from the kitchen.'

'Lovely.'

'Here, I'll cut you a slice, and make us a cuppa, shall I? You got milk in your little fridge?'

'Have I really?' said Molly, smiling at him like he was the son she hadn't seen in years. She took a slice of cake and crammed it into her mouth. 'Are you David?' she mumbled. She had so much jam round her mouth it looked like she'd put her lipstick on in the dark.

'No, Molly. I'm not,' Henry said. 'I've heard from him though. He's in Cardiff, nice and safe in a shelter. I went to see him, and he's doing alright.'

'Is he really?'

'He wanted you to know that.'

'Did he really?'

'Yes he did.'

'Who did?'

'Your son, David. I went to see him in Cardiff. He said he's doing better than he was.'

'You know my son, David?'

'I've known him for a long time. We were at school together.'

'Were you really,' Molly smiled. The vision of her son as a young lad clear in her eyes. 'Were you friends?'

'Not exactly,' Henry laughed. 'Actually he and his friends made my life a misery.'

'Did they really?' Molly said. 'Why?'

'I think it was just because they could,' Henry said. 'Nothing more complicated than that.'

'I'm sorry.'

'It's alright. My mum had a word with you and you gave him a clout. Things were a lot easier after that.'

Henry watched as a distant memory rippled across her face. 'That was you?' Molly brought her hands to her mouth. 'Little Henry? Oh your mum was a lovely lady, Beth, isn't it?'

'That's right.'

'But she died, didn't she. Such a shame. And your dad? Yes, but no. He wasn't such a lovely man. No. He wasn't there was he? Not when she died.' She reached out and held Henry's forearm. 'It's hard not to have a mum.'

'It is,' Henry said. 'I think she'd be your age now, if she was still around. I still miss her and talk to her in my head sometimes. She doesn't always answer,' he grinned. 'I thought if it's OK, maybe I could talk to you about something. You knew my mum and if she was here I'd be able to talk to her. But she isn't.'

'Have you a wife, Henry? She'd be good to talk to.'

'I have an ex-wife.'

'Oh. Having an ex-wife is different to having a wife.'

'That's the thing I want to talk about.' He hid his face, grinning. 'It's complicated. I haven't really got anyone to talk to who wouldn't be funny about it.'

'Boy and girls stuff is never easy.' Molly smiled. 'They used to call me Yo-yo Knickers when I was young.'

'That is too much information,' said Henry.

'It was the Sixties, see. It was different then.' There was brightness in the old woman's eyes suddenly, briefly, but then they stilled and dulled and the bleakness reappeared. 'You are so long alone afterwards.' She looked back out towards the sea, and Henry knew that's she'd left him.

'I better take these back to the kitchen,' he said, collecting up the plates and cups. 'Sister Georgina would give me a clout if I left them with you.' Molly turned and looked at him blankly. 'Anyway, it's been good to see you. I'm sorry it's been so long.' He looked out of the window at the greyness of Swansea Bay. To the west Mumbles lighthouse stood stark against the sky. 'I've been caught up in my own stuff. Bit one dimensional sometimes.' Beyond the lighthouse a vast tanker headed eastwards up Bristol Channel. 'I think I forgot that the world goes on and everyone else has lives going on too. It doesn't matter what muppetry I get up to.' It began to rain. Not light drizzle, but large drops, suddenly pounding against the glass.

'I like the rain,' Molly said, brightening. 'Do you want to sit and watch it with me?'

Henry looked at his watch. He had to be at... ah, well, what did that matter. 'Yeah, I'd like that,' Henry said. He put the crockery on the table and perched on the edge of her bed, smiling as she took his hand.

'Do you remember when you were young, David. Watching the storms across the water with me and your Dad.'

'I do,' Henry said, though his memories included a different set of parents.

'And the fireworks in St Helen's in November,' Molly said.

'And the hooters on the ships in the Bay on New Year's Eve.' Henry watched her face, her cheek muscles working as the scenes drifted by.

'I don't suppose they're allowed to blow their hooters anymore,' she said.

'I don't suppose they are,' Henry nodded. 'I don't suppose they are.'

Chapter Thirty Six
Early evening Saturday 15th March 2008

Tim Korkenhasel huddled in a corner of First Class carriage as the train pulled into Newport Central. He had his black Abercrombie overcoat buttoned tight, the collar flipped up around his neck, but he still felt cold.

Tim sighed. He pinned back the navy blue curtain and peered out onto the platform. He'd been dreading the wave of drunks joining the train in Cardiff, but apparently Wales had beaten France that afternoon to win the championship with a Grand Slam, so he reassured himself that most of the potential idiots would be staying in the pubs long into the night.

When the train slowed on its approach to Cardiff Central, Tim's heart sank as he saw all the people on the platform were wearing red shirts, and, worse still, they were singing. He eased himself further down into his coat, took off his glasses and slipped the glasses into his inside pocket. He closed his eyes and pretended to be asleep.

As the people got on, the cloying smell of beer and the ammonium-sharp stench of stale sweat seeped along the carriage.

A group of girls dressed as nurses with tinsel-rimmed cowboy hats clambered into the carriage. They swung their Bargain Booze plastic bags thoughtlessly as they rushed to grab the empty seats across the aisle from Tim. A heavily tattooed man slumped into the seat opposite. His knuckles carried damp abrasions caused so recently that they were yet to scab over. He stared out of the window, his face set in fury as the girls teased and taunted him to join in their fun.

'Wha's the matter with 'im?' said one nurse to another.

'Too much booze, innit.'

'Oh, joio, fair enough. No, serious, mind. Wha's the fucks the matter with him?'

'I don' know. Don' ask me. He in't my nutter.'

Slit-eyed, Tim watched another group settle into the seats at the other end of the carriage. There were about half a dozen of them; one in a wheelchair, a woman, two girls and a couple of men. One of the girls held a small rugby ball close to her chest. They spread sandwiches, cakes and tins of pop over the table, their voices rising in delight as they talked about the game.

Tim leant his head against the curtain. He peered into the darkness, licking his lips as he thought about Konnie.

The train drifted through Bridgend where the nurses got out, and then Port Talbot, heading steadily westwards and very slowly home. The family were singing songs that even Tim recognised as Max Boyce.

The train slowed as it neared Tim's stop at Neath. He wriggled out of his seat, picked up his bag and shuffled down the aisle. He slipped his glasses back onto his nose as he neared the group, looking beyond them towards the exit. This was going to be awkward. One of the men who'd been leading the singing, was crouching now, feeding a cake to the man sitting in the wheelchair. Tim looked down at him and grimaced as he saw it was Henry Antrim. He looked back up the carriage to see if he could get out another way and he felt his cheeks reddening.

The woman and the girl were talking by the window; '...47/8 it was. Shaney scored twice and so did Lee Byrne. They're both Ospreys, aren't they Dad? And Ryan Jones was a mountain. He's hot too isn't he?'

'Sexiest man in Welsh rugby, survey said,' the woman grinned. 'Fitter than Gav, any day.' She winked at the young girl. 'Looks a bit like your dad, if you ask me. Younger, of course, but still!'

'Hey Tina, your mum fancies my dad,' the girl laughed, elbowing her friend who sat beside her.

'Well he better take care of her,' Tina said. She and Henry exchanged a long look and then Henry smiled, hands on knees as he stretched and stood up. He turned to Maddie, to say something, but she was looking down the train and her face was white.

Henry followed her gaze and saw his boss standing awkwardly a few feet away. 'No way, Timbo...,' he laughed and then his voice faded as he looked first at the Director and then back at Maddie. 'You know him don't you?' Maddie nodded. 'Not the ketchup bottle guy?' She shook her head, glanced quickly at Tina and then back again at Henry. 'The guy from County Hall when you ran off?' and she nodded.

Tim stopped, tried to turn, but there was no dignified way to escape.

'Excuse me,' Tim said, trying a smile, as he began to ease himself around the wheelchair. 'Exciting about the rugby, yes?' He felt the coldness of the eyes upon him. 'Terribly sorry.' He glanced at the faces blankly and then again with a little more interest, as each of the others seemed vaguely familiar. 'Oh. Hello?' he said to Carlo, half recognising him as someone from the golf club. 'How are you?' Another smile failed, and he stood in silence halfway around the wheelchair.

'This is Mr Korkenhasel,' Henry said to no one in particular. 'He's a friend of Konnie's, you know?'

'Konnie?' Tim said.

'Ah come on now, don't be bashful,' said Carlo. 'Konnie the Pole? I heard you know her well?'

If Tim flinched it was only for a second. 'Ah, Konnie,' he turned to Henry. 'What of her?'

Henry laughed. 'Man, you have nerves of steel.' He shook his head. 'You're not embarrassed at all?'

'Embarrassed? Well, I... Why should I be embarrassed? I know a lot of people who need help. She is one of them. It is what we do in the social services, isn't it?' He looked again around the group, his eyes resting on the woman by the window. 'Sometimes we help in unconventional ways, isn't that right, Henry.' The woman's face was familiar too, though it took a moment to place her, and then he did and his stomach tightened. 'Why shouldn't I be involved with a project for vulnerable young women?' he said, and he looked directly at Maddie.

'Yeah, of course we know what you mean,' Henry spat, conscious of the five pints of Brains in his belly and aware that his fists had clenched. The hairs on his scalp prickled for a fight. 'That's a good one!' In his minds-eye Tim was already flat on his back, toothless and bleeding. 'Quick thinking, that. Nice one, Tim. Now I don't give a shit what you do, but reputations are everything up at the Club, I'll bet. Maybe I'll get Konnie down from Cardiff. Get her to run some sort of training for the Team. What do you say?'

'Career down the drain for you, I'd say,' said Carlo, 'when this gets around.' He reached for Henry's arm.

Tim shrugged, outwardly cool. 'I do a lot of work for charity, and I'm not the kind of man who likes to talk about it. Silence is a good thing on certain matters.' He glanced again at Maddie. 'As I am sure some of you would understand. We come across all sorts of people from all walks of life. Some of whom have secrets they would prefer to keep secret.' He glanced first at Tina, then at Karina and then back again at Tina who looked more like Maddie than Karina did. And then he smiled at Maddie. 'If you know what I mean.'

'Of course, of course.' Henry nodded. He looked at Maddie, see how she was coping, and she smiled at him. His defence of her was involuntary. He'd made his choice.

'I was reviewing Megan Atkins's medical notes,' Tim said. 'Very interesting reading.' He looked at Henry, hoping to see him crumble.

'You really are a piece of work,' Henry laughed. 'Legendary!'

'FUCKER,' Dan said. 'FUCKER,' and he grimaced up at Tim, the dribble on his stubble shining like dew.

'This is Dan Franken,' Henry said. He was beginning to enjoy himself. Tim had played the Megan Atkins/Tramadol card and who gives a shit. In his head his voices said; Wales won the Grand Slam! We fucking won it, and no one is going to take this away from us, least not you, you twat! 'Dan Franken. I'm not sure if you'll remember him?'

'Of course,' Tim said. 'How are you?' Dan growled and turned away. 'Such a shame about that nasty business,' Tim nodded. 'Such a shame. Well, I hope things worked out in the end.' Tim's optimistically jovial tone faded as, quite slowly, the young girl by the window rose to her feet.

'Sit down Karina,' Henry said, but she saw his grin and ignored him.

'Don't worry, Dad,' she winked. 'Been to anger management class, haven't I. I can control it now.' Her voice was like steel. 'I know you too,' she leaned towards Tim as Henry, Carlo and Maddie reached to hold her back, while Dan and Tina burst out laughing. 'When my mum was carrying me, you were Dad's college mentor,' she pushed the others away. 'I know what you told him,' her voice rising.

Tim took a step backwards, glancing at Henry. 'I don't think I told you anything, did I Henry?' he said. 'I'm pretty sure you came to your decision on your own. It's well known I'm a supporter of adoption when two unsuitable people are due to become parents. I'm sure it wasn't me that suggested an...'

'You're a piece of shit,' Karina hissed, her eyes as bright as the Port Talbot tower fires which burnt in the darkness behind her. 'My dad came to you when he needed help.' She pointed at him, mocking. 'You can say what you want now, Mr Korken-fucking-big-dog, but I know you and I know the truth. And so do YOU.' She stood up, banging her fist down on the table, the beer cans crashing into Dan's lap.

Tim stumbled and fell over as the train came at last to a halt, and then he scrambled backwards, away from this girl, away from all of them, leaving behind any shred of dignity as he cut towards the exit and safety outside the train.

And as he fled, as he gulped back great sorrowful tears of humiliating fear, Tim was followed not by the sound of determined pursuit; of feet pounding along the platform behind him, but by the altogether more crushing sound of laughter and he knew he was broken.

Chapter Thirty Seven
10.30am 17th March 2008

'Here we go again,' Henry sighed and stretched with his hands behind his head and he yawned. After the best weekend in years, Monday comes and it's back to the stuffy meeting room, the bright fluorescent lights with the obligatory humming tube, and the effusive welcome from the organisers to the End of Life Care Conference.

The weekend really had been the best. From the Grand Slam to Maddie's farewell glance as they said goodbye at Swansea station after the kiss that was more than just a 'thank you for a good day' kind of a kiss.

And now it was back to reality: weak, tepid tea, week-old custard creams and Scottish bottled water imported three hundred miles though the water in the taps was equally drinkable.

'But maybe today's different,' he murmured as he turned to look around the room.

A row of county councillors dozed in the back row. Later, they'd agree what a worthwhile day it'd been and how valuable it was to meet the people as if the people were a rare and alien race. They'd shake hands all round and agree to do all that they could to help. 'Of course, you must understand we can't change policy ourselves, but we can pass on your views and needs to those that can.'

A youthful, balding Assembly Member sat below the window. His shiny dome gleamed as he grinned and clapped at every opportunity. It was the first time the group had seen him since just before the last election. 'I will do all I can to help,' he said when called upon to comment, 'of course I will. I am here for you, elected by you to represent your views and needs. I can't change policy on my own, of course,' he stood up, leaning forward and edging from one foot to the other, 'but...'

Tim Korkenhasel's PowerPoint presentation said very little but Henry didn't mind. It was all bollocks anyway and his delivery had even less enthusiasm than usual. Henry had zoned away, back to the station and to Maddie's smile, the gleam in her eye and the briefest moment when her soft, warm lips meet his. And then the ribbing from Dan, Carlo and Karina all the way home.

'I'm so pleased,' Cathy had said when Carlo told her, and then Carlo had pulled her away with a laugh.

'Leave him be,' Carlo said. 'Leave the poor boy alone. You might have given up your seat so Tina could go too, but that doesn't give you the right to swamp him.'

Henry stretched and smiled. It felt nice to be wanted, not just needed. He looked round the room, caught the Director's eye and blew him a kiss, chucking as the Director stumbled over his words. Yep, it had been a bloody good weekend.

'...a strategy of strategic outreach partnerships inclusive of all viable tri-sector stakeholders to facilitate devolution of power meaningfully from the centre,' said Tim despondently, the heads of the audience nodding in soporific hypnosis. 'We are in the preliminary stages of scoping a consultation exercise relating to the future of End of Life care... facilitate a multi-strained approach...' it was like the drone of bees in a field in summertime.

When he finally finished, Tim switched off the projector and readied himself for questions, but before they could come he shook his head and stepped off the stage with a weary tread, more tired than he'd ever felt. He slid up his sleeve, looked at his watch as he sloped away towards the door, head down, no point in trying to hide it, he'd do anything to be away from these people. He'd do anything to be away from here, away from everyone.

Chapter Thirty Eight
1st April 2008

'Who's the BIG DOG now!' read the title of the email in Henry's in-box. He smiled as he opened Carlo's brief message: 'Remember what your mother said; God will never throw at you more than you can handle. Good luck in the big seat old friend. And KEEP IT REAL! Carlo.'

Henry glanced towards the window, pondering his reply and then his phone rang. 'Hello, Antrim speaking,' he said. He leant in close to the in-laid leather on the large oak desk as he spoke into the monitor. 'In the absence of the Director who's gone off his noodle and onto long term sick-leave, this is Senior Social Worker Henry Antrim holding the fort.'

'Henry?'

'Hi Gaye. I knew it was you,' he laughed. 'Just mucking around. What is it?'

'You mustn't do that,' Gaye said. 'One time you'll get it wrong and be in awful trouble.'

'Sorry Gaye,' Henry said. 'I just can't get over it, that's all. I've never believed in happy endings. Anyway, what can I do for you?'

'Are you on hands free? It echoes when you lean in close.'

'Oh, sorry,' Henry lent back away from the desk. 'Is that better?'

'There's two things, Henry. There's a message from someone on the National Appeals Panel who wants you to ring them back.'

Henry frowned as he wrote down the officer's name and telephone number. 'Has he been in touch before,' he asked, 'I mean when Timmy was still here?'

'I saw a letter from him. It's in the pile on your desk. Something to do with a study of assisted suicide within the authority.'

'Assisted suicide?'

'Dating back to the '80s. Tim wanted an independent external team from the Welsh Assembly to look into it.'

'You are joking?'

'I thought it was strange that he'd call for a historical review of his own department.'

'I'd say.'

'Well, anyway. Here they are, report done, feeding back.'

'And it came through after Tim had gone?'

'That's right.'

'OK.' Henry glanced at Carlo's email on his computer monitor. 'So, what was the other message? You said there were two things?'

'It was your dad. He left his number. Said he wants to talk to you.'

'My dad?'

'Yeah.'

'Is this an April Fool or something,' Henry laughed.

'I don't think so. He said he's staying at the Marie Curie Hospice in Penarth.'

'Marie Curie? That's cancer, right?'

'Henry, I'm so sorry...'

'Fuck! Oh, sorry, Gaye. I mean, *cancer*?'

'I've got his number,' said Gaye and the phone went quiet. 'Henry, you still there?'

'Marie Curie?'

'That's what he said.'

'Are you sure this isn't an April Fool?'

'It wouldn't be a very good one would it.'

'Not really.'

'I've got the number.' Gaye waited. 'Henry? Are you there?'

'Sorry.'

'What do you want me to do?'

'Well I guess you'd better give me the number.'

'OK.'

'Jesus, Mum,' Henry murmured as he dialed the number. '"God will never throw at you more than you can handle?" Bet you lot are having a right old laugh about this one up there in heaven.' His hand went to his pocket, feeling for the rosary. 'Dad?' he said. 'Yeah, it's Henry. So, what? It's been like thirty years?'

The End

Acknowledgements

The author wishes to acknowledge the award of a Writer's Bursary from Literature Wales for the purpose of starting this book, and also from the Literature Wales Critical Service with the purpose of finishing it.

Thank you to Billy Bragg for permission to use his song lyrics.

Thank you to Gwen Davies and the other willing (and not so willing) readers and editors who helped along the way. Without your help it would have been a lot longer.

Thank you to Chris Jones, David Thorpe and everyone else at Cambria Books. It's been a stress-free joy to work with you.

Special thanks to my family.

And also to everyone involved at Clynfyw.

Thank you for reading.
If you enjoyed this story (and it made you think) there is more information about Welshrats, back stories and discussions on my *'Welshrats'* Facebook page.

Lightning Source UK Ltd.
Milton Keynes UK
UKOW06f0400230416

272804UK00015B/413/P